"Be still, my Agatha-Christie-loving beating heart."
—Bustle

"Jumping between past and present, Johnson's novel is deliciously atmospheric, with a sprawling cast of complex suspects/ potential victims, surprising twists, and a dash of romance. As in her Shades of London books, Johnson remains a master at combining jittery tension with sharp, laugh-out-loud observations."
—*Publishers Weekly* (starred review)

"Remember the first time reading Harry Potter and knowing it was something special? There's that same sense of magic in the introduction of teen Sherlock-in-training Stevie Bell. Parallel mysteries unfold with cleverly written dialogue, page-turning brilliance, and a young sleuth just as captivating as Hercule Poirot."
—*USA Today* ★ ★ ★

"A suspenseful, attention-grabbing mystery with no clear solution. The versatile Johnson is no stranger to suspense, and this twisty thriller will leave plenty of readers anxious for more."
—ALA *Booklist*

Praise for
THE VANISHING STAIR

"In this second installment, a few major mysteries are satisfyingly solved, but other long-standing riddles remain tantalizingly indecipherable. Readers, hang tight: There's one more round to come, and if the signs are right, it'll be to die for."
—ALA *Booklist*

"Throughout this volume, Johnson's compelling would-be Sherlock proves to be as bad at personal relationships as she is adept at solving mysteries. Teen angst soars as Johnson delightfully conjures up more nefarious deeds from the mountain mist."
—*Kirkus Reviews* (starred review)

"Take it from the world's most impatient reader: If the Truly Devious series is basically one long mystery book, *The Vanishing Stair* is a middle part so enjoyable you won't even want to skip to the end."
—*Entertainment Weekly*

"In this second installment of her marvelous Truly Devious series, Maureen Johnson offers thrilling suspense, sly wit, a memorable cast of characters, and more pieces of her deliciously intricate puzzle."
—*Buffalo News*

"Waiting for the next installment of Maureen Johnson's Agatha Christie-Sherlock Holmes classic mystery homage series was torture, but *The Vanishing Stair* is oh so worth it."
—Bustle

Praise for
THE HAND ON THE WALL

"The final, riveting chapter of the Truly Devious murder series. Throughout this intricately woven, fast-paced whodunit, Johnson demonstrates how proximity to wealth and power can mold and bend one's behavior, whether with good or—here largely— devious intent. A richly satisfying, Poirot-like ending for Johnson's inspired and inspiring teen sleuth."
—*Kirkus Reviews* (starred review)

"In this hotly anticipated trilogy finale, Johnson pulls out all the stops, filling the thrillingly nimble narrative with classic mystery conventions. A striking foray into an examination of what mysteries can ever truly be solved, and a satisfying send-off for a series that will be missed."
—ALA *Booklist*

"This will be essential reading for the many fans of the first two books. This trilogy ender is fun, satisfying, and a genuine treat for teens and adult mystery fans."
—*SLJ*

The HAND on the WALL

The
HAND
on the
WALL

MAUREEN JOHNSON

 KATHERINE TEGEN BOOKS
An Imprint of HarperCollins Publishers

Katherine Tegen Books is an imprint of HarperCollins Publishers.

The Hand on the Wall
Copyright © 2020 by HarperCollins Publishers
All rights reserved. Printed in the United States of America.
No part of this book may be used or reproduced in any manner whatsoever
without written permission except in the case of brief quotations embodied in
critical articles and reviews. For information address HarperCollins Children's
Books, a division of HarperCollins Publishers, 195 Broadway, New York, NY
10007.
www.epicreads.com

Library of Congress Control Number: 2019953178
ISBN 978-0-06-233812-9

Typography by Carla Weise
22 23 24 25 26 LBC 15 14 13 12 11
❖
First paperback edition, 2020

For Dan Sinker, for teaching me about
making, coping, punk, Disneyland, and tacos.
See you at the Haunted Mansion, buddy.

ELLINGHAM
FOUNDED
EA
1935
ACADEMY
1.
2.
3.
4.
5.
6.
7.
8.
9.
10.
11.
12.
13.
14.
1. Workshop
2. Asteria
3. Genius
4. Artemis
5. Apollo
6. Dionysus
7. Demeter
8. Great House
9. Minerva
10. Eunomia
11. Cybele
12. Jupiter
13. Vesta
14. Juno
NORTH
"CATS KNOW BEST"

FEDERAL BUREAU OF INVESTIGATION

Photographic image of letter received at the Ellingham
residence on April 8, 1936.

LooK! a RiddLE!
TiME FoR FuN!

Should WE uSE
a RoPE oR GuN?

KNiVEs aRE shaRp
aNd GLEaM so pREtty

PoisoN's sLoW,
Which is a PiTy

FiRE is FESTiVE,
dRoWNiNG's sLoW

HaNGiNG's a
RoPy WaY To Go

a bRoKEN hEAd,
a NaSTY FaLL

a caR collidiNG
WiTh a Wall

BoMbs MAKE a
VERY JoLLY NoiSE

SuCh WAYs To
PUNish NAUGhTY boYS!

WhaT shall WE USE?
WE caN'T dECidE.

JUsT LiKE YoU caNNoT
RUN oR hidE.

HA hA.

TRULY,
DEViOUS

December 15, 1932

THE SNOW HAD BEEN FALLING FOR HOURS, DRIFTING PAST THE WIN-
dows, settling on the sill, forming little landscapes that
mimicked the mountains in the distance. Albert Ellingham
sat on an overstuffed chair covered in plum-colored velvet. A
green marble clock sat before him on a small table, ticking
contentedly. Aside from the ticking and the crackling of the
fire, there was no sound. The snow muffled the world.

"Surely we should have heard something by now," he said.

This was to Leonard Holmes Nair, who was stretched
on a sofa on the opposite side of the room, covered in a fur
rug and reading a French novel. Leo was a painter and a family friend, a tall and lanky reprobate in a blue velvet smoking
jacket. The group had been holed up in this private Alpine
hospital retreat for two weeks, watching the snow, drinking
hot wine, reading, and waiting . . . waiting for the event that
had announced itself in the middle of the night. Then the
nurses and doctors swept into action, taking the mother-to-
be to the luxurious birthing room. When you are one of the
richest men in America, you can have an entire Swiss retreat

to yourself for the birth of your child.

"These mysterious affairs of nature take time," Leo said, not looking up.

"It's been almost nine hours."

"Albert, stop watching the clock. Have a drink."

Albert stood and stuffed his hands into his pockets. He paced to a near window, then a farther one, then back to the first. The view was marvelous—the snow, the mountains, the peaked roofs of the Alpine cottages in the valley.

"A drink," Leo said again. "Ring for one. Ring the—ringie. Ringie dingie. Where is it?"

Albert crossed back to the fireplace and pulled on a gold knob connected to a silk cord. A gentle tinkling could be heard somewhere in the distance. A moment later the doors opened and a young woman came in, dressed in a blue wool dress with a prim nurse's apron, a white cap nestled on her head.

"Yes, Herr Ellingham?" she said.

"Any news?" he asked.

"I am afraid not, Herr Ellingham."

"We need glühwein," Leo said. "*Er braucht etwas zu essen. Wurst und Brot. Käse.*"

"*Ich verstehe, Herr Nair. Ich bringe Ihnen etwas, einen Moment bitte.*"

The nurse backed out of the room and drew the doors closed.

"Perhaps something has gone wrong," Albert said.

"Albert . . ."

"I'm going up there."

"Albert," Leo repeated. "My instructions were to sit on you if you attempted it. While I may not be the most athletic man, I am larger than you and I'm entirely deadweight. Let's turn on the radio. Or would you like to play a game?"

Usually, the offer of a game would settle Albert Ellingham at once, but he continued to pace until the nurse appeared again with a tray containing two ruby-colored glasses of hot wine, along with cold sliced sausage, bread, and cheese.

"Sit," Leo ordered. "Eat this."

Albert did not sit. He pointed at the clock instead.

"This clock," he said, "I bought it the other day, when we were in Zurich, from a dealer. Antique. Eighteenth century. He said it belonged to Marie Antoinette."

He put his hands on either side of the clock and stared down at it, as if waiting for it to speak to him.

"Possibly nonsense," he said, lifting the clock. "But for the price I paid, it should be good nonsense. And it has a bit of a secret that is amusing—hidden drawer underneath. You turn it over. There's a little indentation and you press . . ."

Overhead, there was movement. A yell. Hurried steps. A scream of pain. Albert set the clock down with a thud.

"Sounds like the twilight sleep wore off," Leo said as he looked at the ceiling. "Dearie me."

There was more noise—the sharp screams of a woman about to give birth.

Albert and Leo left the cozy study and stood in the much colder anteroom at the foot of the stairs.

"Such gruesome sounds," Leo said, looking up the dark stairs in concern. "Surely there is a better way to bring life into the world."

The cries stopped. All was silent for several moments, then the wail of a baby broke through. Albert sprang up the steps two at a time, slipping at the landing in his haste. In the hall above, the young nurse was standing by the door of the birthing room, prepared for his arrival.

"A moment, Herr Ellingham," she said with a smile. "The cord must be cut."

"Tell me," he said, breathless.

"It is a girl, Herr Ellingham."

"It is a girl," Albert repeated, wheeling around to face his friend.

"Yes," Leo said. "I heard."

"A girl. I thought it would be a girl. I knew it would be a girl. A little girl! I'll get her the biggest dollhouse in the world, Leo. You could live in it!"

The door cracked open, and Albert pushed past the nurse and hurried inside. The room was dark—the curtains drawn against the snow. There were smells of life—blood and sweat—mingling with the sharp tang of antiseptic. The doctor replaced a breathing mask on a hook on the wall and adjusted the level on a tank of gas. One nurse emptied a white enamel basin full of pink water into a sink. Another nurse pulled wet sheets from the bed, while a third replaced them as they slipped away, snapping the clean sheet in the air and letting it fall gently on the woman below. The nurses criss-crossed the room, opening the curtains and swapping the trays of instruments for pitchers of flowers. It was a graceful, well-practiced ballet, and within minutes, the birthing room felt like a cheerful hotel suite. This was the best private hospital in the world, after all.

Albert's gaze fixed on his wife, Iris. She was holding a child in a yellow blanket. He was so full of feeling that the room seemed to distort; the beams of the ceiling appeared to bend down to him as if to catch him should he fall as he made his way to her and the child in her arms.

"She is beautiful," Albert said. "She is extraordinary. She is . . ."

His voice failed him. The baby was bright pink, all balled fists and closed eyes and wails of awareness. She was life itself.

"She's ours," Iris said quietly.

"May I hold her?" said someone on the other side of the room. Albert and Iris turned toward the woman in the bed. Her face was flushed and glazed in sweat.

"Of course!" Iris said, going to her. "Of course. Darling, darling, of course."

Iris gently placed the baby into Flora Robinson's arms. Flora was weak, still half under the influence of the drugs, her blond hair stuck to her forehead. The nurses pulled the sheets and blankets up over her, tucking them around the baby in her arms. She blinked in amazement at the tiny person she had produced.

"My God," she said, looking down into the infant's face. "Is that what I've done?"

"You've done marvelously," Iris replied, peeling some of the damp locks back from her friend's forehead. "Darling, you were a marvel. You were an absolute marvel."

"May I have a moment, please?" Flora said. "To hold her?"

"It is a good idea," the nurse said. "For her to hold. It helps the baby. She will have to nurse soon. Perhaps, Herr Ellingham, Frau Ellingham, you can outside go? For a moment only."

Iris and Albert retreated from the room. Leo had gone back downstairs, so they were alone in the hall.

"She hasn't said anything about the father, has she?" Albert asked quietly. "I thought she might during . . ."

He waved his hand to indicate nine hours of labor and the birth process.

"No," Iris whispered back.

"No matter. No matter at all. Should he ever appear, we will deal with him."

The nurse stepped into the hall, bearing a clipboard with official-looking forms.

"Excuse me," she said. "Do you have a name for the child?"

Albert looked to Iris, who nodded.

"Alice," Albert said. "Her name is Alice Madeline Ellingham. And she will be the happiest little girl in the world."

EXCERPT FROM *TRULY DEVIOUS: THE ELLINGHAM MURDERS* BY DR. IRENE FENTON

Since his wife and daughter's kidnapping, since the murder of Dolores Epstein, all during the trial of Anton Vorachek—Albert Ellingham kept the search going. Vorachek's murder on the courtroom steps didn't slow Albert Ellingham down, even if it appeared that the one person who may have known Alice's whereabouts was dead and gone. Someone knew something. No expense was ever spared. He appeared on every radio show. He spoke to every politician. Albert Ellingham would go anywhere and meet anyone who might know where his daughter could be found.

But on November 1, 1938, the police and the FBI were dragging Lake Champlain, looking for Albert Ellingham and George Marsh. The pair had gone out for an afternoon sail on Albert's boat, *Wonderland*. Just before sunset, a massive explosion ripped through the peaceful Vermont evening. Local fishermen scrambled into their boats to get to the spot. When they arrived, they found fragments of the doomed vessel—pieces of charred wood, singed cushions that had been blown into the air, small brass fittings, bits of rope. They also found something much more disturbing: human remains, in the same state as the boat itself.

Neither Albert Ellingham's nor George Marsh's body would be recovered in their entirety; enough pieces were found to establish that both men had died.

There was an immediate investigation. Everyone had a theory about the death of one of America's richest and greatest men, but in the end, no case could ever be made. That Albert Ellingham had been killed by a group of anarchists seemed the most likely answer; indeed, three separate groups claimed responsibility. With the death of Albert Ellingham, Alice's case began to go cold. There was no father's voice saying her name, no tycoon handing out cash and making calls. A year later, the war started in Europe, and the sad saga of the family on the mountain paled in the face of a much greater tragedy.

Over the years, dozens of women would come forward claiming to be Alice Ellingham. Some could be dismissed right from the start—they were the wrong age, had the wrong physical attributes. Those who passed the basic tests would be seen by Robert Mackenzie, Albert's personal secretary. Mackenzie conducted a thorough investigation into each claim. All were proven to be false.

Passing years have revived interest in the case— not just about Alice but also about the kidnapping and what happened on that terrible day on Lake Champlain. With advances in DNA analysis and modern investigative techniques, the answers may still be within our grasp.

Alice Ellingham may yet be found.

LOCAL PROFESSOR DIES IN TRAGIC HOUSE FIRE

Burlington News Online

November 4

Local professor Dr. Irene Fenton from the University of Vermont's history department died in a house fire yesterday evening. Dr. Fenton, who lived on Pearl Street, was a twenty-two-year member of the faculty and the author of several books, including *Truly Devious: The Ellingham Murders*. The blaze began around 9 p.m. and was believed to have originated in the kitchen.

Dr. Fenton's nephew, who lived with her, sustained minor injuries in the blaze. . . .

THE BONES WERE ON THE TABLE, NAKED AND CHALKY. THE EYE SOCK-ets hollow, the mouth in a loose grimace, as if to say, *"Yep, it's me. Bet you're wondering how I ended up here. It's a funny story, actually. . . ."*

"As you'll see, Mr. Nelson is missing the first metacarpal on the right hand, which has been replaced with a model. In life, of course, he had—"

"Question," Mudge said, raising his hand partway. "How did this dude get to be a skeleton? I mean, here? Did he know he'd end up in a classroom?"

Pix, Dr. Nell Pixwell, teacher of anatomy, forensic anthropologist, and housemistress of Minerva House, paused. Her hand and Mr. Nelson's were lightly intertwined, as if they were considering the delicate proposition of dancing together at the ball.

"Well," she said, "Mr. Nelson was donated to Elling-ham when it opened. I believe he came via a friend of Albert Ellingham's who was connected to Harvard. There are a num-ber of ways that bodies come to be used for demonstration purposes. People donate their bodies to science, of course. That may have been what happened, but I suspect it's not the case here. Based on some of the materials and techniques used to articulate him, I think Mr. Nelson is probably from the mid- to late 1800s. Back then, things were a bit looser in terms of getting bodies for science. Prisoners' bodies were routinely used. Mr. Nelson here was likely well nourished. He was tall. He had all his teeth, which was exceptional for the time. He had no broken bones. My guess—and it's only a guess—"

"You mean grave robbing?" Mudge asked with interest. "He was stolen?"

Mudge was Stevie Bell's lab partner—a six-foot-something death-metalhead who wore purple-colored contacts with snake pupils and a black hoodie weighed down with fifty Disney pins, including some very rare ones that he would show off and explain to Stevie as they dissected cows' eyes and other terrible things for the purposes of education. Mudge loved Disney more than anyone Stevie had ever met and had dreams of being an animatronics Imagineer. Ellingham Academy was the kind of place where Mudges were welcomed and understood.

"It was common," Pix said. "Medical students needed cadavers. People called resurrection men—get it, rise from the dead?—used to steal bodies to sell to student doctors. If he was an old Harvard model skeleton, yes, I think it's likely that he was a victim of grave robbing. This reminds me, I need to send him out to get him rearticulated. I need to get a new metacarpal, and the wire needs repairing here, between the hamate, the triquetral, and the capitate bones. It's tough being a skeleton."

She smiled for a moment but then twitched it away and rubbed her peach-fuzz head.

"So much for metacarpals," she said again. "Let's talk about the other bones in the hand and the arm. . . ."

Stevie knew exactly why Pix had stopped herself. Ellingham Academy was no longer the kind of place where you could make casual jokes about being a skeleton.

As Stevie stepped outside, the cold air slapped her in the face. The magnificent cloak of reds and golds that hung from the Vermont woodland had dropped suddenly, like a massive act of arboreal striptease.

Striptease. Strip trees. Striptrees? God, she was tired.

Nate Fisher was waiting for Stevie outside the classroom building. He sat on one of the benches, with slumped shoulders, staring at his phone. Now that the weather had turned more chill, he could cheerfully—or what passed as cheerfully in Nate-adjusted terms—pile on oversized sweaters and baggy cords and scarves until he was a moving pile of natural and synthetic fibers.

"Where have you been?" he asked as a greeting.

He put a cup of coffee in her hand, as well as a maple doughnut. Stevie assumed it was maple. Things in Vermont often were. She took a long drink of the coffee and a bite of the doughnut before replying.

"I needed to think," she said. "I walked around before class."

"Those are the same clothes you had on yesterday."

Stevie looked down at herself in confusion, at her baggy sweatpants and black Converse sneakers. She was wearing a stretched-out sweater and her thin red vinyl coat.

"Slept in these," she said as a small rain of crumbs fell from the doughnut.

"You haven't eaten a meal with us in two days. I can never find you."

This was true. She had not gone to the dining hall for a proper meal in two days, and instead subsisted on handfuls of dry cereal from the kitchen dispensers, usually eaten in the middle of the night. She would stand at the counter in the dark, her hand under the little cereal chute, pulling the lever to get another Froot Loops fix. She had a vague memory of acquiring and consuming a banana yesterday while sitting on the floor of the library, way up in the stacks. She had avoided people, avoided conversations, avoided messages to live entirely in her own thoughts, because they were many and they needed ordering.

Three major events had occurred to bring on this monastic, peripatetic activity.

One, David Eastman, perhaps boyfriend, had gotten his face punched in in Burlington. He had done this on purpose and paid the assailant. He uploaded video of the beatdown to the internet and vanished without a trace. David was the son of Senator Edward King. Senator King had helped Stevie return to school, with the proviso that she would help keep David under control.

Well, that had failed.

That alone would have occupied her mind entirely, except that on the same night, Stevie's adviser, Dr. Irene Fenton, had died in a house fire. Stevie had not been close to Dr. Fenton, or Fenton, as she preferred to be called. There was one upside to this horrific event—the fire was in Burlington. Burlington wasn't *here*, at Ellingham, and Fenton was identified as a professor at the University of Vermont. This meant that the death wasn't attributed to Ellingham. The school probably couldn't survive if there was another death. In a world where everything went wrong all the time always, having your adviser die in a fire off campus was one of the few "but on the bright side . . ." elements of her confusing new life. It was a terrible and selfish way of thinking about things, but at this point, Stevie had to be practical. If you wanted to solve crime, you needed to detach.

All of that would have been plenty to deal with. But the crowning item, the one that spun through her mind like a mobile, was . . .

"Don't you think we should talk?" Nate said. "About what's going on? About what happens now?"

It was quite a loaded question. *What happens now?*

"Walk with me," she said.

She turned and headed away from the classroom buildings, away from people, away from cameras posted on poles and trees. This was to keep their conversation private and also so no one could see the devastation she was going to wreak on this doughnut. She was hungry.

"Ish olfed decaf," she said, shoving a bite of doughnut in her mouth.

"You want decaf?"

She took a moment to swallow.

"I solved it," she said. "The Ellingham case."

"I know," he said. "That's what we need to talk about. That and the fire and everything else. Jesus, Stevie."

"It makes sense," she said, walking slowly. "George Marsh, the man from the FBI, the one who protected the Ellinghams . . . someone who knew the house layout, the schedules, when the money came in, the family habits . . . someone who easily could have set up a kidnapping. So, here's what happens . . ."

She got Nate loosely by the arm and changed direction, turning them back toward the Great House. The Great House was the crowning jewel of the campus. In the 1930s, it was the Ellingham home. Today, it was the center of the school administration and a space for dances and events. Around the back, there was a walled garden. Stevie walked on autopilot to a familiar door in the wall and opened it. This was the sunken garden, so called because it was once an artificial lake and Iris Ellingham's massive swimming pool. Albert Ellingham had drained it following the disappearance of his daughter, on the word of someone who thought her body was at the bottom. It wasn't, but the lake was never filled again. So it remained, a great big grassy hole in the ground. And in the middle, on a strange little hill that had once been an island in the lake, was a geodesic glass dome. This dome was where Dottie Epstein had met her fate and where, under it, Hayes Major met his end.

"So," Stevie said, pointing, "Dottie Epstein is sitting in that dome, reading her Sherlock Holmes, minding her own business. All of a sudden, a guy appears. George Marsh. Neither one of them expecting the other. And out of all the students from Ellingham George Marsh could have run into, he runs into the most brilliant one, and the one whose uncle is in the NYPD. Dottie knows who Marsh is. The whole plan is ruined, instantly, because George Marsh met Dottie in that dome. Dottie knows something bad is about to happen, so she makes a mark in her Sherlock Holmes, she does the best she can to say who she's looking at, and then, she dies. But Dottie fingers the guy. Flash forward . . ."

Stevie turned in the direction of the house, toward the flagstone patio and French doors outside the room that had been Albert Ellingham's office.

"Albert Ellingham spends the next two years trying to find his daughter, when something . . . *something* jogs his memory. He thinks about Dottie Epstein and the mark in the book. He gets out the wire recording he made of her—we know he did this, it was on his desk the day he died—and he listens. He realizes that Dottie could have recognized George Marsh. He wonders . . ."

Stevie could practically see Albert Ellingham pacing the office, walking across the trophy rugs, from leather chair to

17

desk, staring at the green marble clock on the mantel, trying to figure out if what he had worked out in his mind was true.

"He writes a riddle, maybe to test himself, to see if he really believed it. *Where do you look for someone who's never really there? Always on a staircase but never on a stair.* He's saying, take the word *stair* out of *staircase*. Who's always on a case? A detective. Who's never really there? The person you hired to investigate, the one who was by your side. The one you didn't even think of or notice . . ."

"Stevie . . ."

"And then, that afternoon, he goes out sailing with George Marsh and the boat explodes. People always thought anarchists did it, because anarchists tried to kill him before, and everyone thought an anarchist kidnapped his daughter. But it can't be that. One of them caused that boat to explode. Either George Marsh knew it was all over and took them both out, or Albert Ellingham confronted him and did the same. But it ended there. And I know whoever kidnapped Alice isn't Truly Devious, because I know that note was written by some students here, probably as a joke. This whole thing was just a bunch of stuff that got out of hand. The note was a joke, then the kidnapping went wrong, and all those people died . . ."

"Stevie," Nate said, snapping his friend back to the present, to the cold and marshy grass they stood on.

"Fenton," Stevie replied. "She believed there was a codicil in Albert Ellingham's will, something that said that whoever found Alice got a fortune. It's some real tinfoil-hat, grassy-knoll stuff, but she believed it. She said she had proof. I didn't see it, but she said she had it. She was really paranoid—she only kept paper records. She kept notepads in old pizza boxes. She had a conspiracy wall. She said she was putting something huge together. I called to tell her what I had figured out, and she said she couldn't talk and something about 'the kid is there.' And then, her *house burned down*."

Nate rubbed his head wearily.

"Is there *any* chance that was an accident?" he said. "Please tell me there is."

"What do you think?" she asked quietly.

"What do *I* think?" Nate replied, sitting on one of the stone benches on the edge of the sunken garden.

Stevie sat next to him, the cold of the stone seeping through her clothes.

"I think I don't know what to think. I don't believe in conspiracies, usually, because people are generally too uncoordinated to pull off huge, complicated plots. But I also think that if a bunch of weird stuff happens in one place at one time, maybe those things might be connected. So Hayes died while you were making that video about the Ellingham case. And then Ellie died after she ran away after you figured out that she wrote Hayes's show. And now your adviser is dead—the one you were helping to research the Ellingham stuff—and she died just as you said you figured out who committed the crime of the century. These are all some terrible accidents, or they're not, but I am out of ideas and need to conserve my energy so I can freak out more effectively. Does that help?"

"No," Stevie said, looking up at the gray-pink sky.

"What if—hear me out—what if you told the authorities *everything* you know right now and let all of this go?"

"But I don't know anything," she said. "That's the problem. I need to know more. What if this is all connected? It has to be, right? Iris and Dottie and Alice, Hayes and Ellie and Fenton."

"*Does* it?"

"I have to think," she said, running her hand through her short blond hair. It was standing straight up now. Stevie had not gone to get her hair cut since she had arrived at Ellingham in early September. She had cut it a bit, once, in the bathroom at two in the morning, but lost her vision halfway through. What she had now was an overgrown crop that hung over one eye more than the other and often went right toward the sky like the quiff of an alert cockatoo. She had bitten her nails down to the quick, and even though the school had a laundry service, she wore the same unwashed hoodie almost every day. She was losing track of her physical body.

"So what is your plan, then? You just walk around all the time, not eating or talking to anyone?"

"No," she said. "I have to do something. I need more *information*."

"Okay," Nate said, defeated. "Where can you get information that isn't dangerous or misguided?"

Stevie chewed a cuticle thoughtfully. It was a good question.

"Back in the present," Nate said, "Janelle is showing us a

test run of her machine tonight. She's worried that you're not going."

Of course. As Stevie went down these little lanes in her mind, life was going on. Janelle Franklin, her closest friend here and next-door neighbor, had spent all her time at the school building a machine for the Sendel Waxman competition. It was now complete, and she wanted to show her closest friends the test run. Stevie could remember that much through the haze in her mind—*tonight, eight o'clock. Look at machine.*

"Right," she said. "I'm going. Of course. I'm going. I need to think some more now."

"Maybe you need to go home and take a nap, or shower or something? Because I don't think you're okay."

"That's it," she said, snapping up her head. "I'm not okay."

"Wait, what?"

"I need help," she said with a smile. "I need to go talk to someone who loves to be challenged."

February 1936

"It hasn't come, darling," Leonard Holmes Nair said, wiping the tip of his brush on a rag. "We have to be patient."

Iris Ellingham sat in front of him in a wicker chair, usually used in better weather. She shivered under her white mohair coat, but Leo suspected it was not against the cold. It was a relatively mild day for mid-February on the mountain, just warm enough to go outside to work on a painting of the family and the house. Around them, students from the new Ellingham Academy hurried from building to building, bundled in their coats and hats and mittens, arms filled with books. Their chatter broke the once crystalline quiet of the mountain retreat. This palace—the work of architecture and landscaping—this marvel of engineer and human willpower . . . all of it for a school? It was, in Leonard's opinion, like preparing the most divine of feasts and then taking it outside to watch it be devoured by raccoons.

"Surely you have a *little*," Iris said, shifting in her seat. "You always have *something*."

"You need to be careful. You don't want the candy to get the better of you."

"Enough moralizing, Leo. Give me some."

Leo sighed and reached into the deep pocket of his smock and pulled out a small enameled box in the shape of a shoe. Using his nail, he scooped out a pinch of powder into her open palm.

"That really is all of it until I get a delivery," he said. "The good stuff comes from Germany, and that takes time."

She turned her head and sniffed delicately. When she faced him again, her smile was brighter.

"All better," she said.

"I regret introducing you to this." Leo dropped the container back into his pocket. "A little now and then is fine. Use it regularly and it will take you over. I've seen it happen."

"It's something to do," she said, watching the children. "We can't do anything else up here now that we appear to run an orphanage."

"Take it up with your husband."

"I'd have better luck taking it up with the side of the mountain. Whatever Albert wants . . ."

"Albert buys. It's a terrible situation, I'm sure. There are a lot of people who wouldn't mind being in it, to be fair. There is a bit of a national crisis going on."

"I'm aware," she snapped. "But we should be back in New York. I could open a kitchen. I could feed a thousand people a day. Instead, we're doing what? Teaching thirty kids? Half of them are our friends' children. If their parents want to be rid of them, they could send them to any boarding school."

"If I could explain your husband, I would," Leo said. "I'm just the court painter."

"You're an ass."

"Also that. But I'm your ass. Now hold still. Your jawline is exceptionally placed."

Iris held still for a moment, but then she slumped a bit. The powder had begun to relax her. The perfect line was lost.

"Tell me something," she said. "And I know your position on this, but . . . Alice is getting bigger now. At some point, it will be good to know . . ."

"You know better than to ask me that," he replied, dabbing his brush on the palette and swirling a vivid blue into a gray. If Iris was no longer in focus, he could look at some of the stonework along the roof as it melted into the sky. "I gave you something nice. This is no way to repay me."

"I know that, darling. I know. But . . ."

"If Flora wanted you to know who the father was, don't you think she would have told you? And I don't know."

"But she *would* tell you."

"You are testing my friendship," Leo said. "Don't ask me to give you things I can't give."

"I'm done for the day," she said, pulling out her silver cigarette case. "I'm going inside for a hot bath."

She stood, sweeping her coat around her as she strode across the top of the green to the front door. Leo had given her the powder to help alleviate her boredom—small doses, now and again, the same small doses he took. Recently, he had noticed her behavior was changing; she was fickle, impatient, secretive. She was getting more from somewhere, taking it often, and getting anxious when there was none around. She was becoming hooked. Albert had no idea, of course. That was so much of the problem. Albert ran his kingdom and entertained himself, and Iris spiraled, having too little to occupy her agile mind.

Perhaps he could get back to New York. He and Flora and Iris and Alice. It was the only sensible thing to do. Get her back to a place that stimulated her, get her to a good doctor he knew on Fifth Avenue who fixed these kinds of problems.

Albert would balk. He couldn't stand to be away from Iris and Alice. Even a night was too much. His devotion to his wife and child was admirable. Most men in Albert's position had dozens of affairs, mistresses in every city. Albert seemed loyal, which meant he probably only had one. Perhaps she was in Burlington.

Leo looked up at the subject in front of him, the brooding house with the curtain of stone rising behind it. The late-February afternoon sun was a white lavender, the bare trees etching themselves on the horizon, looking like the exposed circulatory systems of massive, mysterious creatures. He touched the paint to the canvas and drew back. The three figures in the painting stared at him expectantly. There was something wrong, something incomprehensible about this subject.

There is the mistaken notion that wealth makes people

content. It does the opposite, generally. It stirs a hunger in many—and no matter what they eat, they will never be full. A hole opens somewhere. Leo saw it all in a flash in that dying sunset, in the faces of his subjects and the color of the horizon. He examined his palette for a moment, concentrating on the Prussian blue and how he might make a ruinous sky of it.

"Mr. Holmes Nair?"

Two students had approached Leonard while he was staring at the painting, a boy and a girl. The boy was beautiful—his hair genuinely golden, a color poets wrote about but rarely saw. The girl had a smile like a dangerous question. The first thing that struck Leo was how alive they looked. In contrast to the surroundings, they were bright and flushed. They even had traces of sweat at the brow lines and under the eyes. The slight confusion of the clothes. The errant hair.

They had been up to something, and they didn't mind that it showed.

"You're Leonard Holmes Nair, aren't you?" the boy said.

"I am," Leo said.

"I saw your Orpheus One show in New York last year. I liked it very much, even more than Hercules."

The boy had taste.

"You are interested in art?" Leo said.

"I am a poet."

Leo approved of poets, generally, but it was very important not to let them get started on the subject of their work if you wanted to continue enjoying poetry.

"Would you mind very much if I took your photograph?" the boy asked.

"I suppose not," Leo said, sighing.

As the boy raised his camera, Leo regarded his companion. The boy was pretty; the girl was interesting. Her eyes were fiercely intelligent. She had a notebook closely clutched to her chest in a way that suggested that whatever was in it was precious and probably against some rules. His painter's eye and his deviant soul told him the girl was the one to watch of this pair. If there were students like those two at Ellingham Academy, perhaps the experiment was not a total waste.

"Are you also a poet?" Leo asked the girl politely.

"Absolutely not," she replied. "I like some poems. I like Dorothy Parker."

"I'm glad to hear it. I'm a friend of Dorothy's."

The boy was fiddling with the camera. It was one thing waiting for Cecil Beaton or Man Ray to find the right angle, but quite another to wait for this boy, however good his taste. The girl seemed to sense this and lose patience as well.

"Take it, Eddie," she said.

The boy immediately took the photo.

"I don't mean to be rude," Leo said, intending to be as rude as he wished, "but I am losing the light."

"Come on, Eddie, we better get back," the girl said, smiling at Leo. "Thank you very much, Mr. Nair."

The two continued on their way, the boy going one direction, and the girl another. Leo's gaze followed the girl for a moment as she hurried toward the small building called Minerva House. He made a mental note to tell Dorothy about her, which he promptly misplaced on a cluttered side table in his mind. He rubbed between his eyes with his oil-cloth. He had lost his vision of the house and its secrets. The moment was gone.

"Now is the cocktail hour," he said. "That's quite enough for today."

2

"I WANT TO TALK ABOUT HOW I'M DOING," STEVIE LIED.

Stevie sat in front of the massive desk that took up a large part of this room, one of the loveliest in the Great House. Originally, it had been Iris Ellingham's dressing room. The dove-gray silk still hung on the walls. It matched the color of the sky. But instead of a bed and dressing tables, the room was now stuffed with bookcases, floor to ceiling.

She was trying not to look directly at the person behind the desk, the one in the Iron Man T-shirt and fitted sports coat, the one with the stylish glasses and flop of blond-gray hair. So she focused instead on the picture between the windows, the framed print on the wall. She knew it well. It was the illustrated map of Ellingham Academy. It was printed in all the admission materials. You could buy a poster of it. It was one of those things that was always around and you never thought about. It wasn't super accurate—it was more of an artistic rendering. The buildings were massive, for a start, and highly embellished. She had heard that it had been done by a former student, someone who went on to illustrate children's books. This was the illusion of Ellingham Academy—the gentle picture painted for the world.

"I'm really glad you came up to talk to me," Charles said.

Stevie believed this. After all, everything about Charles suggested that he wanted to be fun and relatable, from the signs on his office door that read, QUESTION EVERYTHING; I REJECT YOUR REALITY AND SUBSTITUTE MY OWN, and the big, homemade one in the middle that read, CHALLENGE ME. There were also the Funko Pop! figurines that cluttered Iris Ellingham's windowsills, next to pictures of what Stevie assumed were Charles's rowing teams at Cambridge and Harvard. Because, no matter how bouncy and earnest Charles was, he was highly qualified. Every faculty member at Ellingham was. They came, dripping degrees and accolades and experience, to teach on the mountain.

The thing was, she had not come here to talk about her feelings. Some people were fine with that—they could open up in front of anyone and pour out their business. Stevie would rather eat bees than share her tender inner being with anyone else—she didn't even want to share it with herself. So she had to walk the fine line between seeming vulnerable and showing emotion in front of Charles, because displaying real emotion would be gross. Stevie didn't cry, and she double didn't cry in front of teachers.

"I'm trying to . . . process," she said.

Charles nodded. *Process* was a good word, the kind that

someone who *administrated* as a profession could hook into and work with—and it was clinical enough to keep Stevie from gagging.

"Stevie," he said. "I hardly know what to say anymore. There's been so much sadness here this year. So much of it has touched you in some way. You've been remarkably strong. You don't have to be. That's what you need to remember. There's no need to be brave."

The words almost penetrated. She didn't want to be brave anymore. It was exhausting. Anxiety crawled under her skin all the time, like some alien creature that might burst through at any moment. Stevie became aware of the loud ticking in the room. She turned toward the mantel, where a large green marble clock sat. The clock had formerly been downstairs, in Albert Ellingham's office. It was a fine, clearly valuable specimen, deep forest in color, with veins of gold. The story was that the clock had belonged to Marie Antoinette. Was it just a story? Or, like so many things here, was it the unlikely truth?

Now that Charles was primed and listening, it was time for Stevie to get the thing she came for—information.

"Can I ask you something?" she said.

"Of course."

She stared at the green clock as its delicate, ancient hands moved perfectly around its face. "It's about Albert Ellingham," she said.

"You probably know more about him than I do."

"It's about something in his will. There are rumors that there's something in there, something that says that if someone found Alice they'd get all the money. Or a lot of money. A reward fund. And if she wasn't found, the money would come to the school. I always thought this was a rumor . . . but Dr. Fenton believed it. You're on the board, right? You would know. And isn't there something about the school getting more money soon?"

Charles tipped back in his chair and set his hand on his head.

"I don't want to speak ill of anyone," he said, "especially someone who is recently deceased under such tragic circumstances, but it seems like Dr. Fenton had some issues we weren't entirely aware of."

"She had a drinking problem. It doesn't make her wrong."

"No," he said, nodding in acknowledgment of this. "There is nothing in the will about any kind of reward if Alice is found. There are some funds that would have gone to Alice had she been alive. Those funds will be released. That's how we're building the art barn and some other new buildings."

It was so plain and simple. Like that, Fenton's far-fetched notions seemed to go up in smoke.

Like Fenton's house.

"Now can I ask you about something?" he said. "David Eastman went to Burlington and didn't come back to campus. I didn't want to get you involved in this. You've been through enough. But David's father . . ."

"Is Senator King."

"I assumed you knew," he said, nodding soberly. "It's something we keep very quiet around here. There are security reasons—a senator's son requires a certain level of protection. And this senator . . ."

"Is a monster," Stevie said.

"Is someone with very polarizing political beliefs that not all of us agree with. But you said it better."

Stevie and Charles shared a half smile.

"I'm confiding in you, Stevie. I know Senator King was involved in your return to the school. I can't imagine you enjoyed that very much."

"He came to my house."

"You are close to David?" he asked.

"We're . . ."

She could picture every moment of it. The way they had first kissed. Rolling on the floor of her room. The time the two of them had been in the tunnel. The feel of his curls between her fingers. His body, lean and strong and warm and . . .

"He's my housemate," she said.

"And you have no idea where he is?"

"No," she said. Which was true. She had no idea. He had not returned her texts. "He's not . . . chatty."

"I'll tell you honestly, we're on the edge here, Stevie. If one more thing happens, I don't know how we keep the doors open. So if he does contact you, would you consider telling me?"

It was a fair request, reasonably made. She nodded.

"Thanks," he said. "You know that Dr. Fenton had a nephew? He's a student at the university, and he lived with her."

"Hunter," Stevie replied.

"Well, he has no home now. So admin has decided that, since Dr. Fenton was advising one of our students and had such an interest in Ellingham, he can stay here until he gets a new place to live. And since your house is emptier than normal..."

This was true. The place rattled and creaked at night now that half its residents were missing or dead.

"He'll drive to campus when he needs to. But it seemed like the least we could do as a school. We made the offer, and he accepted. I think, like his aunt, he has an interest in this place."

"When is he coming?"

"Tomorrow, when he's discharged from the hospital. He's doing fine, but they kept him for observation and so the police could speak to him. He lost all his things in the fire, so the school is helping out to get him some basics. I've had to cancel trips to Burlington because of David, but I could authorize a trip to have you get him some things he'll need? I imagine you might be better at picking out things he might like than someone old like me."

He opened up his wallet and removed a credit card, which he passed over to her.

"He needs a new coat, some boots, and some warm things, like fleeces and socks and slippers. Try to keep it under a thousand. I can have someone from security take you to L.L. Bean, and you can have an hour in town. Do you think a trip to town might help you?"

"Definitely," Stevie said. This was an unexpected and very welcome turn of events. Maybe opening up was the way to go.

The moment Stevie was outside, she pulled out her phone and texted a message.

Coming to Burlington. Can you come meet me?

The reply came quickly.

Where and when?

It was time to get some real information.

3

BURLINGTON, VERMONT, IS A SMALL CITY, PERCHED ABOVE LAKE Champlain, a body of water that stretches between Vermont and New York. The lake is picturesque and vast, flowing up toward Canada. In better weather, there is sailing. Indeed, it was on this body of water that Albert Ellingham had taken his fatal sailing trip. The city around it was once serious and industrial; in recent years, it had a more artistic bent. There were studios, lots of yoga and new age shops. Everywhere there were hints of winter sports. This was especially true at the massive L.L. Bean, and its stock of snow shoes, snow-poking sticks, massive jackets, skis, and big boots radiated the message: *"Vermont! You won't believe how cold it gets here! It's messed up!"*

Stevie was deposited in front of the store, clutching the credit card she had been handed an hour or so before. It was more than a bit weird to be shopping for a guy she only sort of knew. Hunter was nice enough. He lived with his aunt while he went to college. He studied environmental science. He was fair-haired and freckled and was actually interested in the

Ellingham case. Maybe not as much as Stevie or his aunt, but enough. He had even allowed Stevie to look through some of his aunt's files. Stevie hadn't seen that much, but she had gotten the hint about the wire recording from them.

The rest, now, were literally up in smoke. All of Fenton's work, whatever she had gathered, whatever she knew.

Anyway, Stevie had to quickly buy some stuff for a guy she barely knew. Charles had given her a short list with sizes, leading with a coat. There was no shortage of black coats, all of them costing way more than Stevie had ever spent on anything. After a confused moment of going from rack to rack, looking at the prices and fills and temperature ratings, she grabbed the first one on the end. Slippers always seemed like kind of a nonsense item until she came to Ellingham and felt the bathroom floor on the first proper day of wintry weather. Once skin touched tile and part of her soul died, she knew what slippers were for. She grabbed some fuzzy-lined ones that sort of looked like shoes and had nonslip bottoms— Hunter used walking aids sometimes because of his arthritis, so having traction would be safer. She took the whole pile to the register, where a friendly clerk tried to talk to her about skiing and the weather, and Stevie stared blankly until the transaction was over. Fifteen minutes and several hundred dollars later, she walked out the door with an oversized bag that banged against her knees as she walked. She had little time to do what she had come to do.

Even though it was only late afternoon, the streetlights of Burlington winked to life. There were holiday lights strung over the pedestrianized Church Street. Street vendors sold hot cider and maple popcorn. There were dogs everywhere, pulling their owners along. Stevie cut a path through the crowds to her destination—a cheerful little coffee shop next to one of the street's many yoga and outdoor shops. Larry was already there when she arrived, sitting by himself at a table in his red-and-black-checked flannel coat, his expression like stone.

Larry, or to use his full name, Security Larry, was the former head of security at Ellingham Academy. He had been let go following the discovery of Ellie's body in the basement of the Great House. What happened to Ellie was certainly no fault of Larry's, but someone had to pay. In his previous life, before Ellingham, Larry had been a homicide detective. Now he was unemployed but looking stern and sharp. He had no drink in front of him. Larry, Stevie surmised, was a man who had never paid over two dollars for a cup of coffee and wasn't about to start now. Stevie felt self-conscious taking up the table and not buying anything, so she went to the counter and got the cheapest coffee they had—plain black in a plain mug, no foams or nonsense.

"So," he said as she sat down. "Dr. Fenton."

"Yeah."

"You okay?"

Stevie didn't like black coffee, but she sipped it anyway. Occasions like this called for bitter, hot drinks you didn't necessarily like. You just had to be awake.

"I didn't know her well," she said after a moment. "We

only met a few times. What happened? I know you have to know something."

Larry inhaled loudly and rubbed at his chin.

"Fire started in the kitchen," he said. "It seems that one of the gas burners on the stove was partially turned. The room was full of gas, she lights a cigarette . . . they said the kitchen went up in a fireball. It was bad."

Larry did not soft-pedal anything.

"It would have been hard not to notice a thing like that," he said, "but Dr. Fenton had a known problem with alcohol. From the amount of empty bottles found on the front porch, this was still an issue."

"Hunter told me that," Stevie said. "And I saw the bottles. Plus, she said the smoking killed her sense of smell. Her house stank. She couldn't smell it."

"The nephew was lucky. He was upstairs, on the other side of the house. He came down when he smelled smoke. The flames were spreading through the first floor. He tried to get into the kitchen, but it wasn't possible. He got some burns, inhaled some smoke. He stumbled outside and collapsed. Poor kid. Could have been worse, but . . ."

They sat in silence for a moment, the awfulness settling in.

"She had cats," Stevie said. "Are they okay?"

"The cats were found. They went out through a flap."

"That's good," Stevie said, nodding. "It's . . . not good. I mean . . . it's good about the cats. It's not . . ."

"I know what you meant," Larry said. He leaned back

in the booth, folded his arms, and regarded her with the icy stare that must have freaked out suspects for two decades.

"Luck only holds out for so long," he finally said. "Three people are now dead—Hayes Major and Element Walker up at the school, and now Dr. Fenton. Three people associated with Ellingham. Three people you know. Three people in as many months. That's a lot of death, Stevie. I'm going to ask you something again: Would you consider leaving Ellingham?"

Stevie stared down at the oily, swirly sheen on the top of her coffee. The people a few tables over were laughing too loudly. The words were there, on the tip of her tongue. *I solved it. I solved the crime of the century. I know who did it.* The words came close to the opening of her mouth, touched the back of her teeth, then . . . they retreated.

Because this was not something you said out loud. You didn't tell someone in law enforcement that you knew who committed one of the most infamous murders in American history because you found an old recording and had some strong hunches. That's how you blew your credibility.

"What is it?" he asked. "What aren't you telling me?"

Since she was going to keep her biggest piece of information to herself, she looked around for the next available offering, something worthwhile. Her mind seized on the closest bit of information and shoved it forward before she could consider whether she wanted to share.

"David," she said. "He got himself beat up. He left."

"I saw the video," he said.

"You did?"

"I have a phone," he replied. "I'm old but follow along with things related to Ellingham. What do you mean *got himself* beaten up? And left?"

"I mean," she said, "he paid some skaters to do it. He filmed it. He uploaded it himself, right there and then. I was there. I saw it happen."

Larry pinched his nose thoughtfully.

"So you're telling me he got himself beaten up and uploaded the video right then?"

"Yes."

"And took off into Burlington."

"Yes."

"You mean just as Dr. Fenton's house burned down."

"Those things don't go together," she said. "He didn't even know Dr. Fenton."

Even as she said the words, something occurred to her. Had she not been so preoccupied, she would have put it together before. While David did not know Dr. Fenton, he had just met her nephew, Hunter. Hunter and Stevie were walking together. *You work fast*, he'd said. *Your new buddy. I'm very happy for you both. When will you be announcing the big day?*

Was David jealous? Enough to . . . burn down Hunter's house?

No. The way he'd said it was so flat, like he felt like he had to be sarcastic. Right?

Larry put on his reading glasses and got out his phone. He watched the video of David, freezing it at the end.

"Stevie," Larry said, holding up a shot of David's bleeding face, "someone willing—as you're telling me—to pay some-one to do this to him and then put the footage up online is capable of lots of things. The King . . ."

He lowered his voice quickly.

". . . that *family*, there's trouble there."

"He did that"—Stevie pointed at the phone—"to get at his dad."

"You're not helping his case," Larry said. "Look, I feel for the kid. He's not all bad. I think the dad's the problem. But he always acted out. I know he was good friends with Element Walker. I bet he took it hard when she turned up dead and he found the body. That does something to a person."

It had. David had broken down completely, and Stevie, unable to process what was happening, had freaked out. She'd let him down because she could not handle it all. Guilt crept around the edges of everything—the taste of the coffee and the smell of the room and the cold coming from the window. Guilt and paranoia. She felt the thrumming in her chest, the engine of anxiety rumbling, making itself known.

"Do you have any idea where he might be?"

She shook her head.

"Have you been in touch?"

She shook it again.

"You willing to show me your phone and prove it?" he asked.

"It's the truth."

"You need to promise something to me right now—if he

gets in touch, you tell me. I'm not saying he had anything to do with the fire—I'm saying he could be a danger to himself."

"Yeah," Stevie said. "I promise."

The room was starting to throb a bit, the edges of things jumping out in her vision. There was a panic attack just under the surface, and it would arrive quickly. She surreptitiously reached into her bag, grabbing at her key ring. She kept a little screw-top vial on it. She got this off with a shaking hand and poured the contents into her palm under the table. One emergency Ativan, always there if needed. Breathe, *Stevie. In for four, hold for seven, out for eight.*

"I need to get back," she said, getting up.

"Stevie," Larry said. "Promise me you'll be careful."

He didn't need to say what it was she needed to be careful about. It was everything and nothing. It was the specter in the woods. It was the creak of the floors. It was whatever was underneath all these accidents.

"I'll keep in touch," she said. "I'll tell you if I hear from him. I promise. I just have to use the bathroom."

She grabbed the bag and stumbled back toward the restrooms. Once inside, she popped the pill into her mouth and stuck her face under the faucet for a swig of water. She stood up, wiped the dripping water from her mouth, and looked at her pale face. The room throbbed. The pill wouldn't work immediately, but it would work soon.

She left the bathroom but waited in the hallway for Larry to leave. As she waited, her eyes ran across the community bulletin board, with its cards for yoga instructors, massage therapists, music lessons, pottery classes. She was about to turn and leave when something about the blue flyer at the bottom right caught her eye. She stopped and read it more carefully:

BURLINGTON CABARET VON DADA DADA
DADA DADA
Come see nothing. Have a noise. Dancing is mandatory
and forbidden. Everything is yum.
Burlington Art Collective Action House
Every Saturday night, 9:00 p.m.
You are the ticket

There was a picture of a person painted gold and blue playing a violin with a carving knife, another person with cardboard boxes on their feet and fists, and, in the background, holding a saxophone . . .

Was Ellie.

April 4, 1936

ELLINGHAM ACADEMY WAS RICH IN DYNAMITE.

There were boxes of it piled high, beautiful, dull beige sticks with warnings on the side. Dynamite to blast rocks and flatten mountain surfaces. Dynamite for tunnels. Dynamite ruled her heart. Not Eddie. Dynamite.

When she'd first arrived, Albert Ellingham teased her with a stick and then laughed at her interest. After that, Francis kept watch. There was less of it now that most of the campus was built, but every once in a while she would hear a workman say the word, and then she would trail along behind him. It was during one of these walks that she heard someone inquire about what to do with some bits of wood.

"Throw them down the hole," his coworker replied.

She watched as the man went over to a statue. A moment later, he sat on the ground and was lowering himself into an opening.

Francis immediately investigated when the coast was clear. It took her some time to work out where the man had gone. Just under the statue, there was a bit of rock. This, she was sure, was a hatch in disguise. It took her some time to work out how it opened—Albert Ellingham liked his games and architectural jokes. She found it and the rock dropped, revealing an opening and a wooden ladder to aid her descent.

The space she entered had the look of an unfinished project—much like the time Francis's mother decided she wanted a music room before she remembered that she neither played nor particularly liked music. The half-finished idea, the first blows of the chisel before the sculptor decided that the subject and the stone were not to their liking . . . rich people did this. They left things unmade.

This project was grander in scale than her mother's music room. The first part of the space was hollowed out and walled up in rough rock to look like a cave. This space narrowed at the end and turned. There was a rough doorway made of rock. Once she passed through this, she found herself in an underground wonderland—a grotto. There was a vast ditch dug out, about six feet deep. Inside of this there were bags of concrete and piles of brick waiting to be used. Along the back wall was a fresco, that Eddie would later identify as being a painting of the Valkyrie. In the far corner, there was a boat in the shape of a swan, painted in gold and red and green, which was tipped over on its side. Half-constructed stalagmites and stalactites lined the area, so it looked like a mouth full of broken teeth. There was garbage strewn about the place—beer bottles, broken shovels, cigarette packs.

For months, the rock had been frozen over, but now the ground was yielding and Francis could introduce Eddie to the lair. They slipped into the grotto several times a week to go about their secret activities. There were the physical ones, of course; the grotto's privacy was also very useful when working on their plan.

On the day they decided to leave Ellingham for good, it would be Eddie's job to get the guns. Shotguns were easy to get—there were loads of them stored around the school. Francis would see to the dynamite. They would steal a car from the garage behind the Great House to make their initial escape, but they would quickly get a new one in Burlington. They got maps and spread them out on the ground of the grotto, plotting their route out of Vermont. They would go south through New York, Pennsylvania, West Virginia, Kentucky . . . cut through coal country. Start with small towns. Get in at night—blow the safe. No bloodshed if they could avoid it. Keep going until they got to California, and then . . .

. . . jump off, maybe. Even Bonnie and Clyde hit the end of the road down there in Louisiana, when the cops ambushed and filled their Ford Deluxe with bullets until it was more hole than car. Bonnie and Clyde got it. They were poets, Eddie said, and they wrote with bullets.

All of this planning went into Francis's diary: possible routes, homemade explosives, tricks she learned from reading true-crime magazines.

On this April afternoon, Francis and Eddie had come down into their secret place once more. Eddie set up a ring of candles on the ground and drew a pentagram in the dirt. He was always doing things like that—playing at paganism. This

47

affectation annoyed Francis; this was a hideout, not some kind of subterranean temple. But Eddie had to have his fun if she wanted to have hers, so she tolerated it.

"Today," she said, setting down a bag of supplies, "we play."

"Oh. I like that." Eddie rolled himself flat on the ground in the circle and pulled up his shirt a bit. "What game did you have in mind?"

"Today we're playing Let's Scare Albert Ellingham."

"Oh?" Eddie pushed up to his elbows. "Not what I was expecting, but I'm listening."

"He was rude to me," Francis said. "When he showed me the dynamite. He laughed at me, as if I couldn't handle explosives because I'm a girl. So we're going to have a little fun with him. We'll make him a riddle. He likes riddles. Only one like this."

Francis reached into the bag and produced a pile of magazines. She pulled one off the top called *Real Detective Stories* and opened to a page with a folded corner with a picture of a ransom note made of cutout letters. Eddie rolled onto his stomach to examine the magazine.

"A poem," he said.

"A warning in the form of a poem."

"All good poems are warnings," he said. (Francis resisted an eyeroll.) "We could start it, *Riddle, riddle, time for fun . . .*"

Francis got out her notebook and wrote this down. *Riddle, riddle, time for fun.* A perfect start. Eddie was good at this sort of thing.

"Then we could do something like Dorothy Parker's poem 'Resumé,'" Eddie went on. "It's a list of ways to die. We could do ways to kill."

"Shall we use a rope or gun?" Francis offered.

Lines were added . . . *Knives are sharp and gleam so pretty* . . . *Poison's slow, which is a pity* . . . Ropes, car crashes, broken heads . . . The signature: *Truly, Devious*, that was both of them.

Then the second part began. She spread out the magazines and newspapers on the ground. She had collected them for weeks, pulling things out of the garbage, taking items from the library, snatching them from Gertie—*Photoplay*, *Movie News*, the *Times*, *Life*, the *New Yorker*. She removed the sewing scissors she had stolen from her mother's maid while she was home at Christmas and a pair of tweezers. The paper and the envelope were from Woolworth. Magazines, scissors, paper, glue. Such simple, benign things.

They worked carefully, clipping each letter and word, dabbing it with glue, placing it just so on the page. It took several hours to find the right letters, to place them at the right angles. Francis insisted they wear gloves. It was unlikely the letter would be fingerprinted, but it was sensible to take precautions.

When it was done, they left it to dry and harden, and they busied themselves with each other, the thrill of the work pushing them on. There were certainly other couples who had had sex on the Ellingham campus—one or two. Those people did it giddy, bashfully, and wracked with terror. Eddie and Francis came to each other without fear or hesitation. When your future plan is a crime spree, getting caught together is of no concern, and the hideout was literally underground, under a rock. There was nowhere more private.

When they were finished and sweating, Francis picked up her clothes and shook them out before dressing.

"It's time to go," she said.

"I refuse."

"Get up."

Eddie got up. He was reluctant, but he did as Francis said.

When she was finished dressing, Francis repacked the supplies. Then, after putting on gloves, she folded the piece of paper.

"I have someone to mail it for us," she said, lowering it gingerly into the envelope. "It will be postmarked from Burlington."

"How will we know he got it?"

"He'll probably tell Nelson. He tells her everything. Speaking of, I have to get back now. Nelson always has her eyes on me. She doesn't trust me."

"She's right not to."

The pair reemerged into the daylight. Francis blinked and looked at her watch.

"We're late," she said. "Nelson will be after me. We'd better hurry."

"Once more," Eddie said, grabbing her at the waist, "up against the tree, like an animal."

"Eddie . . ." It was tempting, but Francis pushed him back. He growled a bit and gave play chase. Francis rushed ahead, laughing, gripping her supplies tight under her arm. The air was full and fresh. Everything was coming together. Soon they would be gone from here, she and Eddie, on their adventure. Away from New York, away from society—toward the road, toward freedom, toward madness and passion, where the kissing would never stop and the guns would blaze.

Once they were back in the more populated part of the campus, Eddie peeled off to greet some boys from his house. Francis continued on to Minerva. While there was more equality here at Ellingham than most places, there were still more rules for the girls. They had to come back earlier to rest, to read, to prepare themselves for dinner.

Francis pushed open the house door and found Miss Nelson sitting primly on the sofa, a large book on her lap. Gertie van Coevorden was there as well, smiling her idiotic smile and reading a movie magazine, the only reading she ever seemed to do. If Gertie van Coevorden had two brain cells, each would be amazed to know of the other's existence. She did, however, have an uncanny sense of when someone else was going to get in trouble, and she made sure to be there to see.

"You're a bit late, aren't you, Francis?" Miss Nelson said as a greeting.

"Sorry, Miss Nelson," Francis said, sounding not sorry at all. She was physically incapable of sounding sorry about anything. "I lost track of time at the library."

"The library is a much dirtier place than I recall. You have leaves in your hair."

"I read outside for a bit," Francis said, brushing her hand lightly over her head. "I'll go wash up for dinner."

She shot Gertie a look as she passed, one that suggested that Gertie better wipe that smirk off her face if she wanted to keep all of her glossy blond hair. Gertie immediately turned back to her magazine.

In the safety of her room, Francis set her things down on her bed. While Albert Ellingham had furnished the rooms well, the furniture was plain. Francis's family had sent her to school with an entire van of personal furnishings—bedding from Bergdorf, a silk dressing screen, fur rugs, tall mirrors, a French chifforobe, a small glass-and-walnut cabinet for makeup and bath oil, a silver dresser set and a dresser to go under it. Her curtains were handmade, as was the lace bed ruffle. She pulled off her coat and tossed it onto her rocking chair and regarded herself in the mirror. Sweaty. Dirty. Her blouse creased all over and the buttons all wrong. It could not have been clearer what she had been doing.

It pleased her. Let them see.

She turned back to the items on the bed. She made sure the magazines were all stashed in the paper bag. She would burn them later. She shoved this under the bed. The notebook was the important thing. It always had to be secured. She scanned their afternoon's work, reading through the riddle with satisfaction and checking the envelope that she had tucked between the pages. But something . . . something was missing. She flipped through the book in a panic.

"Francis!" Miss Nelson called.

"Coming!"

More frantic flipping. Her photographs were in this book. The ones Eddie took of them posing as Bonnie and Clyde. Their secret images. They had come loose from their photo corners and were gone. They must have fallen out in the woods when she ran. Damnable, stupid Eddie! This was why she needed to be in charge. He had no discipline. When you rush, you make mistakes.

"Francis!"

"Yes!" Francis shot back.

There was no time now. She opened the closet door and got down on the floor and pulled back a bit of molding. She shoved the notebook into its place inside the wall and pushed the piece of wood back. Then she smoothed herself as best she could and went back to face the world.

4

THE BURLINGTON ART COLLECTIVE ACTION HOUSE WAS A TEN-minute walk from the coffee house on Church Street, or a seven-minute race-walk with a giant bag of coats and boots. Stevie was very careful not to check the time, because it would inevitably be too short. She had no clearly articulated reason for going, except that something needed to be done, so the fewer impediments (like practicality and basic self-preservation) the better.

She didn't have to check the house number to know she had arrived in the right place. The Art Collective was in the same general area as Fenton's house—a neighborhood of large Victorians in various states of repair, some owned by the college, some turned into apartments. While the basic size, shape, and style of the Art Collective house matched that of its neighbors, everything else singled it out. The house was painted in a deep, somewhat dirty lilac, with a sunbeam of purples on the gabled roof. The front porch sagged. A dozen or more mobiles hung from the porch roof beams; these were made of tin cans, broken bits of glass and pottery, rusty cogs and machine parts, and, in one case, rocks. There was a macramé plant hanger that suspended a mannequin head, which spun gently in the wind. The leg part of the mannequin stood alone in the far corner of the porch and was used to support an ashtray. A wooden box by the door contained a snow shovel and cat litter.

Stevie pulled back the screen and knocked on the inner door, which was painted wine red. A shirtless guy in a pair of patchwork pants and a massive knit hat opened it.

"Hi," Stevie said, almost blanking for a moment as she realized that she had come to a very strange house to talk to strange strangers about something she had not clearly defined in her mind. Having no prepared statement, she held up the flyer and pointed at Ellie in the photo.

"Ellie was a friend of mine, and I think she came here. . . ."

The guy said nothing.

"I was wondering if . . . I . . . I just wanted to find out . . ."

He stepped back and held open the door for her to come inside.

The Burlington Art Collective Action House was a big place. One wall was full of bookshelves from floor to ceiling, packed solid with books. There was a small stage in the back, with an old piano and a pile of other instruments. In every direction, there was *stuff*. There were feather boas and top hats, half-formed pieces of pottery, drums, yoga mats, art books, a stray flute sitting in an empty fish tank . . . Off to the side, there was a mattress on the floor with loose bedding; someone called this living area their bedroom. The second floor was open, with a large balcony sealed off with a white wrought-iron rail, from which several painted sheets were hung. The smell of sage lorded over the space.

Also, there was a tree in the house. It didn't seem to be a live tree—rather one that had been cut down and somehow brought into the house whole. It dominated one corner of the first floor and stretched up over the second floor. Stevie had no question in her mind that these were Ellie's friends. This was what the inside of Ellie's head must have been like.

"So, I . . ."

The guy pointed at the second-floor loft. Stevie cocked her head in confusion.

"Should I . . ."

He pointed again.

"Up there?" she asked.

He nodded.

"Go? I should go up there?"

He nodded again and pointed toward a small spiral staircase in the back of the room, then he walked over to one of the walls and went into a headstand. As Stevie climbed the stairs, she noticed there were paper tags hanging from the tree branches with words on them, things like, "Think the sky," and "This isn't the time; this is the time." Upstairs, sitting on a pile of cushions, was a girl. For one moment, Stevie almost mistook her for Ellie. Her hair was in small, matted bunches. She wore a stretched-out T-shirt that read *Withnail and I* and a faded pair of Mickey Mouse leggings. At Stevie's approach, she looked up from her laptop and pushed her headphones off her ears.

"Hey," Stevie said. "Sorry."

"Never say sorry as a greeting," the girl replied.

This was a good point.

"The guy downstairs let me in. He said to come up. Or, he pointed . . ."

"Paul's in a silent phase," the girl said, as if this explained everything.

"Oh. I'm Stevie. I am . . . was . . . a friend of Ellie's. . . ."

Stevie barely had the words out when the girl sprang from the floor and wrapped her in an embrace. The girl smelled of a sweet mix of body odor and incense. Her body was taut from what was probably daily, intensive yoga. It was like being wrapped in a warm, stinky garden hose.

"You came to us! You came! She'd be so happy! You came!"

Stevie had not known what kind of reception she would get in the Art Collective, but this was not on the list of possibles.

"I'm Bath," the girl said, stepping back.

"Bath?"

"Bathsheba. Everyone calls me Bath. Sit. Sit!"

This was weird, because when Stevie first met Ellie, Ellie got into the bath with all her clothes on to dye her outfit pink, probably for this very cabaret. The word *bath* would always remind Stevie of Ellie.

Bath pointed at another pile of cushions on the floor. They looked faded and stained and vaguely bedbuggy, but Stevie sat down anyway. Once on the floor she noticed that almost one entire wall of the upstairs was lined with empty French wine bottles with melted candles in them.

"From Ellie," Bathsheba said, sitting cross-legged on the bare floor. "Of course. French wine. French poetry. German theater. That was my girl."

With these words, Bath broke into tears. Stevie shifted on the cushions and fussed with the bag for a moment.

"I'm glad you came," Bath said as she sniffed and calmed down. "She liked you. She told me all about you. You're the detective."

This made something catch in Stevie's throat. Right from the start, Ellie had taken Stevie seriously when she said she was a detective. Ellie seemed to have so much confidence in Stevie that Stevie had more confidence in herself. Ellie had taken her in, made friends with her from the start, much like Bathsheba was doing now. Now that Stevie was looking at Bathsheba, it occurred to her that Ellie may have copied her look a bit, as well as some of her behaviors.

"How did Ellie end up here?" Stevie asked. "This is part of the university, right?"

"Not part of," Bath said. "Most of us who live here go there. The house is owned by a patron who wants to support local arts. It's an open place for artists. Ellie found us the week after she got to Ellingham. She showed up at the door and said, 'I make art. Are you going to let me in?' And we did, of course."

"I'm here because I'm trying to figure out . . ." Such a rookie mistake. Always have your questions ready. Then again, as a detective, you might not always know who you were going to end up talking to. *So talk*, she thought. *Get talking and the rest will come.* ". . . about Ellie. About what she was like, and . . ."

"She was real," Bath said. "She was Dada. She was spontaneous. She was fun."

"Did Ellie talk to you about Hayes?" Stevie asked.

"No," Bath said, rubbing her eyes. "Hayes is the guy who died, right? That was his name?"

Stevie nodded.

"No. She said she knew him, but that was it. And that she was sad."

"Did she ever mention helping him make a show?"

"She helped make a show? Like a cabaret piece? Hey, did you ever see our cabaret?"

"No, I—"

Bath was already on her laptop and pulling up a video.

"You need to see this," she said. "You'll love it. It's one of Ellie's best performances."

Stevie dutifully watched ten minutes of dark, confusing footage of tuneless saxophone, poetry, handstands, and drumming. Ellie was in there, but it was too dark to really see her.

"So yeah," Bath said as the video ended. "Ellie. I haven't been able to do much since she died. I try to work, but I mostly stay in a lot. I know she would want me to make art about it. I've tried. I'm trying. I don't want to let her down."

Me either, Stevie thought.

"When I think of her . . . ," Bath went on, "how she died. I can't."

Neither could Stevie. The idea of being trapped in the dark, underground, with no one able to hear you—it was too horrible. Her panic must have risen as she felt her way down that pitch-black tunnel and realized there was no way out. At some point, she would have known she was going to die. Stevie was thankful for the Avitan gliding through her bloodstream, holding down the pulsing nausea and air hunger she felt whenever she conjured this image in her mind.

Ellie's death was not her fault. It really wasn't. Right? Stevie had no idea there was a passage in the wall or a tunnel in the basement. Stevie certainly hadn't sealed the tunnel. All Stevie did was lay out the facts of the matter in Hayes's death, and she'd done so in public, in a place that seemed perfectly safe.

Bath had reached over and taken Stevie's hand. The gesture caught Stevie off guard, and she almost recoiled.

"It's good to remember her," Bath said.

"Yeah," Stevie replied, her voice hoarse.

She looked around the room for a new point of focus. What did she see? What information was there? Splattered paint, Christmas lights, a guitar, glitter, some laundry in the corner, canvases stacked against the wall, a load of wine bottles . . .

They had done some partying here. And so had David.

That's right. He'd told Stevie that he used to come to visit Ellie's art friends in Burlington. These were those friends. So maybe these people knew something about where he was? Stevie latched on to this.

"I think another friend of ours came here? David?"

"Not recently," Bath said. "He used to come with Ellie."

"But not recently?"

"No," Bath said. "Not since last year."

So, no leads on Hayes, and no sightings of David. All she had really accomplished was making this girl cry and making herself late.

"Thanks for your time," Stevie said, getting up and shaking out a sleeping leg. "I'm really glad I got to meet you."

"You too," Bath said. "Come back anytime, maybe for cabaret? Or whenever you want. You're welcome."

Stevie nodded her thanks and gathered up her things.

"I'm sorry for all you went through," Bath said as Stevie reached the stairs. "With all this bad stuff. And that thing on your wall."

Stevie stopped and turned back toward Bath.

"My wall?" she repeated.

"Someone put a message on your wall?" Bath said. "That was horrible. Ellie was so pissed about that."

Had Bath said, "By the way, I can turn into a butterfly at will, watch!" Stevie would hardly have been more surprised. The night before Hayes died, Stevie had been woken in the middle of the night to see something glowing on her wall—some kind of riddle, written in the style of the Truly Devious riddle. Stevie felt her body physically tremble, partially at the memory of the strange message that had appeared that night.

"That was a dream," Stevie said, ignoring the fact that her phone was buzzing in her pocket.

"Ellie didn't seem to think it was a dream." Bath leaned back, and her tank top revealed a little casual and confident side boob and armpit hair. "She said she was pissed at the person who did it."

"She knew who *did* it?"

"Yeah, she seemed to."

"I thought . . ." Stevie's mind was racing now. "I thought, if it happened at all, maybe *she* did it? As a joke?"

"Ellie?" Bath shook her head. "No. Definitely no. Absolutely no. Ellie's art was *participatory*," she said. "She never worked with fear. Her art was *consent*. Her art was *welcoming*. She wouldn't put something up in your space, especially if she thought it would scare you or mock you. It wasn't her."

Stevie thought back to Ellie bleating away on Roota, her beloved saxophone. She would not have described the sound as welcoming, but it also wasn't aggressive. It was raw and unschooled. Fun.

"No," Stevie said. "No, I guess it wasn't."

"That thing about the wall is messed up," Bath said. "It's like Belshazzar's feast."

"What?"

"The hand on the wall. You know—the writing? From the Bible. My name is Bathsheba. With a name like mine, you end up reading a lot of Bible stories. There's a big feast and a hand appears on the wall and starts writing something no one can understand."

Stevie's knowledge of the Bible was not tremendous. She'd had some Sunday school classes when she was small, but that was mostly coloring pictures of Jesus and singing along while their Sunday school teacher played "Jesus Loves Me" on the piano. And there was a kid named Nick Philby who liked to eat handfuls of grass and would smile his big green teeth. It was not a complete education. But she had a passing memory of words written on a wall.

"Rembrandt used it as a subject," Bath said, typing something on her laptop. She turned it around to face Stevie. There was an image of a painting—the central figure was a man, leaping up from a table, his face bug-eyed with horror. A hand reached out of a cloud of mist and etched glowing Hebrew characters on the wall.

"The writing on the wall," Bath said.

The phone was buzzing again. Stevie put the shopping bag on top of it to muffle the noise.

"But she didn't say who did it?" Stevie asked.

"No. Just that she was mad that someone was trying to mess with you."

Buzz.

Someone projected a message. It happened. And if it wasn't Ellie, who? Hayes? Lazy Hayes who did nothing on his own? Who else would even care enough about her to want to get her attention like that?

Only David. David could have done it. And now David was gone.

"Yeah," Bathsheba said, nodding to herself. "Ellie always talked about the walls."

"The walls?"

Buzz.

The phone could have stood up and walked over to her at this point. It could have exploded. It would not have mattered.

"Yeah. She said that there was weird shit in the walls at Ellingham. Things and hollow spaces. Stuff. She'd found things. Shit in the walls."

Shit. In. The. Walls.

She had a clue now, a point of focus. *There were things in the walls.* She wasn't sure what that meant, or what she might be looking for. But so much of this had been about walls. Writing on them. Disappearing into them.

And, at some point, a hand *had* written on her wall.

5

THERE IS DARK, AND THEN THERE IS *DARK*. UP ON THE MOUNTAIN, IT was the second kind.

This was something Stevie had to wrap her head around as fall turned to winter at Ellingham. In Pittsburgh, there was always some ambient light somewhere—a streetlight, cars, televisions in other houses. But when you are on top of a rock that is close to the sky, surrounded by woods, the dark wraps around you. This was one of the reasons Ellingham supplied everyone with high-powered flashlights. When you walked around at night, it could get intense. Tonight, the clouds were rolling in, so there were only a few visible stars; there was nothing between Stevie and oblivion as she walked to the art barn. She stayed on the paths, generally, and even felt a little thankful for the eerie blue glow from the security cameras and outposts that Edward King had installed around the place.

It had been a slightly uncomfortable ride back to campus. She had ridden to town with Mark Parsons, the head of grounds and maintenance. Mark was a big, serious man with a square head and a John Deere tractor jacket. He drove an SUV with one of those phone mounts on the dash so he could monitor and reply to a seemingly endless stream of texts about pipes and materials and people coming and going from work. Her lateness had screwed up his day, and she tried to make herself very small and apologetic in the passenger seat.

Stevie got around the lateness by saying that she had to take an emotional moment and walk around Dr. Fenton's neighborhood. Lying like that was gross and weird, but again, these were not normal times. She had to do what was necessary. Much like Rose and Jack at the end of the movie *Titanic*. The door was not a great raft, but when your choices are a door or the deep, cold ocean—you take the door. (Stevie's other big interest, outside of crime, was disaster, so she had seen *Titanic* many times. It was clear to her that there was plenty of room on that door for two people. Jack was murdered.)

So, for the whole twenty-minute trip, Stevie tried to act sad until Mark couldn't take the palpable awkwardness in the car anymore and turned on the radio. There were reports of snow coming. Lots of snow. Blizzards and whiteouts.

"The storm that's coming in a few days is going to be huge," he said as they turned up the steep, winding path through the woods to the school. "One of the biggest in twenty years."

"What happens up here in giant storms?" Stevie said.

"Sometimes the power goes out for a little while," he said, "but that's why we have fireplaces and snowshoes. And that's why I had to go to town for some extra supplies and why I need to get back."

There was an implied *"And now I am late"* at the end of that.

Mark deposited Stevie on the drive, and from there Stevie began her walk to the art barn, where she was due to watch Janelle's test run. She crunched along the path in the dark, walking past the statue heads. There were the night sounds that Stevie had still not come to grips with—the rustling on the ground and above, the hooting of owls—things that suggested that far more happened here at night than during the day. (And yet, Stevie had yet to see the one creature that had been promised in sign after sign along the highway, the ones that read MOOSE. One moose. That's all she wanted. Was that so much to ask? Instead, there were these suggestions of owls, and all Stevie ever heard about the owls was that they liked shiny things and would eat your eyes given half a chance.)

She was so caught up in her swirling thoughts about Ellie and walls and owls and moose that she didn't notice someone coming up behind her on the path.

"Hey," said a voice.

Stevie lurched off the path and spun, half raising her arms in defense. Behind her was a person who looked like they might be part owl—wide, wondering eyes and a sharp, tight expression.

"So," Germaine said, "your adviser died."

Germaine Batt didn't mess around with niceties. Stevie

had a case to solve; Germaine had stories to follow. She got into Ellingham because of her journalism, and her site, *The Batt Report*. *The Batt Report* had gone from a small blog to a medium-sized one on the strength of Germaine's inside stories about the deaths of Hayes Major and Element Walker, and the general bad luck at Ellingham Academy. She, like the owl, hunted in the dark and the shadows, looking for something new that would get her more clicks.

"It was an accident," Stevie said.

"That's what they said about Hayes until you said differently. Lots of stuff happens around you, huh?"

"Around us," Stevie said. "And yeah. Stuff happens."

She continued toward the art barn, and Germaine fell in alongside. Even though she didn't really feel like being pummeled by Germaine's questions, she had to admit, if only to herself, that it was good having company through the woods.

"I heard you're getting a housemate," Germaine said.

"You heard that? Where?"

Germaine shrugged to indicate that sometimes we will simply never know where knowledge comes from. Perhaps the wind.

"Not a student. Some guy."

"His name is Hunter. He was Fenton's nephew."

"Fenton?" Germaine asked.

"That was her name. Dr. Fenton."

"So why is this guy who isn't a student getting to live here?"

"Because the school feels bad," Stevie said.

"Schools feel bad?"

"This school does," Stevie said. "Dr. Fenton wrote a book about this place. And I guess it looks good for us to support the community or something after . . ."

"People keep dying here?" Germaine said.

Stevie let this go and focused on the warm lights of the art barn up ahead.

"You want a story?" she said. "Janelle's going to test-run her machine. Report on that."

"I don't do human interest," Germaine said. "What about David? Everyone's saying he went home for some family thing, but that seems like bullshit. You guys are dating or something, right? Where is he?"

"I thought you just said you don't do human interest," Stevie replied, walking faster.

"I don't. He got beaten up, and now he's gone, and no one really knows where. Here, that can mean something. The last person who just went away ended up dead in the tunnel. So where is he? Do you know?"

"No idea," Stevie said.

"And he was friends with Ellie. Do you think David could be in a tunnel too?"

Stevie tapped her ID on the door panel and pushed her way into the art barn silently, leaving Germaine in the dark.

The workroom in the art barn was now home to a large, strange contraption. Vi was hanging a wooden sign that read "RUBE'S DINER," while Janelle moved around, checking things with a level. Janelle had taken the budget the school had granted her and also raided the castaways from the dining hall to create her machine. The poles had been put into place to make a frame that held gently tipped shelving, on which stacks of plates and cups and been glued into carefully calculated arrangements. There were small tables, deliberately angled chairs with more piles of plates and cups balanced on them. There were several old toasters and a board painted to represent a soda dispenser. Everything was connected by some plastic tubing that looked like the circulatory system of this diner version of a Frankenstein's monster.

Nate looked up from his computer.

"That was a long talk you had," he said.

"I went to Burlington."

"How? They cut off the coaches since David did his beatdown and run."

"Okay!" Janelle said. "I'm ready to start."

Vi came over and sat next to Nate and Stevie. Nate looked at Stevie anxiously, but Stevie turned her attention straight ahead.

"Okay," Janelle said, nervously knotting her hands together. "So I'm going to do my speech and then I'll run the machine. So. Here we go. The point of engineering is to make something complex into something simple. The point of a Rube Goldberg machine is to make something simple into something complex . . ."

"Why?" Nate said.

"For fun," Janelle replied. "Because you can. Don't interrupt. I have to do this. The point of engineering is to make something complex into something simple. The point of a Rube Goldberg machine is to make something simple into something complex. The Rube Goldberg machine started as a comic. Rube Goldberg was a cartoonist who was also an engineer. He created a character called Professor Butts . . . someone's going to laugh at that, right?"

Vi gave a thumbs-up.

"Okay, I'll pause for laughter. A character called Professor Butts, who made ridiculous machines to do things like wipe his mouth with a napkin. People liked the comics so much that Rube Goldberg machines became a feature in his comics and then, later, a regular competition. . . ."

Stevie's mind was already drifting. Was this what murder was? Something simple that became complex?

". . . the dimensions cannot exceed ten feet by ten feet and can use only one hydraulic . . ."

Who put that message on the wall? What was the point of it? Just to mess with her? If Hayes or David had done it and Ellie knew about it, why hadn't she told Stevie?

". . . and this year's challenge is to break an egg."

Janelle delicately placed an egg in a small egg cup on a table by the far wall where a white plastic sheet had been strung up.

"So," Janelle said, returning to the front of the long and winding machine. "Here we go!"

She depressed the lever on one of the toasters, and it popped up a second later, shooting out a piece of plastic bread. This tipped a wooden lever above, which sent a little metal ball rolling down a series of small half-pipes attached to a menu board. The ball kept rolling, continuing over a tray in the hand of a chef figurine. It fell from there, plopping into a bowl on one side of a scale. This raised the opposite side, which triggered the release of another ball.

The machine made so much sense. A seemingly pointless trigger set off the series of events. The ball rolled, knocking each strange little piece into play. *Hayes making a video about the Ellingham case. Janelle's pass being stolen to get the dry ice. The message on the wall. Hayes turning at the last moment on the day they were shooting, saying he had to go back for a minute to do something and never coming back again. Stevie realizing that Ellie had written the show. Ellie running into the walls, then getting into the tunnel and never coming out.*

Another ball was triggered, running down the rims of a stack of cups, which tumbled into the soda dispenser. This began pouring liquid into three plastic pitchers. These weighed something down and . . .

Stevie blinked into alertness as three paintball guns fired off at the same time, all pointing at the egg, which exploded in a blast of red, blue, yellow, and albumen.

Vi screamed in delight and jumped up to embrace Janelle.

"That was pretty good," Nate said.

Stevie nodded absently. Of course, she had missed the event that triggered the gun. She was looking right at *something* but she couldn't see it. *Where do you look for someone who's never really there....*

At some point, the gun placed in act one goes off, usually in the third act.

That was one of the most important parts of being a detective: keep your eye on the gun.

April 4, 1936

DOTTIE EPSTEIN DID NOT MEAN TO START WATCHING FRANCIS AND Eddie that day. She had been minding her business up in the high crook of a tree, bundled in a big brown sweater knitted for her by her aunt Gilda, a book open on her leg. The April weather meant that it was not warm, but the mountain was no longer frozen. You could be free in the space again, and it was good to be in the woods, out in the air. The tree was a perfect place to read, to spend some time with Jason and the Argonauts.

That's where she happened to be, quiet and out of sight, when Francis and Eddie came by. They were close, tight, their heads almost together as they walked. (How did people *walk* like that, heads so close? It was fascinating to see, like something from the circus.) And there was something in the *way* they were walking—silent, smiling, quickly but not fast. It was a walk that suggested they did not want to be noticed.

Unlike the other rich girls, Francis was nice to Dottie. She wasn't like Gertie van Coevorden, who looked at Dottie like she was a walking bag of rags, her eyes lingering on every patch in her clothes. (Dottie's mother had worked so hard on sewing those patches in her coat. "Look, Dot, you can barely see the stitches! Look how good this thread matches up. I got it at Woolworth. Isn't that a good match? I spent all night on it.") Gertie unpicked Dottie's mother's seams, judging her whole family, her entire reason for being in one sweeping glance of her small, blue eyes. "Oh dear, Dottie!" she would say. "You must be so cold in that thing. Wool isn't *quite* as warm as fur. I have an old one I can lend you."

It might have been different if Gertie had actually lent her the fur. But that was part of it. They mentioned things, and they forgot. It was a tease.

Francis, however, was the real kind of nice—she left Dottie alone. That was all Dottie really wanted. When they did talk, which wasn't often, it was about something good, like detective stories. Francis loved to read, almost as much as Dottie did, and her passion was crime. That was, in Dottie's opinion, a noble interest. Francis also liked to sneak about. Dottie heard her moving around at night and would peek out her door to see Francis creeping down the hall, or sometimes going out the window.

It was this quality that caused Dottie to slip out of the tree, almost automatically, and loosely trail them. Perhaps, she thought, it was because of her uncle the policeman. "Sometimes, Dot," he said, "you just know. Follow your instincts."

Francis and Eddie went back, to the raw, wild part of the grounds, where thick tree cover was cut through with only the roughest paths. They wended back to the place where the rocks were still being worked off the face of the mountain. There were massive piles of stone, some of which looked like it was in the process of being broken down into smaller pieces for building materials. The path was extremely uneven, cutting up sharply. Dottie followed, as silently as she could, using the trees to pull herself up the rocky steps. Francis and Eddie were two flashes of color in the landscape, and then—they were gone.

Just like that. Gone. Gone in the trees and the rock and the brush.

Clearly, they had disappeared into one of Mr. Ellingham's little hidey-holes, one Dottie herself had not yet found. She was filled with fear of discovery and the thrill of the mystery in equal measure. She considered going back to her reading spot, but she knew she would not be able to do it. So she backed up a few steps, to a point she knew they could not have vanished into, and tucked herself behind a tree.

She waited there for over two hours. She had actually gotten back into her book when she heard the crunch of their steps and ducked down just in time. They came out, whispering, laughing, hurrying. Francis had a book under her arm.

"Oh God, we're so late," Dottie heard Francis say.

"Once more, up against the tree, like an animal . . ."

"Eddie . . ." Francis pushed him off with a laugh and hurried on. In their sport, a few things fell from Francis's book, small, the size of leaves. Once they had gone, Dottie went to the spot and picked them up. They were photographs. One was of Francis and Eddie posing. Dottie knew what they were doing at once—everyone had seen this pose before. It was like that famous photo of Bonnie and Clyde, the gangsters. Dottie was posed as Bonnie, holding what must have been a toy shotgun (or maybe it was a real shotgun from one of the crew?) directly at Eddie's chest. Her arm was extended toward him, her fingertips not quite touching his shirt. Eddie had a strange half smile and wore a hat tipped back on his head, looking at her with longing. It was so much like the real photograph that the tiny differences stood out in deep relief. They were not Bonnie and Clyde but wanted to be so much that Dottie could feel it.

The other photograph was of Leonard Holmes Nair, the painter, standing on the green, brush in hand, looking perhaps a bit annoyed at the interruption. A painting of the Great House was on the easel in front of him. The photos were a bit sticky. Some glue seemed to be on the edges.

Dottie leaned against the tree and studied the images for several minutes, drinking them in. These shimmering clues into other people's lives—they pointed the way for her. To where, she did not know.

It was time to go. It would be dinner soon. She put the photos in her pocket and hurried home to Minerva. Once inside, she considered slipping them under Francis's door. They belonged to her.

But no. It would be odd to do that. It would give everything away. And for some reason—she needed these for her collection. She went into her room and shut the door, then got down on the floor and pulled back the baseboard.

Francis had told Dottie about using the walls to hide things she didn't want anyone else to see. The molding came back easily. This was where the rich girls kept their gin and cigarettes. Dottie stored her tin there—her collection of the wonderful things she had found. She tucked them away and stashed the tin back into its space.

She would return the photos at some point, she decided. Soon. Maybe before the end of school.

There would always be time.

6

*LAY IT OUT. PUT IT DOWN ON PAPER. WORK IT OUT. WRITE WHAT
you remember. Write your first impression, before your memory gets
a chance to play with it and switch it around, putting a leg where
an arm used to be.*

Stevie opened her desk drawer and pulled out a handful
of off-brand sticky notes (that she'd nabbed from the Edward
King campaign supplies in her parents' home office). Her
wall was currently in use—she had attached several stick-on
hooks, so her coat and clothes hung there. She took these
down and started putting up the notes. The victims from the
1930s, on yellow ones:

Dottie Epstein: head trauma
Iris Ellingham: gunshot
Alice Ellingham: condition unknown

And then, on the other side, people from the present, in
light blue:

Hayes Major: CO_2 poisoning/dry ice
Ellie Walker: exposure/dehydration/immurement
Dr. Irene Fenton: house fire

She sat on the edge of the bed and stared at the six squares, letting her mind go blank and her eyes blurry.

There was a pattern here, something that she wasn't seeing. She got up and looked at the spines of her mystery books. She pulled one from the shelf—Agatha Christie's *The Murder of Roger Ackroyd*. This was a notorious book when it came out, featuring Hercule Poirot as the detective. Poirot's method was to use his "little gray cells" to solve the crime—to sit and think, to contemplate the psychology of the murderer. . . .

Stevie turned back to the wall and looked from note to note, repeating the information in order, lingering on the ones from the present. Dry ice, immurement. Fire. Dry ice had that echo of a locked room mystery, where the weapon is ice and the murderer is never there. Immurement—walling in. Another locked room. Fire, where the weapon is the building itself.

Stevie began to see a line running through these things; it was almost literally visible, like a piece of string on a conspiracy wall. The psychology of the murderer. That was what she was seeing. These two sides weren't just separated by time—they were separated by *separation itself*. Dottie's death had been brutal and direct. Iris had been shot. These were hands-on weapons, with blood, where the assailant had to be there, to stand over the victim. But Hayes, Ellie, and Fenton had all died in contained spaces, where someone could set the trap and walk away. Hayes walked into an underground room full of carbon dioxide. Ellie went into a tunnel and the exit was blocked. Dr. Fenton—well, maybe she did forget the gas and lit a cigarette. But maybe someone had been there with her, talking. Someone turned on the gas and shut the door behind them. Then, Dr. Fenton, nose blind and a confirmed smoker, lit up.

Wind it up and let it go, like Janelle's machine. Depress the toaster lever, and in the end, the gun goes off.

This was someone smart. Someone who planned. Someone who perhaps didn't want to get their hands dirty. And all these things, they were deniable, almost. Hayes walked into that room on his own, not knowing about the sublimated dry ice that had poisoned the space. Ellie crawled into that tunnel on her own. And Fenton lit the fuse that set her own house ablaze. Three things that seemed like accidents, that happened when someone else was nowhere around.

Who was smart? David.

Who played tricks? David.

Who would be able to lift Janelle's pass and get the dry ice? Who knew about tunnels and secret places? Who was in Burlington on the night of the fire? David.

But there was no reason at all that Stevie could see for him to do these things. None. He had no strong feelings about Hayes. Ellie was his friend. Her death devastated him. He had broken down in uncontrollable sobs when he found her. He didn't even know Fenton at all. Unless David was some kind of serial killer who killed for sport, there was no way he did this.

Then who?

And the note on the wall? How did that fit?

What was more frustrating was the fact that Stevie had barely gotten a look at that message on the wall that night. It appeared as she slept. She heard a noise, looked up from her bed, and saw a glowing message. She hadn't written it down because she had first gone to the window to try to see who did it. Then she'd experienced a massive panic attack and gone to Janelle's room. After that, she assumed it was a dream—or tried to convince herself it was, because the truth was too creepy. That was a lot of time for her mind to work, to make things up, but maybe she could recover some of it.

She closed her eyes and let her breathing go even and steady. In for four, hold for seven, out for eight. She let thoughts come and go and kept setting her attention back on the breathing. After several minutes, she opened her eyes a bit and focused on the wall where the message had been, where the sticky notes now were. This blank, unassuming stretch. What had been there?

She resisted the urge to get up and move around. Breathe. In and out. What had she seen that night? It was there, hints of it, somewhere in her mind, like a trace of perfume on the wind. What had it *looked* like?

Cutout letters, ransom-note style, like the Truly Devious letter.

Be more specific, Stevie. How did they look?

Glowing. Large. Some in focus, some not. The light in the window was coming in from an angle, stretching itself, landing on that bit of wall next to the fireplace.

Riddle, riddle, on the wall . . .

Yes, that was the first line. It was easy to remember. This much, she was sure of.

But what happened from there? It had rhymed. It was something with murder. Something murder.

There were images in the message. Bodies. Something about a body in a field. That made sense. A reference to Dottie, who was found half-buried in a bit of farmland. A body in a field . . .

Her mind made noises, tried to lure her this way and that, but she stayed with the bodies. There had been another. A second body. It had to be Iris's, as Iris was the only other body. Yes . . . a lake. A mention of Iris. Something about a lady in a lake.

Now the picture began to assemble itself a bit more clearly. Those cutout letters took on a bit more definition. Murder. Bodies. The message was eerily playful. Something about playing.

Alice, Alice . . .

Alice?

Alice. It had mentioned Alice. By name. What about Alice, she could not recall. But Alice's name was there.

Stevie let her eyes come back into focus and let the meditation go. The light made halos around all the objects in the room as her pupils adjusted. She tucked up her knees and, in doing so, took a better look at herself. She really did need to change. She couldn't go on like this, grabbing clothes off the floor. Maybe a shower would jog her mind into action. She grabbed her bath caddy and dragged herself across the hall, where she slumped against the queasy salmon-colored tiles and let the water run over her, flattening her short hair to her head. She remembered meeting Ellie in the shower once. Ellie walked around proudly naked.

Ellie. Ellie, I'm sorry.

Why was she thinking that? She hadn't hurt Ellie. All she had done was tell the truth about who wrote Hayes's show. But Ellie was gone now. And Hayes. And Fenton. It suddenly didn't seem to matter that she may have put together the pieces of the great Ellingham case. There was something happening right here, right now. Hayes, Ellie, and Fenton—they were linked together somehow. All were dead. Larry was afraid for her.

There was a murderer here.

She wondered if she was afraid. She asked herself the question, and it was surprisingly quiet on the subject.

She turned off the water and let herself shiver, let herself feel.

That message on the wall was someone telling her something. Someone wanted to play with her. So all right. She would play. Maybe she was anxious. Maybe she was untrained. But Stevie Bell knew one thing about herself—once she had bitten in, tasted the mystery—she would not let go. She had gotten herself to this mountain. She could do this. After all, people were doing this all the time now. Citizen detectives, working on cases online, at home, alone and in groups.

She hurried back to her room, and, despite what she had just been thinking about not picking clothes up off the floor, she picked up a pair of sweatpants from the corner of the room. These were pretty clean. Ellingham did your laundry, but you had to put it in labeled bags. Stevie had not been paying enough attention to do that. She made sure to put on an extra thick coat of deodorant. She would smell good, at least. Her hair was now finger-length, sharp blond strands, crisp as wheat. The off-the-shelf bleach was strong stuff. She messed it around with her hands until it landed in basically the right position.

Now she was focused. Now she could . . .

Her phone rang. The number was blocked.

"You were in town today."

The voice wound around her like a snake. It warmed her and chilled her at the same time. It was so close it seemed to come from inside herself.

"Where the hell are you?" she replied.

"So we got the hellos out of the way." Just the sound of David's voice was all Stevie needed to conjure David in his entirety—his curling dark hair, his slightly peaked brows, his ropy, muscled arms, his tattered T-shirts and sagging Yale sweatpants, the busted-up Rolex on his wrist. This reprobate rich boy—the kind of person she thought she would never be able to stand—strange and difficult and maybe a bit self-pitying. Someone who didn't care what the world thought.

Someone funny. Someone dangerous.

"You didn't answer my question," she said, trying to sound even, almost bored, instead of breathless.

"On vacation," he said. "Working on my tan. Doing that thing where you surf with a dog wearing sunglasses."

"David," she said. Even saying the name was hard. It exploded from her mouth. "What is happening? Why did you get yourself beaten up? Are you going to tell me?"

"No."

"*No?*"

"Are you worried about me?" She could hear the smile in his voice, and it both enticed and enraged her.

"No," she said.

"Liar. You are. You are worried about me and my beautiful face. I can understand that. The face is healing. The beating wasn't as bad as it looked. I smeared the blood around."

"What do you want?" she said, her heart racing. "Are you going to tell me what's going on? Or did you call just to be a dick?"

"The second one."

"Seriously . . ."

"Something I should have done a long time ago," he replied. "All further questions should be sent in writing to my lawyer."

Stevie rolled her gaze to the ceiling. To her surprise, tears were forming in her eyes. Of course he was not coming back. Her whole body flooded with feeling. He was the first person she had ever kissed and done . . . other things with. Right here on this floor.

"How did you know I was in town?" she said, coughing out the emotion. "Bathsheba?"

"I have eyes and ears everywhere. I heard about your professor too. Bad shit."

"Yeah," she said. "Bad shit."

"Her house burned down?"

"She left the gas on and lit a cigarette."

"Jesus," he said. "A lot of bad things are happening."

"Yeah, no kidding."

She sat on the floor next to her bed and considered what to say next. Silence pulsed between them.

"So," she said, "what do you want? If you're not coming back. There must be something. Unless you're worried about me."

"You?" he said. "Nothing ever happens to you."

She didn't know what that meant, if it was reassurance or an accusation.

"I'll make you a deal," she said. "I'll be careful if you call me back once a day."

"Can't promise that," he said.

"What, are you in the witness protection program or something? Stop screwing around."

"I'm hanging up so it doesn't get weird," he said.

"Too late for—"

But he was gone. Stevie stared at her phone for a while,

trying to work out what the hell had just happened, only to be startled by an alert that flashed across her phone: BLIZ-ZARD WARNING ISSUED FOR BURLINGTON AND SURROUNDING AREA. STORM DUE TO ARRIVE IN 48 HOURS, ACCUMULATIONS UP TO 24 INCHES EXPECTED.

Stevie put her phone down and kicked it across the floor.

7

At breakfast the next morning, Stevie poked at a freshly made waffle as Janelle typed furiously on her computer. Vi was reading a political science textbook. Nate was consumed by a book with a dragon on the cover.

Stevie should have been reading as well; she had lit class in an hour and was supposed to have read *The Great Gatsby* by now. She had skimmed the first few chapters—something about a rich guy who threw parties and a neighbor who would watch him. She had anatomy later as well, and there was going to be an oral quiz on the skeletal system. Mr. Nelson would be back on the table, and Stevie was supposed to know the names of all his bones. She was six units behind in her self-based math and language work. Schoolwork loomed around behind her, like a big, dumb monster. If she didn't turn around, maybe it wouldn't bother her.

"I sent a school-wide message," Janelle said, snapping her computer shut.

Stevie looked up, and syrup dripped on her hoodie as she did so.

"Huh?" she said.

"I'm doing a demonstration at eight. I'm inviting everyone."

Indeed, even as they sat there, Stevie saw the message come through on some people's phones and computers. Mudge, from across the room, gave her a thumbs-up.

"You know Mudge?" Stevie said.

"Sure. He wants to be an Imagineer and make automatons and robots."

"It's going to be so great!" Vi said. They were dressed that morning in red overalls, with a rainbow half shirt underneath. They had shaved some more from the sides of their silver-blond hair and spiked it high. Vi always looked alert and alive, like they had scored a direct hit off the electrical mains. Maybe that was why they were so good with Janelle. Both lived completely and brightly.

"Have to go," Vi said, picking up their bag. "I'll be late to Mandarin class."

They kissed Janelle on the top of the head and waved to Nate and Stevie. Nate bunched up a napkin and stuck it in his empty juice glass.

"I'd better go too," he said.

"Don't you have a few hours before your first class?" Janelle said.

"Yeah," he replied. "I just want to go back and enjoy having the second floor to myself for a little while before this Hunter dude shows up. Hunter. Is he rugged?"

"He studies environmental science," Stevie replied. "He's nice."

90

"Good," Janelle said. "David's gone, and a nice guy who likes the environment is moving in. Sounds like a good switch to me."

Janelle had never made it a secret that she wasn't fond of David.

"Okay," Vi said. "I'll meet you over there at six and bring you dinner and . . ."

Vi's phone pinged, and they picked it up.

"Oh my God," they said. "Oh God."

"What?" Janelle said.

Stevie's stomach lurched.

Vi held out their phone, revealing a headline that had flashed across the screen: SENATOR EDWARD KING ANNOUNCES PRESIDENTIAL RUN.

"He's running," Vi said. "I knew it. That *dick*."

Stevie had shared the secret with Janelle and Nate—they knew that David was Edward King's son. They both looked at Stevie. Nate grabbed his tray and made a hasty exit.

"Anyway," Vi said, shaking their head. "Six o'clock. I'll bring tacos if they have them."

When they were alone, Janelle ate some fruit salad and looked at Stevie.

"You've been really quiet," she said. "What have you been up to? Ever since we played that recording on that old machine you've been squirrely. And your teacher, the one from Burlington . . . What's going on with you?"

"It's a lot of things," Stevie said. "Do you remember the message that appeared on my wall that night? The dream one?"

"Sure."

"I met a friend of Ellie's in Burlington yesterday. She told me some stuff, like that Ellie knew all about the message and she thought someone put it there. Ellie thought it was real. She may have even *known* it was real."

Janelle drew her head back in surprise.

"But who would do that?" she said. "David?"

"I don't think so," Stevie said. "I mean, the only one who makes any sense at all is Hayes? Because of the video? No one really makes sense for it. But this girl said Ellie was sure it was real and that Ellie knew who did it."

"Well, if we find out," Janelle said, "there will be hell to pay. No one does that to you."

Stevie felt a warm rush. She'd had friends at her old school—people she spoke to and sometimes texted with. But if she was being honest with herself (and she often tried not to be), she'd never really had that IRL connection. Her most real relationships had been with people on her case boards. Ellingham had provided her with that *something*—maybe even the something her parents had talked to her about. Friends who hung out together in pajamas and talked. Friends who listened. Friends who stood up for you.

But she didn't know how to express this or even if she should, so she dipped her waffle piece again.

"Can you look inside of walls?" she asked Janelle.

"Can I personally look inside of walls? I can do anything. But I think you're asking if there is something that can penetrate a wall to show stuff behind it, and the answer is yes. A wall scanner. They're pretty common. They use them to find studs, wires, pipes, things like that. Why?"

"Just . . . wondering."

"Oh! I already got four replies!" Janelle said as her phone pinged. "People are going to come tonight! Oh my God. What if it doesn't work?"

"It works," Stevie said.

"Okay. I have to be calm. I'm going to class, then I'm going to run it a few times. See you there, yeah?"

"Of course," Stevie said.

Janelle grabbed her things and stuffed them into her big orange bag and hurried out. Stevie got *The Great Gatsby* out of her bag and stared at the cover: a midnight-blue background with a woman's face floating in it—a flapper made of light and sky, mostly eyes, with a city dripping in the background like a string of jewels. It was a little like the Ellingham family portrait by Leonard Holmes Nair, the one that hung in the Great House. It was a hallucination of person and place.

Speaking of flappers . . . Maris was just coming into the dining hall. She was wearing a big shaggy coat of fake black fur. Maris had a lot of shaggy, fringy things. She wore lots of darks, smudgy eyeliner and strong lipsticks. Dash was with her in his oversized coat and long scarf.

Maris and Dash were the theater people—Ellingham had only a few, and they were definitely in charge of all things dramatic now that Hayes was gone. It looked like Maris had shaken off some of her gloom after Hayes's death. For a few weeks, she'd walked around like the town widow, wearing black on black with black lipstick, crying in the library and in the dining hall and tending to the impromptu shrine for Hayes that had sprung up in the cupola. It seemed like a lot of mourning for someone you had been dating for about a week, maybe two at the most. Maris had shed the widow's weeds for a yellow dress—a vintage-looking one, which she wore with black fishnet stockings and chunky heels. She was doing blue lipstick now, as she transitioned back to her signature bright red.

On the other side of the dining hall, Stevie saw Gretchen—a pianist with a head of fiery red hair. She had been Hayes's girlfriend last year. Hayes had used her to do his work, to write his papers. He'd even borrowed five hundred dollars from her, which he'd never repaid.

In theory, both Maris and Gretchen would have had something against Hayes. Hayes had screwed Gretchen over in several ways. And Hayes was dating Maris while also having a long-distance relationship with fellow YouTuber Beth Brave. Was that enough to kill? Also, Maris could have helped if Hayes had wanted to project that message on Stevie's wall. Maris was smart. Maris knew theater things, so she would likely have been able to put something together to project a message.

This thing about the message on the wall was nagging at her. What did it even mean? It was a harmless prank at best. Well, not harmless. It had caused her to have a massive panic attack. But in the scheme of things at Ellingham, it was harmless. It had not killed her.

It wasn't the severity of the thing; it was the why. *Why do it?*

She couldn't shake the feeling that if she could figure out the mystery of the hand on the wall, she would understand everything.

Almost all of the incoming class took Dr. Quinn's literature and history seminar, a class in which everyone read a novel and then learned about the historical period and context that surrounded it. *The Great Gatsby* was about the 1920s, a period that vaguely interested Stevie, as it had a lot of good crimes and it butted up against the Ellingham Affair in the 1930s.

"Much is made of the green light at the end of the dock," Dr. Jenny Quinn said. Dr. Quinn was the associate head of the school and a generally terrifying person. She strode around in front of the room. She was dressed in high, glossy pumps, a pencil skirt, and an oversized white blouse that was definitely fancy in a way Stevie could not classify. "Everyone talks about the green light at the end of the dock. But I want to focus on the circumstances around Gatsby's death at the end. About his murder."

Stevie looked up. *The Great Gatsby* was a murder mystery? Why had no one mentioned this before? She looked at her copy of the book in a feverish sweat.

"Stevie," Dr. Quinn said.

Dr. Quinn could smell sweat and fear, probably from at least a mile away if the wind was right. She narrowed her focus to Stevie, who felt her spine shrink under the pressure.

"You're our resident detective. Did you feel that Gatsby's death was expected? How do you feel it served the narrative?"

She had to say something, so she went with what she knew.

"Murders don't normally happen at the end of a book," she said.

"Perhaps not in murder mysteries," Dr. Quinn said. "Otherwise there wouldn't be much for the reader to do. How does the murder function in this story?"

"Can I say something?" Maris said, sticking up her hand.

Stevie felt a wave of gratitude spread over her and in the direction of Maris and her blue lips.

"It's a discussion," Dr. Quinn said noncommittally.

"I felt like his murder was a cop-out."

"How so?"

"I think Gatsby should have had a chance to live through the outcomes," she said. "I mean, Tom—he's a racist and an abuser. He and Daisy, they get to live."

"And Gatsby pays for their misdeeds," Dr. Quinn said. "But what I'm asking is, when do you think Gatsby really died—when the bullet went in, or at some other point in the story?"

It was like all of this was designed to pick at Stevie's brain. When did Hayes actually die? When he decided to follow the path to that room filled with gas? And what about the others? When Ellie first made her way into the tunnel? When Fenton looked at the cigarettes on the table? Everything had been lined up for them by some hand, disembodied as the eyes on the cover of this book . . .

"So what do you say, Stevie?" asked Dr. Quinn.

"I don't know," she said honestly. "I don't know how to tell where it all starts or stops. It's like a loop."

Her answer was sufficiently weird enough to make Dr. Quinn pause and consider her. At first the lingering look predestined a dressing down in front of all her classmates, one that would cause the varnish to drip away from the mahogany bookshelves from the pure shame and embarrassment of it all. But then something changed. Dr. Quinn shifted her weight to her other heel and drummed her manicured hand on the desk. Her examination of Stevie deepened. It felt like Dr. Quinn wanted to pick her apart and examine her clockwork.

"A loop," Dr. Quinn repeated. "Something going around in circles. Something that moves back as it tries to move ahead. Something that returns to the past to find the future."

"Exactly," Stevie blurted out. "You have to make sense of the past to figure out the present, and the future."

Stevie had no concept at all of what Dr. Quinn was saying, but sometimes, quite by accident, you find yourself vibrating on someone else's frequency. You can follow the sense of the thing, if not the literal meaning. Sometimes, this is more important and more informative.

"But are the answers there?" Dr. Quinn said. "That's certainly what Gatsby thought, and look how he ended up. Dead in his pool. Think about this passage, from right before the shot, as his killer approaches: 'He must have looked up at an unfamiliar sky through frightening leaves and shivered as he found what a grotesque thing a rose is and how raw the sunlight was upon the scarcely created grass. A new world, material without being real, where poor ghosts, breathing dreams like air, drifted fortuitously about . . . like that ashen, fantastic figure gliding toward him through the amorphous trees.'"

Even without context as to their meaning, the words hypnotized Stevie. Ghosts breathing dreams like air, a figure of ash moving forward with, if Stevie was following along, a gun. The person seeking meaning in the past ended up dead.

Stevie looked at her teacher, swathed in designer clothes and pedigree. She was a woman who knew a lot of important people, had been offered jobs in presidential administrations—and here she was, teaching *The Great Gatsby* on a mountain. Why turn those things down to teach, to work under Charles, a man she appeared to dislike?

Was Dr. Quinn warning her—sending her a message? Or was Stevie losing her marbles, one by one?

"Read the book next time," Dr. Quinn said, "or you'll be penalized."

Stevie could almost feel the ashen figure at her back.

April 20, 1936

FLORA ROBINSON AND LEONARD HOLMES NAIR STOOD ON THE stone patio outside the ballroom and Albert's office. It had been a week since the phone rang and the world shattered. Albert had spent most of the week in his office with Mackenzie, manning the phones, waiting for news. Nothing had come since the night when he lowered a bag of money off Rock Point, and each day's silence was more ominous.

No one was forcing them to stay, but the outside world was wild and dangerous and full of people who would want to question them, to pick every bit of meat off the bone of the story. So they wandered around the house, smoking and nibbling at the endless platters of sandwiches the kitchen produced for the crowds. Waiting for something to happen. Anything. The police were roaming the grounds, poking the hollows with sticks, putting in phone lines, shooing off the press and the curious.

This evening, they walked along the patio, watching the sun set against the mountains. Leo had grown tired of the silence.

"Iris asked me about the father," he said, drawing his finger along the stone railing. He looked over to Flora, who took a long, anxious drag on her cigarette.

"Obviously, I had nothing to tell her," he went on. "But I've been thinking, Flo, dear . . ."

"It doesn't matter."

"It didn't matter *before*," Leo said. "But things . . . could develop."

"Nothing is going to develop. They'll be found. That's it."

Leonard let out a long sigh and snuffed out his cigarette under his shoe. He came close to his friend and sat on the rail.

"There will be a lot of talk about young Alice," he said in a low voice. "It's going to start soon. They're getting tired of writing the same thing day after day. They'll want more. Her photo is in every newspaper in the world. And people may note that she doesn't look much like Albert or Iris."

"Sometimes small children don't look like their parents."

"Then they'll start asking why Iris went to Switzerland to give birth. . . ."

"To avoid the press, that was the story. . . ."

"And then some intrepid reporter will go to the clinic and start asking questions. No matter how well everyone there was paid—someone will want to sell a story."

"There's nothing wrong with adopting a child."

"Of *course* there's nothing wrong with adopting a child," Leo said. "This isn't about right and wrong. This is about a world that's hungry for a story. She's the most famous child in the world. And since you and I are in this mess together, perhaps you do want to share this one piece of information with me. This is to protect you, and Iris, and Alice. This isn't the world's business. I want to know in case there is someone out there who might also want to make a quick buck off this story. Tell me, because I only want this for you and for Alice. You know this about me. You know I keep everyone's secrets."

Two policemen walked close by, and the pair stopped speaking for a moment.

"It was always all right," Flora said when they had passed, "because here, she would have the best home possible. She would be rich. She would be safe. She would have the best of everything. Albert will pay. Albert will pay and they'll come home. They'll . . ."

Something transfixed Flora's attention below. Leo followed the line of vision. Below them, Robert Mackenzie and George Marsh were walking around the ornamental pond and in their direction. Now Leo saw it. The line of Alice's jaw. Her blue eyes.

So like George Marsh's.

"So he's the one," Leo said quietly. "How did I not see it before?"

"It didn't last very long," Flora replied. "A few weeks. You know how boring it can get up here when the weather turns."

"Does he know?" Leo said.

She shook her head. "No," she said. "He hasn't got a clue."

"Good," Leo replied. "At least *he's* not likely to sell his story to anyone, but better he has no idea."

"Alice will come home," Flora said, mostly to herself. "She'll come home safe and sound and they'll take her back to New York, away from here, and nothing like this will ever happen again. She's safe. I know she is. She has to be. I'd know if she wasn't. I'd *know*."

The sun dropped over the line of the horizon, and the mountain birds made their final circles across the sky for the day. Leo put his hand on Flora's shoulder. He wanted to say that everything would be fine, but that would be a lie. Leo was many things, but a liar was not among them.

"We'll have a cup of tea," he said, hooking his arm through hers. "Maybe something stronger. Let's go inside. It's far too crowded out here."

8

WHEN STEVIE RETURNED TO MINERVA, THERE WERE BAGS IN THE COM-
mon room, including the one she had gotten in Burlington.

"And you're sure you're okay with the staircase to get to
the bathroom?" Pix was saying. "I want to make sure everything is accessible."

"It's no problem," a voice replied. "I can do stairs. Thanks."

There was a single arm crutch leaning against the hallway
wall. A moment later, Hunter emerged from the room that
was once Ellie's, the one next to Stevie's.

Hunter bore little resemblance to his aunt except for his
blue eyes. There was something sunny about him, maybe the
light sandiness of his hair, or his smatter of freckles. When
he saw Stevie he smiled, taking up his crutch in his left arm
and coming into the common room.

"Hey," Stevie said.

"I didn't see this coming," he said. "Moving in. Surprise?"

"Your room is next to mine," she said. It was a simple fact,
but it sounded weird saying it out loud. "Do you need help?
Setting up or unpacking or . . . ?"

"Sure."

She followed him back into the room, number three, at the end of the hall by the turreted bathroom. The room was no longer filled with peacock feathers, colorful clothes and tapestries, paints and colored pencils, art books and cabaret costumes. The bits of French poetry that had been illicitly painted on the walls were still in evidence; the maintenance crew had yet to repaint. One thing Stevie clearly remembered about Ellie's room—she threw her underwear on the floor, proudly. Dirty panties. She could toss them around as easily as a dude threw his boxers on the floor. Where they had been, there were now shopping bags, the new sheets still with the folds from the package.

"I heard you got me some of this stuff," he said.

"Well, the school did. I picked it out."

Hunter picked up the heavy puffer coat Stevie had purchased for him and slipped it on.

"Thanks," he said. "This is a serious coat. We don't have coats like this in Florida. I feel like I'm wearing a mattress. In a good way."

He examined his arms in the coat, then looked around at his scattered belongings. There were not many to speak of. It's easy to pack when everything you have goes up in flames.

"I'm really sorry," she said. "About your aunt. And you. With the fire. Are you . . . okay?"

The words tumbled out of her mouth clunkily, like wooden blocks.

"Thanks," he said. "I'm sore. I have a few burns, but

they aren't too bad. My throat hurt a lot at first, but that's getting better too. I'm supposed to rest this week, so I'll be your neighbor who lies around a lot. I get to live here, at least until the end of the semester. Then the university should be able to get me a place on campus. They're waiving my room and board, and they're letting me keep the tuition discount, which is nice. And in the meantime, I get to live in a place that is super cool that I've always wanted to see. I'm actually kind of making out. . . ."

He pulled off the coat and placed it carefully on the bed.

"That didn't come out right," he said. "Nothing comes out right. I sound like an asshole."

"It's fine," Stevie said, shaking her head.

"No, it's not. . . ." Hunter sat on the edge of his new bed and looked around at the spare, empty room. "I didn't know my aunt very well. I didn't . . . like living there? It was dirty and it smelled bad, and I couldn't help her. I was thinking about going home. The tuition discount wasn't worth it. Obviously, what happened was horrible, but I can't act like we were close. Just so you know, this is where I'm at."

This was the kind of sentiment that Stevie could understand completely.

"You'll like it here," she said. "Pix is nice."

"She's an archaeologist?"

"And anthropologist. She collects teeth."

"Who doesn't?" he said.

"And Nate is a writer, and Janelle makes machines. She's doing a demonstration tonight. You should come."

"I'm staying here," he said. "I don't *go* here. I don't know if I'm supposed to go to stuff."

"You can definitely come," she said. "See something normal for once."

"For once?"

That was probably an odd thing to say. But this was Ellingham, after all.

"Sure," he said. "Okay. Might as well meet my new housemates and their machines."

He smiled at her, and for a moment, Stevie felt like maybe life here could be normal. A balanced, happy guy with reasonable reactions to things—that could make for a nice change. Maybe this was the moment everything would change for her. Maybe now the school year was beginning in earnest.

That was perhaps burdening the moment with more expectation than it could bear, but, Stevie figured, something about this year had to give.

It was a good turnout in the art barn.

Along with Stevie, Vi, Nate, and Hunter, a solid group of around thirty students had shown up to watch, which was impressive, considering that was about 30 percent of Ellingham's student body. Ellingham was the kind of place where, if your classmate was going to an engineering competition, a certain number of people would stop composing music, writing books, singing operas, and doing advanced mathematics to come have a look.

Kaz was there, of course. As the head of the student

union, he offered his support to every project and smiled his astonishing smile, the one like an open-plan kitchen full of white cabinets from a home improvement show.

(After months of being here, Stevie had little idea of what the student union did or even if it was a real thing. This either said something about the student union or about Stevie. She suspected it was both. She had been similarly clueless about the student council in her old school. She knew that elections had taken place and that the winners were four people with good hair. Their campaign promises had something to do with recycling, parking, and vending machines. They got an exemption from daytime phone jail because of their positions; Stevie sometimes saw them walking the halls at a good clip, typing importantly into their phones. Nothing ever changed with the parking or recycling or vending machines, so it seemed like the student elections were a popularity contest draped with the thinnest veil of legitimacy. Perhaps Stevie was just suspicious of politics in general because of her parents. It was an aspect of her own psychological makeup she would explore at some other time, when she had figured out all her anxiety triggers and when she wasn't trying to solve multiple murders. People have limits.)

Maris stretched out on the floor, deep in conversation with Dash. She was, Stevie noticed, fluttering her eyelashes in Kaz's direction. Next to them was Suda from Stevie's anatomy class, wearing a brilliant blue hijab. Mudge was also there, leaning into the corner of the room.

"This is the kind of stuff you guys do?" Hunter said,

looking around at the pipes and dishes and tables. "I mean, my high school was fine, but it wasn't like this."

"Neither was mine," Stevie said.

"This *is* your school."

"My old one," she said, a little more sharply than she intended. "I mean, before. I guess there was stuff, but I didn't know about it. I didn't . . . go to things."

"You must have done something right," he replied. "You ended up here."

This was not a thought Stevie had ever assembled for herself.

When she thought of old Stevie, the one in Pittsburgh, she had two separate ideas that never met up. The first Stevie was antisocial and underachieving. She didn't participate in any clubs, except for one semester in freshman year when she joined glee club and didn't sing. She did not like her own voice, so she mouthed the words. She joined glee club only because of the general pressure to have something to put on an application someday. She didn't do sports; she didn't play an instrument. She could perhaps have joined a publication, but yearbook was about knowing people, and the magazine was about poetry, so both of those were out. She went to one meeting for the newspaper to see if that would work, but it was less about hard-hitting investigative journalism and more about going to sporting events and writing about how many balls went where and who put the balls there. No club seemed to suit her, so it was twelve weeks of pretending to sing along to a melody of Disney songs until her spirit broke and her parents gave her a long lecture about how she was letting them down. That Stevie was the worst.

And yet, there was another, bigger Stevie. This Stevie spent her time online reading everything about murder. She studied criminology textbooks. She believed, really believed, that she could solve the crime of the century. And she *had*.

Stevie had never put these Stevies together to assemble a portrait of herself—her choices had not been failures. They had been choices. It was all one Stevie, and that Stevie was *worthwhile*.

All of this information entered her head at once. Hunter was still looking at her. She became aware that her mouth was hanging open a little bit, as if this profound fusion of identities wanted to make itself known to the world for the first time. She could be like other people—like Janelle, who made things and had interests and also had a relationship with Vi that was romantic and real. Maybe Stevie could be a real person too. Maybe she could express herself and this new, fully aware Stevie could be born, right now.

"Whatever," she heard herself saying in a low voice. "I mean, yeah."

Maybe not.

Behind them, Germaine Batt made her silent, ever-watchful way into the room. She was wearing her semi-professional-looking clothes again—the black pants and blazer. She had pulled her long hair into a low ponytail that hung down her back. She looked around, saw Hunter and

Stevie, and sat down next to them. She had her phone out, with the recording function on.

"You going to report on this?" Stevie asked.

"No. I hate human-interest stories. You're the nephew of that woman who died, right? You were in the fire."

Hunter blinked in surprise.

"Oh my God," Stevie said. "Really?"

"I was," Hunter said.

"Would you consider being interviewed?" Germaine asked.

"I . . . guess?"

Stevie wanted to stop this slow-motion train wreck, but Janelle was stepping to the front of her machine and looked about ready to start. She was wearing her lemon-patterned dress with her hair wrapped up in a cheerful yellow scarf. She always wore her lemons for luck.

"So," she began, "thank you for coming out to see my machine! Let me tell you about Rube Goldberg. He was an engineer who became a cartoonist . . ."

Stevie's thoughts began to drift, following the twists and turns of the tubes and dishes and plates. They were taking an unexpected course. David was gone. David could never really be gone, because he kept coming into her mind over and over. Maybe she needed something to push him out. Was that something Hunter? Was that what people did? Got interested in someone new? She didn't know how she and David had gotten together in the first place.

". . . so he made a character called Professor Butts, who . . ."

It had been like magnetism. It could honestly not be explained. But once Stevie was around David, something in her became wobbly. The lines and edges blurred. Even now, she wrapped her fingers around her phone. Maybe he would call again.

"So," Janelle said, "here's the Danger Diner!"

She reached down and depressed the lever on the toaster. The balls began their journey around the cups and saucers and plates, down the half-pipes, over the little chef. The room responded well, with noises of appreciation and some laughs. Janelle stood to the side, her hands tightly wound together. She nodded as each part of the process functioned exactly as she had designed it, as each weight, each stack, each tube did its part. The last ball was coming to the end. The soda dispenser was triggered. The three plastic pitchers began to fill. This time, Stevie would be ready when the gun went off and the egg was shot down by a series of paintballs. She focused.

Except . . .

What happened next happened so fast that Stevie barely had a chance to register it. There was a loud clanking, a hissing. Something was moving, flying. There was an earsplitting shattering as the plates fell all at once, and some object was rocketing toward them. She fell back on someone as a scream broke out throughout the room.

When the clanking finally stopped, Stevie looked up from the pile of people she had landed in. A small canister was rolling on the floor. Aside from that, there was a heavy, confused quiet. Parts of Janelle's machine lay in ruins, piles of glued-together plates and cups were shattered. From across the room, once voice cried out in pain. Then a few more gasped in alarm.

Stevie looked down at herself. There was some fine glass powder on her hoodie, but otherwise she was no worse for wear. Nate, Hunter, and Vi were all the same, more stunned than anything else. Vi immediately ran to Janelle, who stood in mute, confused horror.

Suda, the girl in the emerald-blue hijab, leaped up. She immediately ran to the hurt people and started assessing injuries. She proceeded quickly to Mudge and knelt down at his side. Stevie's tall, goth friend, who always helped her in anatomy, was bent over his arm and weeping quietly.

The demonstration was over.

9

"SO," HUNTER SAID, BREAKING THE SILENCE. "WEIRD NIGHT, HUH?"

"Not really," Nate replied, picking through the bottom of a large bowl of popcorn, looking for any fully popped pieces that weren't hard kernels in disguise. "This is pretty much how it goes. Something terrible happens and we all come back here and talk about how terrible it is. We don't learn."

Stevie elbowed him gently, but firmly, in the ribs. She sat next to him on the sofa, while Hunter was in the hammock chair, tacking softly from side as the fire crackled in the fireplace. On the other side of the room, Janelle sat with Pix. She had been crying almost nonstop all the way back to the house.

"They're standard paintball-gun canisters," she said tearfully.

"It's okay," Pix said, her arm over Janelle's shoulders. "It's not your fault."

"It *is* my fault," Janelle said, tears flying as she spat out the words. "I built it. I'm responsible for what I build. The tanks were correctly pressurized. The regulators were set at a very low level. I don't understand what happened. Everything about this machine was safe. It's all benign. I tested it dozens of times."

Pix couldn't think of anything to reply to this with, and for a moment, neither could anyone else. Then Hunter stepped in.

"Carbon dioxide canisters are really common," he said. "People have them in their kitchens. Those home seltzer things?"

"Carbon dioxide canisters?" Stevie said.

"Is that what you were using?" Hunter asked. "Or some other kind of canister?"

"Carbon dioxide," Janelle said. "Yeah, people use them for making *seltzer*."

Stevie began to quake a bit.

"Be right back," she said.

She stumbled frantically back to her room and pulled down the coat and robe and other clothes from the hooks, the clothes that were hiding the sticky notes she had put up the night before. She looked at the blue ones.

Hayes Major: CO_2 poisoning/dry ice
Ellie Walker: exposure/dehydration/immurement
Dr. Irene Fenton: house fire

She reached for the blue sticky notes and added one more.

Janelle's machine: CO_2 tank accident

There could be no doubt about it now. There was some hand in this—some quiet hand that tipped things in the wrong direction. It moved the ice, shut the doors, turned the knob, and now, perhaps the hand altered Janelle's machine.

Why the hell would anyone want to ruin a Rube Goldberg machine? She glared at the four notes, demanding that they speak to her, that they make the picture clear. What did Hayes, Ellie, Dr. Fenton, and . . . some *random students* have in common?

Well, in two cases, Janelle.

Janelle's pass had been used to take the dry ice. Janelle had that access because she was building her machine, a machine that was now destroyed. But those two things had no connection to what happened to Ellie or Dr. Fenton, unless there was a killer out there with the goal of messing up a few Ellingham student projects.

Stevie pulled off a few more sticky notes, listing all the things that played on her mind.

Janelle's pass
The message on the wall
CO_2 accidents

There was a light knock at her door, and Nate slouched his way in. Stevie grabbed her robe and some towels and made a half-hearted attempt to hang them back up to cover the wall, but Nate had already seen it.

"You don't think that was an accident," Nate said.

"Whenever you leave a room like that it means you think the bad thing that just happened wasn't an accident. It's your move."

"Do you?" she said, giving up and tossing her robe across the room, where it missed her bed by several feet and splayed dramatically on the floor.

"No," Nate said, coming in and sitting down in her squeaky desk chair. "I don't think anything is an accident anymore. Even I'm not that fatalistic. I do think it's weird how someone or something hates this building in particular. It feels like we're living in a parable."

"What's the message of this parable?" Stevie asked.

"I don't know." Nate spun the chair. "Don't go to school?"

"It's right here and I can't see it," Stevie said, shaking her head. "We're famous for being the school with the murders. There's all this *legend* around the place. Isn't it easier to do bad things in a place where bad things are supposed to happen? All these people died here, and there's a reason. Maybe even the same reason. Maybe there's a line right from 1936 until now."

She opened up her dresser drawer and pulled out the battered tea tin she'd found in Ellie's room, the tin that had broken the Truly Devious case open for her. She opened it carefully and pulled out the contents, setting them on her dresser next to her brush and her deodorant.

"A bit of a white feather," she said, holding it up. "A lipstick tube. A shiny clip. This little enamel box that looks like a shoe. A piece of torn cloth. Photos. And a poem. Someone collected these things back in 1936 and hid them. It's junk. But that's what clues are. Clues are junk. They're things that fly off the car when it gets into an accident. Murder is messy, and you have to use garbage to figure out what's going on. Somehow this shit takes us all the way to now, and these accidents with carbon dioxide and fire and people getting trapped. This school isn't cursed. There's no such thing. Unless money is a curse."

"It kind of is," Nate said. "Not that I have any. Well, I have some. From the book. Actually, I do. I don't know what to do with it. I have to pay *tax*."

"Money," Stevie said. "The kidnappings were for money. If Fenton was right, if there's something out there in a will that says someone gets a fortune if they find Alice dead or alive . . ."

"But didn't Charles tell you that didn't exist?"

Stevie stared at the items on her dresser. The beads glistened. She rolled the lipstick under her finger, back and forth.

"There's something big that sticks all this stuff together," she said. "I don't know how to find it. I don't know what to do. I don't know how to investigate a case. I mean, I've read about it, but I don't have a forensics lab. I don't have access to police databases or the ability to question people. I can look at stuff in the past, but I'm not sure how to do this in the *now*. This is real. It's ongoing."

"Tell someone," Nate said.

"Tell them I think a bad big murderer is sneaking around and show them all my Post-its?"

"I guess?"

There was a knock, and the door creaked open a bit. Hunter's tawny blond head stuck in, and he bit his lip nervously.

"Can I come in?" he asked. "I feel weird because Janelle is really upset, and I don't want her to think I'm ignoring her or staring at her . . ."

"Sure, sure . . ." Stevie stepped in front of her sticky notes and tried to do a casual lean. Hunter had seen the tin before, so that was no problem—but the conspiracy wall of death was something he might not be prepared for.

"I guess this machine thing is going to be a problem," he said.

"Maybe not," Stevie replied. "The school has had to deal with worse. It's not like before, when everything was in the news and there was a lot of pressure. As long as—"

"Does this count as news?" Hunter asked.

He held up his phone. The headline was loud and clear:

ANOTHER ACCIDENT AT ELLINGHAM: A *BATT REPORT* EXCLUSIVE

"Germaine," Stevie said. "*Germaine.*"

The bottom line came via a school-wide text that landed at seven the next morning, buzzing Stevie out of her restless sleep. She had gone to bed in her hoodie and sweatpants again, the phone loose somewhere in the blankets, demanding her attention. Before she could fish it out to see what it wanted, Janelle was at her door in her cat pajamas, her eyes flooding with tears.

"Oh my God," she said. "I shut down the school."

"Huh?" Stevie managed.

Janelle dropped down next to Stevie on the bed, pushed over her own phone, and burst into tears.

School-wide meeting at 9:00 a.m. Attendance is mandatory. All classes are canceled. Please meet in the dining hall.

A short while later, the small group from Minerva joined the migration across campus. Janelle had only just stopped crying. Nate's hands were so far into his pockets that they must have touched his knees. Vi was waiting by the front door to accompany them. They were dressed in a shirt and tie, and they had made Janelle some paper flowers to cheer her up. Hunter walked with them as well. He was not a student and did not have to come. He was still feeling new and awkward and wasn't quite sure how to fit in, so he trailed along.

"This is all my fault," Janelle said, sniffing. "Whatever is about to happen."

"It's not," Vi said. "And it's probably nothing. They're probably going to put some new policy in place, or maybe it's about the snow. This storm is going to be huge."

They pulled out their phone and quickly scanned through the forecast.

"Listen," they said. "Updated forecast, up to thirty-six inches, with high winds, so expect high drifts. Snow will begin tomorrow morning, initially two to three inches per hour, intensifying rapidly."

"This is my fault," Janelle said again.

As the group prepared to cross the green, Hunter paused.

"I need to take the path, if that's okay," he said. "I'll meet you."

"Why don't we take the green," Vi said to them, giving them a knowing look that said, *Give me a few minutes with her*.

"Sure," Stevie said. "We'll take the path and meet you two over there."

Vi and Janelle crossed the grass, and Hunter, Nate, and Stevie turned to go around the drive.

"Sorry," Hunter said, "my crutch gets stuck in the grass a bunch."

"Don't apologize," Stevie said. "I think they needed to talk anyway."

"What do you think is going on?" Hunter asked.

"Nothing good," Nate said. "There's no such thing as a good emergency school assembly. Not here."

All of Ellingham was in attendance in the dining hall. A fire was crackling in the big fireplace in the front of the space, in the cozy study area with the chairs. Most people sat there, draped over every surface, some still in pajamas and hoodies. There was a high pulsing energy in the room. Teachers milled around with cups of coffee. Vi and Janelle were sitting at a table. Vi was trying to tempt Janelle into eating some pancakes, but it wasn't working. A few tables over, with her face close to her laptop screen, Germaine Batt was watching something intently.

"I'll be over in a second," Stevie said to Nate and Hunter.

She approached Germaine's table and sat down. Germaine did not look up.

"Don't," Germaine said.

"Don't what?"

"Don't tell me I shouldn't have posted it. I didn't say it was Janelle's fault."

"You said her machine blew up," Stevie said. "Which isn't even true."

"Did you see that thing go? It broke Mudge's arm."

"But it didn't blow up. It . . ."

Germaine shut her laptop firmly and stared at Stevie. "Look," she said. "I know Janelle is upset. I told the story. That's it. Just like you looked into Hayes's death. And how did that turn out?"

It was like Stevie had been punched in the face. She almost physically reeled from the blow. She leaned back, then got up, walking back to the group table in a daze. Call Me Charles and Dr. Quinn came briskly into the room. They conferred with a few teachers by the door, all their expressions serious.

"Not good," Nate whispered to Stevie.

Charles went to the middle of the study area and stepped up onto a low table made of heavy wood.

"Can everyone gather or look over here?" he said.

The room went quiet very quickly. Stevie could hear the fire crackle from a good distance.

"We asked everyone to come here this morning so we could all talk," he began. "This semester has been one of the hardest in the school's history. We've never experienced anything quite like it, at least not in our lifetimes. We mourn the loss of two of our friends. Those losses brought about some very serious conversations—conversations about safety, both physical and emotional. We felt that the school and all of you would benefit from continuing the semester. However . . ."

However was bad. Very bad.

". . . and I want to stress this is no one's fault . . ."

Janelle coughed back a sob.

". . . we've come to the very difficult decision that this semester should be brought to a close."

The ripple that went through the room was a sonic event the likes of which Stevie had never experienced. It was a collective intake that seemed to suck away all the air, followed by a yelp, then a cry, an "oh shit" and several "oh my Gods."

"What? What are we going to do?" This was from Maris. She was sitting on the floor by the fire, curled up like a cat in a pair of velvety black pajama bottoms and a massive fuzzy sweatshirt. She gazed up from her position like a tragic heroine in a silent movie.

"Here's what we're going to do," Charles said. "First, you don't need to worry about your academics. We're going to work out a way for all of you to finish the semester remotely. None of your academic credit will be affected. None of it."

One relieved sigh from an unknown corner of the room.

"Normally, we would want to give you time to process, to talk, but there is a complicating factor. I'm sure you've heard about the storm coming in. It's looking to be a big one. By this time tomorrow, the roads will be impassable. So, unfortunately, we're going to have to start the moving out tonight...."

Everything was spinning a bit. The room seemed to elongate. Stevie looked up at the peaked roof with its wood beams, the ones that made this building seem like a ski lodge or some kind of Alpine retreat. She could smell the warm maple syrup, the fire, and that strange funk that all cafeterias possess no matter how hard they try not to.

"I realize that is not much time," Charles said. "You do not need to worry about any travel—we will arrange and pay for all of it. For those of you who need flights, we're already getting them set up. Planes are still taking off from the airport this afternoon and this evening, which is why we had to meet this morning. For those of you who are within driving or train distance, we have set up that as well. You don't need to worry about packing all your things. Take the things you need for this week, and we'll get everything else to you. We're going to text each one of your travel—"

"Are we coming back?" someone else asked.

"That remains an open question," he replied. "I hope so."

He went on for another five or so minutes, talking about community and emotions. Stevie heard none of it. The room continued to distort, and her pulse raced. She had not thought to bring her bag with her medication, so she closed her eyes and breathed. In for four. Hold for seven. Out for eight.

Pix was coming in as they were going out. She embraced everyone, except Nate, who did not hug.

"I have a flight to San Francisco at two," Vi said, staring at their phone.

"Mine's at four," Janelle said.

The two held each other. Stevie felt the buzz in her pocket but refused to look.

"I'll meet you all at home in a few minutes," Pix said. "I'm sorry. It's all going to be okay."

But it wasn't, of course.

They made their way back to Minerva in a slow, silent procession. Vi came along with them, walking hand in hand with Janelle. Stevie had memorized that sentence from *The Great Gatsby* that had so transfixed her. She hadn't meant to—she just read it several times and now it was stuck, running through her head as she looked up: *He must have looked up at an unfamiliar sky through frightening leaves and shivered as he found what a grotesque thing a rose is and how raw the sunlight was upon the scarcely created grass.*

She still didn't know exactly what it meant, but the words scared her. They made her aware that there were echoey hallways inside herself that she had not yet explored, that the world was big, and that objects changed upon examination. These are not the kinds of things you want to think about when your dreams of school and escape and friendship have— at long last—properly exploded. Everything was the last. The last time as a group walking back from the dining hall. The last time touching her ID to the pad. The last time pushing open the big blue door. The last time looking at the weird snowshoe spikes, and the moose head, and David sitting on the saggy purple sofa. . . .

David. Was sitting there. Hands folded in his lap, a massive backpack by his feet, wearing his two-thousand-dollar Sherlock coat and a knowing smile.

"Hey, everybody," he said. "Miss me? Shut the door. Not a lot of time."

September 1936

IT WAS VERY ODD SEEING A LAKE GO AWAY. HOUR BY HOUR, IT SANK from view. At breakfast, Flora Robinson had gone out to its bank to wish it good-bye. After lunch, it was not looking itself and had revealed a mossy, slimy border of rock. By four, one could hear a whooshing sound as it continued to sink. Leaves congealed on the contracting surface. By sunset, it was gone.

The lake met its fate because a famous physic had called the *New York Times* and told a reporter that Alice Ellingham had never left home at all; that she was at the bottom of the garden lake. Albert Ellingham did not believe in psychics, but after four sleepless nights, he told Mackenzie to call up the engineers and drain it anyway. This was not hard to do. The lake was fed by a series of pipes that brought water down from a higher point on the mountain; another pipe ran down-hill and into the river. All that needed to be done was to close the feed and open the drain and . . . good-bye, lake.

As went the lake, so did Flora's life, drained of beauty and fullness. Wherever Flora went, she was "that woman who was there that night," or "a speakeasy hostess known to the family." Never what she was—a friend. The friend. Iris's best friend in the world. The one who actually mourned her. The world may have seen pictures of Iris's New York relations as they made public spectacles of themselves at the funeral service at Saint John the Divine, of the greenhouses' worth of roses and irises and the great bunches of lilacs (her favorite scent) that filled the church. There were movie stars who flew in from California to pay tribute to the wife of their employer. Members of the New York Philharmonic played by her casket, and the mezzo-soprano Clara Ludwig sang "Ave Maria." Everyone wept.

Many photographs were taken of the cortege of Rolls-Royce Phantom limousines with black crepe that wound through Central Park to the luncheon at the Plaza. From there, the mood turned over countless glasses of champagne and towers of finger sandwiches. It was a fulsome summer's day, with the hot breeze coming in through the windows. The mourners compared dresses and stock portfolios and vacation plans. So many of them had come in from their summer houses. How terrible to face the city in this heat!

Flora moved like a ghost. She did not eat finger sandwiches or drink champagne. She wore black and sweated in it and twice went to vomit. When the show was over, she and Leo walked numbly through Central Park. The day was endless, refusing to give way to the evening. The sky seemed to swell overhead, and a small pack of photographers trailed them at a distance until they left the park and escaped in a cab to Leo's studio. Leo gave her something to help her sleep.

Months later, she was still that ghost. Now she watched the last of her friend's lake disappear into a pipe, leaving a big, empty cup of rocks. She shivered and shut the curtains. She turned to George Marsh, who was sitting on the other side of the room, reading a newspaper. He folded back the top and looked over it at Flora.

"Is it done?" he asked.

"It's done."

"I was already out there twice. We'll go over it inch by inch, but I don't think there's anything to find in there."

Flora went into the great hall, where Leonard Holmes Nair was sitting on a divan by the large fireplace. A novel dangled from his fingertips, but he didn't seem to be reading. His focus was on the second-floor balcony.

"Something's going on." He nodded toward the balcony. "For the last few hours there's been a trail of crates and boxes coming in. Albert's supervised them all, and they all went to Alice's room. Some of them were massive. I went to go see what they were but he shooed me away from the door. It's the most excited I've seen him in ages. He was *smiling*."

Flora sat next to her friend and looked up. This was a strange, not entirely welcome development. Albert Ellingham soon appeared, leaning over the rail.

"Flora, Leo, come see. Bring George. It's ready." Albert was almost giddy. "Come to Alice's room."

Flora had not been in Alice's room since the kidnapping.

It was perfectly kept. The lace curtains were drawn every morning and closed every night. Fresh sheets and blankets were regularly put on the bed. The stuffed animals waited in a line. The dolls were dusted and settled in their chairs. New clothes in larger sizes had been brought in every season to be ready for Alice's reappearance. All of that, Flora knew about. But there was something else now, something that dominated the center of the room, almost filling it. It was a replica of the house she stood in—the Great House, rendered in miniature.

"It was made in Paris," Albert said, walking around the house and looking in the windows. "I had it commissioned two years ago, and it's finally arrived. Marvelous, isn't it?"

Leo tried to mask his horror with a blank stare, but he wasn't able to pull it off. Albert didn't seem to notice. He went to the side of the massive toy house, flipped a latch, and swung it open. The interior of the Great House was spread out in front of them, like a patient on a surgical table, insides exposed.

"Look," Albert said. "Look at the detail!"

There was the massive front hall, shrunk down, its stairs and marble fireplace faithfully re-created. Tiny crystal knobs gleamed on hand-sized doors. There was the morning room with its silk paper and French decor, the ballroom with its motley walls. In Albert's office, the two tiny desks had stamp-like papers on them and telephones that Flora could have balanced on her thumbnail. Upstairs, the same—Iris's dressing room in morning gray. Room after room, including the one they stood in now. The only thing the dollhouse missed was a miniature of itself.

"I had them work from photographs, and by God, what a job they've done. I told you, Leo. I said when she was born that I would get her the best dollhouse in the world."

"You did," Leo said, his voice sounding dry.

"What do you think, Flora?" Albert asked.

"It's a marvel," she said, fighting down the rising bile in the back of her throat.

"Yes." Albert stood, his hands on his hips, regarding the sight as a whole. "Yes. Yes, it is."

Something in his elevated manner suggested that this dollhouse would somehow change things. Alice was not here, but the dollhouse had come—and if the dollhouse had come, Alice must follow. Giddy, funhouse logic, distorted.

"You know," he said, "I was building something quite wonderful for Iris as well, for her birthday. She was so enamored of what we saw in Germany, I thought . . . Well. It doesn't matter now. What matters is that Alice's gift is here."

"You know, Albert," Leo said, looking to Flora and Marsh for support, "I think this calls for a celebration. Why don't we go downstairs and have something to eat? What do you say?"

"Yes," Albert said. "I suppose I should eat something. Montgomery can scare me up a ham sandwich or two."

He clapped Leo on the back to usher him from the room.

Flora wanted to leave, but the presence of the dollhouse transfixed her. George was squatting, examining the small furniture from the office.

"Be there in a moment," she said. "I want to look some more."

"Do . . . do!" Albert said. "Look away!"

When Albert and Leo had gone, George Marsh straightened up and turned to Flora.

"Look at this," he said, pointing at the top bedroom.

Sitting on the bed, neatly and in a row, were three china figures—one of Albert, one of Iris, and one of Alice, sitting between them.

"Dear God," she said.

"Yeah. I wish I could set fire to this thing."

He must have been feeling the same queasy strangeness, this mockery of reality. That must have been it—this warping—that made her speak so suddenly.

"Alice," she said. "Do you know? Did they ever tell you?"

"Tell me what?" George replied.

Flora rubbed her hand across her brow.

"It's a secret, but I thought you would know. They never said?"

"Said what?"

"She's Albert and Iris's child, but she's . . ." Flora waved her hand in the air for a moment. "Iris didn't give birth to her."

"Who did?"

"Me," she replied.

She waited a moment as this information made contact. George cocked his head.

"Think about when she was born, George," Flora said. "Think. Four years ago."

George blinked once, very slowly, then turned back to the dollhouse for a moment.

"Are you sure?" he said.

"There's no doubt," Flora replied. "One morning I woke up, and I threw up right into the wastepaper basket. I hadn't been out the night before. I went to the doctor, and he confirmed it. I told Iris. She had always wanted a child, but she hadn't been able to have one of her own. It was the perfect solution, for everyone. The child would want for nothing. So we all went to Switzerland together. There are clinics there— private ones—where everyone knows how to keep a secret. It wasn't that there was any issue with Alice being adopted. They just wanted privacy. They didn't want the whole world telling her. It was all so perfect."

The tiny chandeliers twinkled as a stray beam of sunset struck its crystal droplets. George sank his hands into his pockets and looked at the house, not moving or speaking for some time.

"I would have married you," he finally said. "That's what you do."

At this, Flora laughed—a strange barking sound.

"Did it ever occur to you that I wouldn't want to marry *you*?" she said. "We had fun, George, but you were never seriously interested. Neither was I."

"I have a daughter," he said.

"No," she replied. "*I* have a daughter. And I made sure she was safe. Or I tried to."

She wound her arms around herself and rubbed at her sides. She felt cold and confused. She had never meant to have this conversation. Now that she had spilled the knowledge, she had nothing more to add. She walked out of the room, her heels clicking hard against the wooden floor.

George stood alone, staring at the dollhouse. He reached inside, like a giant, and removed the tiny porcelain Alice. Even in this form, he could see the resemblance. She had his eyes.

He had let his own child be kidnapped.

She was missing, somewhere out there in the world, with the men he had hired. The men who had killed her mother.

George Marsh had always wanted to find Alice, but in that moment, that task became the sole focus of his life.

10

THERE HAD BEEN SEVERAL OCCASIONS IN THIS MATTER WHEN ONE OF the King family—either Edward or David—decided to turn up suddenly in Stevie's life. Each time, she felt like metal clamps came out of the floor and wrapped around her feet, locking her in place.

"Who are you?" David said. "We met, right? Are you the new me?"

This was to Hunter, who was staring at the person he had last seen getting his face bashed in on the street in Burlington. The bruises around his left eye were still dark and angry, some green, some blue-black. The cut that ran from his temple to his cheek looked like it had needed stitches but had not gotten them, and it gaped a bit where the new flesh was knitting itself together. But his wide smile was the same, and the bruising brought out the deep color of his eyes.

"Yeah, I have no idea what's happening," Hunter replied.

"What are you doing here?" Janelle asked. "I thought you left."

"I came in through the bathroom window," he said, as if this was obvious.

"Oh, the last thing we need today is your bullshit."

"Normally, I would agree. But today I have something that's really important, and we need to talk fast, and not here. Upstairs."

"The school is *closing*," Janelle said.

"I know. That's why I came. Seriously. Can we go upstairs, right now? You can yell at me or whatever, but I have something really, really important to talk to you about."

"We need to—"

"I'm not sure if Stevie told you this, but Edward King is my dad."

This was a surprise to Vi, and certainly to Hunter, who was having a strange introduction to life at Minerva.

"Shut up," Vi said.

"I'm serious. Look at my face." David ran his finger along his noninjured jawline. "See it? See the resemblance?"

"Oh my God," Vi replied.

"Yeah. My reaction too. Do you want to stop a bad man from becoming president? If you want to know more, follow me. If not, pack your shower gel."

This resulted in silence from the group.

"I have your attention?" David said. "Good. Upstairs."

He got up, slinging the massive backpack over his shoulder. It made a loud clunking noise. He went off down the hall, leaving everyone else.

"What is he talking about?" Janelle asked Stevie.

"I have no idea," Stevie replied. "But I think we should find out."

Maybe it was the nervous energy of having been told the school had closed, but there was a kind of group movement—a magnetic pull to stay together. They went one by one up the curved, creaking stairs, Janelle looking after Vi, Stevie still thrumming at the sight of David, Nate because . . . well, because the tide pulled him. Upstairs, in the dark hallway, David unlocked his door. Everyone followed him inside. Stevie had been in David's room before. It was stark, full of expensive but impersonal things. Gray sheets and bedding. Nice speakers that he didn't use. Some gaming systems. She had been on that bed, up against the wall. They had . . .

She couldn't think about that.

"No one knows I'm here," he said, sitting on the floor.

"No one knows?" Janelle said. "What about all those security cameras your dad put in?"

"Ah," David said, smiling. "I shut those off for a while. I can explain everything but—"

"You just . . . *shut them off*?"

"Here's the thing about my dad you need to understand," David replied. "He seems like the big bad, like he's scheming all the time and knows exactly what he's doing, but a lot of his solutions are quick and dirty. The security system isn't that good. And the installation wasn't great either."

Stevie felt his gaze linger on her for a moment, so she looked down to examine her shoes.

"It was a good system," she said. "He came to our house and showed us the information on it."

"What information was that?" David said, cocking his head slightly to the side.

"I saw . . . the specs," Stevie said. She used the word *specs* because it sounded technical but immediately regretted it. She had not seen specifications. She had no idea why she'd said it. Stick to the truth.

"He had all these . . . shiny folders."

"Oooh. Shiny folders, huh?"

Stevie's face flushed.

"To get the system up and running in a week, they used a plug and play," he said. "It's not hardwired. The day they brought it in, I lifted a base station when they were unpacking. I stashed it and set it up."

"Where?" Janelle asked.

"Doesn't matter for the purposes of this conversation. I hid it. All I had to do then was establish myself as a system admin. Since he bought it, he had user profiles made for himself and his staff. So I set up additional identity on his staff server. My name is Jim Malloy. I'm from the Boston Malloys. Went to Harvard for my MBA. Very impressive. All I have to do is log in and switch the network over to the other base station, which does nothing at all. System goes down. Easy. Easy for me to come and go. I went home because I needed to get these."

He reached into his pocket and produced a handful of flash drives.

"Behold," he said. "The keys to the kingdom."

"What's on those?" Janelle said.

"No idea. But these drives were in the safe in the floor under our dining room table, the one he thinks no one knows about."

"You broke into his safe?" Stevie asked.

"What I have on these drives is information regarding my father's campaign activities. I need help reading it all. Which is why I came to you," he said to Janelle.

"First of all," Janelle said. She was the only one who seemed willing and able to steer this conversation. "Whatever you have there has got to be illegal."

"Illegal how? Is it even stealing if I took it from my house?"

"Yes," Janelle said. "That's campaign information. People go to jail for things like that. It's not a box of cereal or a TV."

"What, are you a lawyer?" he countered. "And how did you know about the cereal?"

Janelle seemed to rise from the floor a bit.

"Kidding. You think my dad could afford those cereal carbs? That guy lives on hard-boiled eggs and human misery. The legalities of it aside . . . the risk incurred is my own. All I'm asking is for help looking at it. Looking at something is not a crime."

"Yes, it probably is," Janelle said. "I'm going—"

"Nell," Vi said. "Wait."

"Vi," Janelle said. "No. We can't."

"I just want to hear," Vi said. "If we have to tell the police, the more information we have, the better."

"Vi is correct," David said, waving his hand graciously. "When you narc on me, be in possession of all the facts! Hear me out."

"You're suggesting we stick one of those radioactive things in our computer and . . ."

"I would never," he said, putting his hand to his heart. "What kind of monster do you think I am? I have with me . . ."

He opened the massive backpack, pulled out some rolled, soiled clothes, including some checkered boxers, which Stevie tried not to look at. (God, it was so hard to look away from someone's underwear when it was stuck unexpectedly in your field of vision. Especially this underwear. Why, brain, why?) He pulled out a small stack of banged-up laptops and two tablets, plus some kind of router or base station.

"All freegan or fifty bucks at most. I've disabled their network connectivity. You couldn't get online with these pieces of junk if you tried. I will put the content onto these devices, and I will set them down roughly in the range of your vision. I'll even scroll the pages if you want. All you have to do is read, which all of you can do, very fast. I'll wipe these things down and dump them in Lake Champlain when we're done. I'll strip them to parts. They never existed."

"One problem," Nate said. "We're leaving in, like, an hour."

"Which is why I showed up when I did to present my radical plan. Don't. Go. When they come to get you, be somewhere else. Shut off your phones. Wait. Eventually, the storm will start and the coaches will go."

The idea was so simple, Stevie almost laughed. Just don't go. Stay.

"Imagine it," he said. "All of us, together for the best snowed-in weekend in a mountain hideout. There's plenty of food, blankets . . . syrup. If nothing else, don't you want to leave Ellingham in style? What are they going to do? Kick you out for not leaving when the school shuts down? How is it your fault if you were in another building saying good-bye and lost track of the time? Not yours. There is nothing they can do to you."

"My parents would kill me," Nate said. "There's that."

"Mine too," Janelle said, but her tone had shifted very slightly.

"Again," David said, "we, us, right here, right now, have the ability to stop a bad, bad person from becoming president. Think about what you could be stopping—someone who uses racist policies to hurt or kill people. Someone who could do untold damage to the environment. Someone who could start an illegal war to distract from his political problems. You know, Vi, that he's capable of that."

Vi inclined their head slightly.

"Stevie," he said, looking directly at her at last, "your parents help with his campaign. You could undo all they've done and more. And I will happily go down in a column of flame for it, except I won't because I'm his son and I'm a rich, white asshole, so I'll get a slap on the wrist or sent to school in God knows where, but it will be worth it. Because believe it or not, this is the right thing to do. It's not easy. But it's right. So what's the bigger deal? What's *worth* it?"

"How do you even know he's doing something illegal?" Janelle asked. "Something that would stop him? Because people have tried to block him before."

"Because he is my dad," David said. "I know how he lives. And like I said, he likes a quick-and-dirty solution."

The group was silent for a moment.

"Well, I'm convinced," Hunter said.

"Can we trust this guy?" David asked.

"Too late on that front," Hunter replied. "But I hate the dude, and I'm not going anywhere anyway."

"I'm staying," Vi said.

"Vi . . ." Janelle went over to her partner.

"David's right. This is worth it, if he really has something. This is about the greater good. And me. This is the kind of person I am. I want to stay and do this, because it's right. Stay with me."

The wind whistled and snapped at the windows.

Janelle let out a long exhale through her nose and looked at Stevie.

"Stevie?" she said, her voice pleading.

Stevie's body had gone numb from overload. She looked to David, at his peaked brows, the swing of his coat, the curl of his hair. Larry's words echoed hollowly through her mind—he's not right; he was in town; be careful . . .

"I . . . yeah. I'll stay."

David's mouth twisted into a smile.

"Nate?" he asked.

Nate waved a dismissive hand. "I got nowhere to be. Might as well. I'm sure it's only sort of illegal. What's a few years in federal prison?"

All eyes were on Janelle now. She shifted from foot to foot and rolled her shoulders back, struggling with herself.

"God help me," she said. "Fine. Okay. Fine. Let's do this. Because someone with some sense should be here."

"Right." David rubbed his hands together and smiled. "Time to go underground."

11

"Okay, campers," David said, putting everything back in his bag. "Pix is going to be back any minute, so we need to go. Time to hide."

"Where?" Vi asked.

"The gym," he said. "Already scoped it out. It has the least security and it's probably going to be the first building they lock up and the last place they'd look for anyone. We'll go around the back way, through the woods. We'll stay there until everyone's gone. Let's go."

"Now?" Nate said.

"Now," he said.

"What should I do?" Hunter said, looking around. "I'm allowed to be here."

"You can do whatever you want. Just don't narc."

"Wait," Janelle said. "If we're going to strand ourselves here, we're going to do it *safely*. Everyone brings a flashlight and an extra layer, water, snack bars . . ."

"We have to *go* . . . ," David said.

"Snack bars," Janelle repeated slowly. "There's a box in the kitchen. I'll go and get it."

"We don't need those. We'll be back—"

"We need"—Janelle fixed him with a stare that could have blown a hole in a wall—"food, water, flashlights, and extra layers."

Everyone was given a few minutes to run to their respective rooms. Stevie hastily shoved stuff into her backpack—her computer, the tin, her medication, and her copy of *And Then There Were None*. She wasn't sure why she grabbed the last item, but she knew it had to come along. She pulled on her coat—the heavy one she never really used—and shoved gloves in her pockets. Janelle was gathering things as well but seemed to be moving at a much slower pace, picking through her scarves, putting a sweater into her bag, then her computer, looking at her phone. Vi rocked from their heels to their toes impatiently.

"Thanks for the help, Freckles," David said to Hunter. "We'll meet you when the coast is clear. Keep Pix distracted for a few minutes when she gets back, okay?"

"Are you seriously going to call me Freckles?" Hunter replied.

"Give me all your IDs," David went on. "The security posts can ping them as you pass. I don't want them showing up when I turn the system back on."

Again, Janelle looked very hesitant, but things were moving now. They passed over the cards. David dropped them into Janelle's bath caddy.

"The security system is about to go down. Ready? Three, two, one."

He put his phone back in his coat pocket. It was impossible for Stevie to ignore the fact that security-shutting-off David was sexy.

"It's off. Time to move."

They pushed open the door and stepped out into a world of gently falling snow. The sky was an extraordinary color, a kind of pink steel. It had barely been an hour, but already about two inches had gathered on the ground and the trees, and this was not even the storm itself. Stevie could hear the coaches and the voices of fellow students carried on the wind, as people said good-bye and cried and began to go.

A little flash ran through her mind—this had happened here before. In April 1936, the morning after the kidnapping, when Albert Ellingham ordered all the students to be evacuated because of the events of the night before. Just like this. Perhaps Ellingham was never meant to be. Perhaps it was always designed as a place that had to be abandoned because of death and danger.

"We're going the long way around," David said, waving them toward the back of Minerva.

The group walked past the circle of stone heads, then veered toward the woods, away from the yurt. They kept along the line of the woods, tramping over rocks and sticks. They passed a statue of a man in a classical stance. This was the statue Ellie had climbed on their first night here, as they went to the party at the yurt. She had painted THIS IS ART on his torso. It had been scrubbed clean, but Stevie suspected that if she got up close, she would be able to see the outline of the letters.

Every contact leaves a trace.

David went ahead, leading the way. Vi and Janelle, normally entwined and constantly talking, now walked side by side in silence. Janelle's gaze was fixed firmly and miserably ahead; Vi had their chin up defiantly.

"I'm trying to figure out if this is the stupidest thing I've ever done," Nate said as he kept up the rear with Stevie. "I don't think it is, and that worries me."

"It probably isn't."

"I mean, the thing with the files is crazy. I honestly don't even know if I'm going to look at them."

"Then why did you stay?" she asked.

"Because," Nate said, tipping his head toward David, "when you and he get together, something bad happens to you."

Stevie swallowed down a lump in her throat. She wanted to reach over and grab Nate's hand at that moment, except that Nate would probably receive the gesture with as much enthusiasm as a handful of spiders.

"Are you going to tell him what you told me?" he asked. "About how you solved the case?"

"I don't know," Stevie said as her breath puffed out in front of her like a feather of frost. "No. I don't know. Maybe.

No. And if I stay, it's more time to get what I need—anything I can find to bolster the case."

"Well," Nate said, "now that we belong to *The Shining* reenactment society, you might as well go for it. Last chance."

There is one thing about talking about doing something—and then there is going into the mountain woods as you see your classmates carrying their bags out and going to coaches and crying and hugging each other. Stevie got to see a little bit of this as they hid among the statuary. In particular, she could see Maris, in a flash of red, running from person to person. Dash was with her, in his long, sweeping coat. Stevie had known them a bit—had experienced a death with them—and now, she would likely never see them again. Mudge was there as well, getting help, as his right arm was casted and slung over his chest. All of them departing, while she and her friends were here in the trees.

They wound behind the art barn, walked into the woods opposite the maintenance road, past the entrance to the tunnel that led to the dome. From there, David waved them down sloping, uneven ground laced with tree roots and filled with leaf pits of unknown depth. They slid and stumbled down to the river, which was running low and fast. Through the bare trees, on the rise above, Stevie could see the top of the library, and a bit of Artemis and Dionysus, the gym. Three coaches were making their way past the entrance sphinxes and around the drive.

"This way," David said, leading them around the back of

the building where a window had been propped open. They each climbed through, Stevie awkwardly throwing her leg over the sill and getting her pack jammed as she pressed her way inside. It was not a graceful way for any of them, but it was an entrance.

"System is back on," David said once they were all securely through the window.

"Now what?" Janelle said.

"We bunk down. I recommend the pool-supply room. I slept there last night. Very private. Lots of towels. And pool noodles. Did you know we had pool noodles?"

Stevie hadn't spent much time in Dionysus. She had been here on the tour on the first day of school and had made a few quick trips to the costume room upstairs. It was a strange building. The theater was there—a small space with a painted entrance wall that looked like a temple. There was a modern room full of exercise machines with rubber matting on the floor, and some changing rooms. The building smelled of chlorine.

"We're going to go upstairs," Vi said. The message was clear—Janelle and Vi needed some more time to talk.

"We'll be in the pool," David said. "Don't leave without us. No phones."

Nate, David, and Stevie continued on to the pool area, which encompassed most of the ground floor of the building. The pool was accessed by a beautiful old wooden door, with the original POOL written on it in gold paint. The room was tiled in a vibrant aqua with white. There were additional decorative smiles with bas-relief faces in them—gods or goddesses or assorted Romans or Greeks peering out like silent lifeguards. The room had a magnificent glass roof that curved down, the top of which already had a white cap of snow. Snow nestled in the crook of every square of glass. There was a mosaic of Neptune at the bottom of the pool. He stared up at them through the water.

"In here," David said, his voice booming as it bounced off the tiles.

Their hiding place was the supply closet, stacked with blue towels, hampers, jugs of chemicals, and safety equipment. There was a small nest on the side—David's sleeping bag, with a pile of towels serving as a pillow. There was a bag of food and remains—sandwich wrappers, Doritos, packaged cupcakes, and what seemed to be several containers from the dining hall.

"How long have you been here?" Nate asked.

"Only since last night. Welcome. Get comfy. The towels are very plush. I recommend them."

Stevie and Nate found space on the floor away from the sleeping bag. She grabbed a few towels to sit on.

"All good?" David asked. "Okay."

He switched off the lights.

"Seriously?" Nate said.

"In case they search the building or look in the window."

David crossed the room, his feet bumping into Stevie's leg as he passed.

"So," he said. "How's everybody been?"

"I hate this," Nate said.

"Nothing new there. How's the book?"

"I'm leaving," Nate replied.

"Nate . . . ," Stevie said.

"There has to be somewhere else. A trash room or something."

"Nothing this nice," David replied. "Sit. We have to play this out. I'll be good. Promise."

Silence.

"So how are *you*, Stevie?" David said.

"It's been busy," she replied.

Nate sighed loudly.

"Why don't you tell me more about what you've been doing?" Stevie said. "That seems more interesting."

"Well," he said. "After I got beat up, my friend drove me to Harrisburg. I slept in our neighbor's shed. Got into the house. Took what I needed. Got back. Crawled up through the woods like a goddamned mountain man, slept in the pool room, and then got you guys. And now, here we are."

"What about those tablets and stuff?" Nate said.

"I've been picking those up for a while. An operation like this requires advance preparation. Ideally, I wanted some more time, but I heard about the accident last night and about the storm that was coming—seemed like things were about to go really wrong here. So I had to improvise."

"You didn't improvise that speech back there," she said. "How long were you working on that?"

"Day or two. Got a bunch of it from *The West Wing*. That

was the only show I was never allowed to watch when I was a kid, so it's my favorite. I wonder who my dad will have as VP if he gets into the White House? I'm rooting for a cloud of bats. What about you, Stevie? You know him better than I do."

"Anywhere," Nate said. "A boiler room? Something connected with sewage?"

After about a half hour, Vi and Janelle rejoined them. Whatever they had been doing upstairs, it had not resulted in things being worked out. They came into the tiny pool room, Janelle taking a seat next to Stevie and Vi pressing in by Nate. Janelle insisted on turning on the light, which almost blinded Stevie.

"Good to have you back," David said, holding up his hand to his eyes.

"Here," Janelle said, passing out snack bars and small foil packets.

"What's this?" Nate said. "Tinfoil?"

"Mylar blankets," she replied. "The kind they give people after marathons."

"Why do you have Mylar blankets?" Nate asked.

"I wasn't coming up a mountain without proper safety gear," she replied. "Besides, they're cheap and about as big as a pack of tissues. They're for when the power and heat go out in here, which they probably will."

Janelle's powers of anticipation were almost beyond comprehension.

"I have more questions," she said. "Like how did getting

yourself beaten up help? Doesn't that make your dad want to find you?"

"That's what would happen in your family, probably," David said. "My family is different. My dad expects the worst of me, so that's what I gave him. I ran off, got into a fight, put it online to make sure he saw that I was a loose cannon, and vanished, into what I am sure he assumed was a cloud of vape smoke on a pile of beanbags somewhere. I wanted to make myself a little radioactive so he wouldn't seek me out, at least for a few days."

This entirely checked out with things David had told Stevie about his parents.

"And thanks, Stevie, for taking part."

"What?" It erupted from her mouth.

"You think you walked in on that beatdown by accident?" he said. "I needed you to see it. I followed you to Burlington and paid those dudes. Then I made sure we were in your path and started the beating right on time. That way you could let everyone know that not only did I get beat up and take off, but I paid people to do it and uploaded it myself. That's a double layer of weird and crazy. It would keep everyone wondering for long enough. I needed to seem all . . ."

He jazz-handed around his head.

"And why do you think there's something on those drives?" Janelle said.

"I have my sources," he said. "Now, who wants a tablet? We need to get started."

"Me," Vi said loudly.

David passed them one, along with a device to connect the drive.

"Nate?"

"I'm good for now," Nate said. "I'd like to do this one violation at a time."

David shrugged expansively as if to say, "Suit yourself."

"I'm assuming that's a no, Janelle, or . . ."

"It's a no," Janelle said, looking at Vi, who was already working away on the tablet.

"Fine, then. Let's get to it."

"What about me?" Stevie asked.

"Oh, you want one?" David said. He got out one of the tablets and held it toward Stevie, but as she reached for it, he drew it back.

"Maybe you shouldn't," he said.

He put it back in his bag. Nate put his head down so hard it looked like he was trying to crawl into his computer. Janelle shook her head.

"You're better off," she said.

And so, each member of the group turned to their own task in the little closet near the pool, while the snow fell and the wind blew and Ellingham emptied. Stevie reached into her bag and got out *And Then There Were None*, the story of ten strangers gathered on an island and murdered one by one.

It was, perhaps, a little too close to reality at the moment.

February 18, 1937
New York City

GEORGE MARSH PUSHED OPEN THE DOOR OF MANELLI'S RESTAU-
rant on Mott Street. Manelli's was like many joints in the
area—spaghetti and clams, veal, decent red wine, rapid-fire
Italian spoken all around. At ten o'clock on a snowy night,
it was still thrumming quietly, a haze of cigar smoke hanging over the tables and laughter puncturing the rhythm of
forks and knives hitting plates. He took a stool at the bar and
ordered a glass of whiskey and a plate of salami and bread.

"I'm looking for two guys," he said as he tore into the
small loaf.

The bartender wiped down some rings on the bar.

"Lots of guys around here. Pick any two."

George reached into his pocket and put a hundred-
dollar bill on the bar. The bartender blinked, then slid
the bill off the bar and into his apron pocket. He lingered
by George, polishing the zinc bar top in circles. Even in a
place like this—a place where rackets were managed and
numbers run, where small fortunes were passed back and

forth in paper bags and cigar boxes—a free hundred-dollar bill would get attention and a friendly ear.

"These guys have names?" he asked casually.

"Andy Delvicco and Jerry Castelli."

The bartender nodded as if George was talking to him about the weather.

"Yeah, I may know these guys," he said. He shoved the rag in a sink below the bar, rinsed it, then wrung it out. "Might take a day or two."

"This is my phone number." George pulled a nub of pencil from his pocket and wrote it down on a napkin. "In case anything comes to mind. If you have something useful for me, that fella I gave you has plenty of friends."

He polished off the whiskey and the last bite of the salami and slipped off the barstool. Once outside, George turned up his coat against the falling snow, which glowed pink and blue in the light of the neon signs. He walked slowly to give anyone who wanted to follow him a chance to catch up.

Each night for the last ten nights, George Marsh had followed the same routine. He went to a known wise-guy hangout, had a chat with the bartender, and dropped a hundred. The bartender usually said he'd ask around. George would leave his phone number. So far, no one had called. He'd had one or two slow tails, but it seemed to George that they were more casual—mob guys always liked to take a look at anyone coming in, and everyone knew who George Marsh was. No one was going to go after Albert Ellingham's man. Too much trouble. They just wanted to have eyes on him, and George wanted to be seen. He wanted it *known*: Andy Delvicco and Jerry Castelli were wanted men, and there was money for anyone who could turn them up. Ellingham money. Bottomless money. Easy money.

Easy money. That was the start of most of the trouble in this world. It was certainly the start of his trouble. . . .

George had always played cards. Nothing serious—a game here or there, at the station, at someone's house on a Saturday night. He liked a little dice now and again, or a trip to the races. Things got a bit more exciting when he started running in Albert Ellingham's circles. Suddenly there were nights at the Central Park Casino, weekends in Atlantic City, trips to Miami, Las Vegas, and Los Angeles . . . places with bigger and better games, more glamour, more excitement, more money.

It had happened quickly, the debt. People were happy to front him credit, as he was such a good friend of Albert Ellingham's, and George was always sure he would win it back. It was nothing at all to be five thousand dollars in debt, then ten, then twenty. . . .

He could have asked Albert for the money, of course. He thought about it. But the shame was so great. What if Albert said no? Then there was no money, no job, no credit, no friends—the life he had made for himself would be gone. He had to get the money. Twenty thousand.

About the amount that Albert Ellingham regularly kept in the safe in his office to pay the workmen at the school . . .

The plan had been so simple.

Andy and Jerry were two nitwits he knew from his days

as a cop—wannabe made men who never quite made much of themselves, but perfect for a straightforward job like this. On the day of the job, they would get the signal from him and wait on the road for Iris Ellingham to drive by in her Mercedes. They were to grab her and hold her for a few hours in a farmhouse while George did the rest. After that, they would get paid and go home, have a steak dinner. Easiest money they'd ever make. No one would be hurt. Iris would laugh when it was over. She would tell the story forever. She loved adventure. This was her kind of thing.

The first problem was that Alice was there. Alice didn't usually go along with her mother for her car rides. Iris probably got defensive because of her daughter—she probably fought back to protect Alice. Iris somehow got dead and wound up floating on Lake Champlain.

And then there was the kid—little Dottie Epstein. She should never have been in the dome that day. No one was. And she had jumped down that hole herself, out of fear. She busted her head in the fall. It was horrible to see. George had no choice but to finish the job.

And Andy and Jerry proved to have a little more upstairs than he had given them credit for. They jumped him when he turned up that night to get Iris and Alice and bring them back. They had hidden them away, and they wanted more money. The whole thing was out of control from the start. Two people dead, and Alice still missing.

Alice. His kid. Not Albert Ellingham's. *His* kid.

Andy and Jerry had done a good job of hiding themselves

for almost a year. There had been no sightings of them at all. Then, out of nowhere, one of George's sources had called him a week ago to tell him that he'd seen Jerry near Five Points. George had come back to New York at once and had been working street by street. If you spread enough paper around Little Italy, someone would know something.

He took a taxi back uptown to Twenty-Fourth Street, where Albert Ellingham had one of his many Manhattan pieds-à-terre. Albert Ellingham bought apartments and houses in the way other people bought fruit. This one had been a rumored haunt of Stanford White, before he was shot on the roof of Madison Square Garden during the performance of a musical called *Mam'zelle Champagne* in 1906, over thirty years ago now. White was a creep who deserved what he got. The guy who shot him was a creep too. So many creeps in this town.

The apartment was small but perfectly outfitted. There was a handsome bedroom, a safe for cash, a modern little kitchen that never got used, and a first-rate radio. George turned this on the moment he came inside. The sound of a symphony filled the room. He didn't care what was on—he just couldn't handle the silence. He sat down in the dark room, coat and hat still on, lights off, and watched the falling snow. He ran through it again in his mind, for the thousandth time.

If Alice had not surfaced, there had to be a reason. Of course, she could have died with her mother, but that felt wrong to him. It would be easy to keep a kid, especially a kid like Alice who was small and gentle. You couldn't ask for a sweeter child. He had played with her often. She showed everyone her toys and dolls, and always gave a hug and a kiss. She would take his hand and follow him around the grounds sometimes. She would be easy to hide somewhere. She wouldn't even have to be very well hidden. Change her clothes, cut her hair, she could be any kid at all.

Little Alice. Now, his every memory of her had new meaning. His daughter. He had put her in harm's way. It only made sense that he, her father, would come and rescue her again.

George Marsh fell asleep in the chair, watching the snow. When he woke, it was light again. The morning radio program was a history lecture about President Lincoln. It had snowed quite a lot during the night; the bathroom windowsill had at least four inches.

As he was still wearing his coat, there seemed little point in showering and changing. He would go right to the corner diner for breakfast instead.

As he approached the front door, he noticed there was something pushed underneath. It was a postcard. On one side was an illustration of Rock Point in Burlington, the place where he and Albert Ellingham had lowered a massive amount of marked bills down to a boat—a boat which then disappeared. He flipped over the card and read the following words, written in a blocky scrawl:

KEEP YOUR MOUTH SHUT IF YOU WANT HER.

George smiled grimly. The fish was tugging on the bait.

"Wakey, wakey."

Stevie opened her eyes, but she was still in the dark. There was a hand shaking her shoulder. It took her a moment to process that the hand and the voice belonged to David. Stevie had dozed off leaning against the closet wall in her stack of pillows, *And Then There Were None* open in her hand. She shook her head hard and tried to seem alert and together, though she strongly suspected she had been drooling and snoring. There was a stiff crustiness to her whole body, the kind you get from wearing the same clothes for a few days because you've been preoccupied, then spending a winter's day inside a pool closet with a bunch of chemicals.

"Up and at 'em," David said. "Time to go home."

"Home?"

"No point in hiding now," he said. "That just makes them look for us and cause trouble."

Stevie stepped out of the closet into the pool room. The glass ceiling was heavy with snow. Nate was looking up at it worriedly.

"I know it's probably built for this weather," he said. "But that is a lot of snow. Not to be a big baby or anything, but I don't want to die in a shower of glass shards."

The first thing they found was that they could no longer open the door; a foot of snow had already blocked it. They left through the window they had used to come in. The snow was pouring down. It was so heavy that Stevie couldn't see the other buildings, just outlines in a white and night-pink world. The view was a bit magical—the Great House framed against the sky, with a white blanket set all around it. A few lights were on, glowing against the fierce, weird weather. The rest of Ellingham was dark. Nothing stirred in the library or the classrooms or the houses. Neptune was slowly being buried in his fountain, consumed by another form of water, which had slipped out of his control. The snow muffled everything. That was maybe the strangest part. Stevie realized that even though it was quiet up here, there was always a low, gentle current of noise—trees rustling in the wind, creaking wood, animals. Tonight, nothing but the operatic whistle of the wind. Their voices were flattened by the thick coating all around them, making each word stand out.

Not that they could say much. Walking was hard. Each step demanded that she pull her leg out of the almost knee-deep accumulation, lift up the other foot, and plunge it down through the snow. It was heavy and aerobic. She sweated from the effort of the walk, and the sweat created a halo of cold all over her body. It wasn't long before her feet began to burn and go numb. By the time they had gotten back on the path to Minerva House, Stevie would have faced anything or anyone to get inside.

Minerva was deliciously warm when they trudged back in. There was a cheerful fire going, tended to by Hunter, who poked at it threateningly, in case it decided to get out of hand. He was wearing the fleece and slippers she had picked out for him. Pix was next to him, on the beaten-down sofa, wrapped in her massive brown fuzzy robe. Though she was dressed like a teddy bear, she had the look of a much more frightening creature on her face as she stood up.

"Everyone get changed so you don't freeze to death," she said. "Then you come right back here so I can yell at you. Because I am *pissed*."

Stevie stumbled into her room, which was darker than normal as the snow had piled on her windowsill and blocked the window halfway. She knocked on the light switch with a raw, burning hand and peeled off her wet clothes. Everything hurt as her body came back up to temperature. Instinctively, she grabbed her robe and staggered across the hall to the shower. Even the hottest water felt cold against her skin. She huddled in the corner against the tiles until something approaching warmth took over again. Her feet were the last to come back online. She went out, numbly pushed her way back into her room, and grabbed at whatever clothes were closest and softest and warmest. Then she put on more— more socks, another sweatshirt on top of the first, then a blanket around her shoulders. Finally, covered in so many layers she had to shuffle, she went back to the common room. Janelle was there, in her fuzzy cat-face pajamas. Vi was wearing another borrowed pair covered in rainbows. David must have had one spare set of clothes in his big bag—the sloppy old Yale sweatpants that used to be his dad's. He had been wearing them on the night they first kissed.

"Okay," Pix said once everyone was seated. "I'm going to be really, really clear about some things. Everyone is under house arrest. Nobody leaves here until the snow clears. The school may be closed, but that doesn't mean that there's no way to enforce this. You want good recommendations at your home schools? Do you want any chance of coming back if we ever reopen? Do you want to go to college? You stay put until I say otherwise. Except you, Hunter. You can do whatever you like."

"I can't go anywhere either," he said. "The snow is nuts."

"No. But I have to say that you're free to do whatever."

"Fine," David said, kicking back and putting his feet by the fire. "Nowhere to go anyway."

"We're not even going to get into where you've been," Pix said. "Only because it's probably not even relevant anymore."

"I went on a quest," he said.

Nate shot him a look that seemed to say, *"Don't joke about quests, jackass."*

"All of you," Pix said. "Have you called home yet?"

"I don't have a signal," Vi said.

"Yeah, me either," Nate said.

Stevie pulled out her phone. No signal.

"I have a landline upstairs," Pix said. "We'll take it in turns. Who wants to start?"

No one wanted to start, so somehow Stevie ended up going first. In all the time she had been at Ellingham, she had not been in Pix's private apartment, which took up the space above the common room and kitchen, and also the area down the hallway opposite the upstairs rooms. She had painted the walls a clay color. There were beautiful Middle Eastern and African objects—brass teapots with long spouts; low, hexagonal tables topped in azure and white tiles; delicately carved wooden animals; tin and brass hanging lanterns with colored insets. There were reproduction hieroglyphics printed on vellum hanging alongside Pix's other passion: her 90s music. She had at least a dozen original concert posters from bands like Nirvana. Nirvana was the only one Stevie recognized.

Of course, there were bones too. There were Pix's precious teeth in the little craft organizer. Her mantel was decorated with some bones that were *probably* fake—a femur, a skull, a knee joint mounted on a little board. The rest of the place was filled with books—books in all directions, piled into bookcases and into stacks along the walls. Books next to her little sofa, books by the hallway and books on the table.

Pix handed her a landline phone. Stevie braced herself against Pix's treadmill and dialed. Her mom answered.

"Hey," Stevie said. "I'm sorry. I missed the coach. It all happened really fast, and . . ."

"You're all right! Oh, Stevie, are you okay? Are you warm?"

To her utter amazement, her mom did not seem angry. The school had to have said something mild, that she had missed the coach or something—not that she had run and hidden in a pool until nightfall. This seemed like Call Me Charles's work; it was his job to smooth the rough and make it seem like Ellingham wasn't a total death trap. In his defense, he had done a pretty good job. All the bounciness and platitudes had some good effect.

"You stay in," her mom said. "Stay safe, stay warm. As soon as the snow clears, you'll come home."

"Sure," Stevie said, unsure of how to feel. When her parents were understanding about things, it always made her feel like a toad, like she was misjudging them.

"We love you," her mom added.

What was this love stuff? It wasn't something her parents and she did. They all felt it, but they didn't go around *saying* it.

"I, um . . . yeah. We're fine. We have lots of food, and, like, popcorn and stuff. And blankets and firewood."

What was she saying? She must have been trying to build some mental picture of what a cozy weekend indoors in a cabin was like. Which, to be fair, was a pretty accurate picture. They did have food and popcorn and blankets and firewood. It would be cozy.

When she was done with the call, she handed Pix the phone.

"You seem confused," Pix said.

"I thought they'd kill me," Stevie replied.

"Surprise, Stevie. Your parents just want you to be safe."

Pix put the phone back on the charging base and leaned against the wall.

"You guys are morons, you know that?" she said. "Out of all the houses, I got the most boneheaded. But I'd be lying if I said I wasn't happy you're all still here. Now come on. Let's get all the calls out of the way and then we can eat. I raided the dining hall when I realized all of you were still here."

The mood in the room lifted a bit as everyone made their calls and then the food started coming out of the kitchen. Pix had come back with a solid haul—trays of mac and cheese, plastic bowls of salad and fruit, lasagna, chicken, roasted potatoes, grilled tofu . . . whatever had been prepared for the day's lunch, plus milk and juice and all kinds of drinks. There was too much of it to fit in the fridge, so Pix had put some of it outside, under the kitchen window. Nature had provided the refrigeration. There were plenty of the normal things like hot chocolate and popcorn and cereal. Really, they had all the makings of an amazing weekend in. One great last hurrah together. They all dug into the food enthusiastically.

"Who else stayed?" Janelle said. "Not just you, right?"

"You mean aside from you maniacs?" Pix said. "Mark from maintenance. Dr. Scott and Dr. Quinn. Vi, I'll make up the upstairs room for you." The upstairs room was Hayes's room, but no one was going to say that. "You two"—she indicated both Janelle and Vi—"separate rooms."

Vi and Janelle passed a silent look. Even Pix picked up on it.

"It's nice to be back," David said. "I'm going to go to my

room, read. Enjoy the snow. See you all in the morning."

"I think I'll do the same," Vi said. "I'm pretty tired."

"It's so weird not to be the first person who wants to go to bed and read," Nate said, when those two had gone to their respective rooms. "Anyone want to play a board game or something?"

"I'm not really in the mood for a game," Janelle said. "Night, everyone."

Pix looked at the rapidly dwindling group at the table.

"Okay . . . ," Nate said. "Well, the game I had in mind is better with a bigger group, so maybe I'll call it a night too. Work on my book or something."

Things had gotten dire. Now it was Stevie, Hunter, and Pix. Stevie knew that the right thing to do was sit and talk to Hunter. But she heard the footsteps overhead—David was once again in the house. After this storm, they would all be blown in different directions across the map. She would not be able to talk or focus. The best idea was to go the way of the others and try to go to sleep.

After an awkward good-night, she shuffled back to her room. She climbed into bed and stared at the wall, unable to turn out the light. It was unlikely any message would appear there, but she had an uneasy feeling that someone was watching, someone not in the house. This was impossible. The snow was driving down hard and the school was empty. She got up anyway and went to the window. It took a bit of effort to open; the cold had half frozen it shut. Once she did, arctic air and a blast of snow shot into her face. She picked up her heavy-duty flashlight and shone it out.

They were alone. Deeply, unnaturally alone, in a rugged, very serious way.

Stevie fought the wind to pull the window shut, then shivered and brushed the snow off herself. She climbed back into her bed.

She did not see the figure that reemerged from the shadow of a tree just outside.

13

It didn't work. It was never going to work.

First of all, it was frigid in her room, and Stevie kept having to get up and put on more clothes—warmer pj's, then a second pair, more socks over her socks, her black hoodie, and then her robe. She got into bed, squashed into all of these layers like a human burrito.

Then there was the noise—the whistling outside. It was like being in a room with a dozen teakettles going full blast, spitting steam and hot water. The blizzard had arrived, and its rage startled Stevie. The wind put its fingers through the edges of the window. She put in her earbuds and tried to listen to a podcast to distract herself, to bring herself back to some kind of normal, but the familiar voices felt strange. The walls of her room made her nervous.

Why had he denied her a tablet? Why come back and then not let her do the one thing he needed everyone to do? Was this a test? A game? A lesson? All of the above?

She itched from it.

It would be a mistake to go upstairs. That's what he wanted. It was also what she wanted.

Why were humans wired like this? Why were we built with a current that could short out our powers of reason and judgment at any time? Why were we filled with chemicals that made us stupid? How could you feel so excited and enraged and like you were being pierced with a thousand emotional needles in the brain all at the same time?

She would not go upstairs.

She would just get up, that's all. But she would not go upstairs.

She would go to her door, but no farther.

Definitely no farther than the hallway.

Bottom step of the stairs. That was the limit.

Halfway. Top of the stairs, then turn back.

So she was at his door in the dark of the hall. There was no light from underneath the door, no sound inside. She strained, trying to pick up any noise, any sense of what was going on. There were no other voices. She shifted from foot to foot, her body coursing with anticipation.

No. She had to go back to her room. *Don't give in to this.*

"Why don't you come in?" she heard him say.

She heard a sharp intake of breath and was surprised to find that she was the source of the noise. Bodies, constantly betraying us. Stupid meat sacks. She put her hand on the doorknob, cursed everything, everywhere, and cracked open the door. David was on the bed, on top of the covers, fully dressed, bent over a tablet.

"You want something?" he said.

She didn't know what she wanted. She had come with some vague notion that once she arrived in David's doorway, all would become clear. Nature would move her, and him. Words would not be necessary. But nature had missed the memo, so she found herself wobbling in the threshold like a vampire.

David's room was filled with things ordered from catalogs by someone who didn't look at prices. These items created a blank canvas that set off all the things that were evocative of him. The battered backpack, the lingering smell of illicit smoke, his Sherlock coat flung carelessly on the floor, a cup of ramen noodles, his banged-up phone. She was looking for clues to explain him, and everything she found made her synapses dance with activity.

"You didn't give me a tablet," she said.

"That's right."

"Why?"

"You're so busy," he said placidly. "I don't want to keep you."

The glass rattled in the pane. The light from the tablet was enough that she could see the contours of his face, the hollows of his cheeks, the sharp peaks of his eyebrows. She wanted to walk over to the bed now, stretch out next to him. Do something. Anything.

She took a few more steps forward, hesitantly. He set the tablet down in his lap.

"Oh, did you want to make out?" He folded his hands

neatly on the tablet and crossed his legs at the ankles. "Really go for it? *Hit those bases?*"

There was no edge in his voice. This was a dull knife.

"Could we . . ."

"No," he said. "We couldn't."

"What did you come back here for?" she said. "You could have read this stuff on your own."

"Where's the fun in that?" he replied. "And I'm slow. Better to get a few big brains on it."

"Bullshit," she said.

"You think I came back to see you?" he said. "Is that it? You, the person who worked for my dad, who came back to spy on me—"

"I didn't spy on you," she said. "I don't like your dad either. My *parents* work for him, and I do everything I can to stop that. . . ."

"Yes, you told me. You put SeaWorld on the call list. Well done."

"Your dad," she said, "put a giant, racist billboard up down the street from where we live. You think I'm going to work for *that guy?*"

David remained in his same casual pose—legs long, body relaxed. But his manner grew tense.

"Let's run through the facts," he said. "My dad brought you back here on his plane, with the agreement that you would keep an eye on me, keep me on the straight and narrow. I trusted you. I confided in you. I told you about my mom and my sister, what my dad did to us."

"After lying to me," she said. "A lot. Telling me your family was dead . . ."

"And I apologized for that. Clearly not enough. I did everything I could. I put myself out there."

He had. This was all true. He had told Stevie all about his life that night in the tunnel. And when they found Ellie, he sobbed. He laid himself bare. And in response, Stevie had panicked, spit out all the information about how his father had made a deal with her—she could come back to the school if she helped keep David on the level.

"The thing with your dad—I told you, I wasn't spying. He brought me back. That's it. I don't even really know what he wanted from me."

"Something he thought you could give," David replied. "That's how he works. My dad can sense where people are weak. That's how he's gotten to where he is. It's also how I know that if I look through his stuff, I'll find something. See, devious malcontents spawn devious malcontents. The evil eat their own. I needed some smart people, people who know stuff about politics, like Vi. That Hunter guy was a lucky find too. People who give a shit about making a difference for the future. Whereas you . . ."

She couldn't see his expression that well in the dark, but she felt the smirk.

". . . want to solve the great crimes of the past so that everyone will think you are Nancy Drew. And in the process, what? Ellie dies, and—"

Here, he cut himself off. But the knife had already gone

in. It didn't matter that she had given Edward King nothing. Edward King saw weakness in her.

"I think it would probably be better if you went downstairs," he said. "Keep warm. It's going to get colder, I hear. A lot colder."

February 24, 1937

FOR FIVE NIGHTS, GEORGE MARSH KEPT WATCH OUTSIDE OF MANELLI'S Restaurant.

Someone had gotten the word to Andy or Jerry that George was in town and looking for them. They had been spooked enough to try to warn him off. When you tell someone to stay back, it's because you're going into a corner and can't get out. The postcard told him that at least one of them was in New York, and whoever it was was frightened. He would wait and watch, as long as it took.

It was too risky to stand out on the street. There was a grocery across the way on the diagonal that accepted two hundred dollars a night to let him sit inside and look out the window. Additional funds went to a few guys who sat at the bar at Manelli's all night and listened, reporting back anything of interest. Money had no meaning now—it was just something he handed out, small fortunes in a city rocked by the Depression. He would pay everyone on Carmine Street if he needed to.

Right after nine o'clock on an icy night, as he was opening a new pack of cigarettes and the owner of the shop was sweeping up, George saw a figure walking toward Manelli's, head down but casting furtive backward looks. Whoever it was had a scarf wrapped high, covering his face. It was a very poor attempt not to be noticed. The person went to the door of Manelli's, looking in both directions before going inside.

"Sal," George said, never taking his eyes off the window, "dial Manelli's for me, huh?"

The shopkeeper set the broom aside and dialed the phone, then passed the receiver to George. The bartender picked it up after a few rings.

"A guy just walked in," George said, as a greeting. "If that's Andy or Jerry, say 'You gotta come downtown. No delivery.' Otherwise, say 'Wrong number.'"

After a pause, the bartender said, "Yeah, no delivery. Come downtown if you want it."

George handed back the phone.

About a half hour later, the door to the restaurant opened and the same figure hurried out with his hat down and a scarf wrapped around his face. George stubbed out his cigarette into an ashtray on the grocery counter. When the figure reached the end of the block, George began to trail him. The snow helped—it was fresh and clean, so it was easier to track the newest set of prints as they turned left. He caught sight of the figure weaving between cars and heading for an alley. George quickened his pace but stayed out of the man's sight. It wasn't for nothing that George Marsh had been so decorated a police officer and that he was now in the FBI. These were his streets, and he knew how to work them.

The man stopped by a car and was in the process of opening the door when George made his move.

"Hello, Jerry."

"Jesus, George," Jerry replied, already out of breath with fear. "Jesus."

George punched him in the face, sending him crashing into some trash cans. When he was down, he flipped Jerry on his back and slapped a pair of cuffs on his wrists, pinning his arms behind him. George quickly patted him down, pulling a gun from his waistband and a switchblade from his sock. Then he hauled Jerry to his feet.

"George . . . ," Jerry began. "I—"

George removed his own coat and threw it over Jerry's shoulders, concealing the cuffed wrists.

"Walk," he said. "You run, you scream, I shoot. You so much as look funny, I shoot."

"*Jesus*, George . . ."

"And you shut up."

On the morning he'd arrived back in New York City, George purchased a car from a reliable thief down by Five Points. George had busted him many times as a cop, but the man held no grudges and was happy to supply a vehicle for a paying customer. It was a good, solid car that George had outfitted with blankets and extra lights. It was toward this car that George pushed Jerry now. Once he got Jerry inside, he bound his ankles together with rope, then tied him to the seat. When he was fully secured, he walked around and got in the driver's side.

"The girl," he said. "Alice."

"George, I . . ."

"The girl. Is she alive?"

"I could never kill a kid, George. We didn't even mean to kill the woman. And I never wanted you to get beat down. That was all Andy . . ."

"Where is she?"

"She's alive," Jerry said eagerly. "She's alive. We left her with some people to watch her."

"Where?"

"Up in the mountains, on the other side of the lake. The New York side. These people have a cabin up there. Nice people. Family people. We told them she was my sister's kid and we were trying to keep her out of a bad situation. Nice people, George. We were just keeping her up there until we figured it all out."

"Where?"

"Somewhere up there in the woods. Some cabin. I forget where."

George punched Jerry in the side of the head.

"*Jesus*, George . . ." Jerry was sweating profusely, despite the cold.

"You kidnapped a girl and forgot where you left her? Here's what I'm going to do in that case: I'm going to attach you to an anchor and throw you in the East River."

"Jesus, George!"

"You remember where the cabin is," George said calmly. "You think about it."

"Maybe if I saw a map or something I could remember."

George had prepared for this. He had a large selection of maps next to his seat, maps from all over the country. He was prepared to drive to California if he had to. He held them up.

"New York," he said, unfolding the map. "Assume that I'm going to kill you. You can only improve your situation. Impress me. Look at this map. Tell me, where are we going?"

14

STEVIE STOOD IN THE DARK OF THE UPSTAIRS HALLWAY AND CONTEM-plated how she had managed to ruin her life.

She had snatched defeat from the jaws of victory. And so easily too! She had jumped right into that gaping maw. She had solved the case—she had done the impossible thing—and now, she was a freezing reject in a hallway, the world crashed, her limbs numb with sadness.

All the badness in the world swirled around her head. She had just pulled her last Ellingham stunt in staying here. Her parents would not only not let her come back here, they would likely never let her go anywhere again. They might take college money off the table, if they had any. Ellingham itself would probably tank her grades. She would go back to Pittsburgh and be hopelessly lost, stuck forever.

For what? The chance to spend a few nights in a snow-storm with someone who hated her.

And the Ellingham case? What if she was completely delusional? She had the tin—she had some concrete proof that the Truly Devious letter wasn't connected to the kidnapping.

That was something. But her other conclusions—they were all conjecture. And what did it matter, really? Maybe she could try to show that the letter had been written by two students. Was that worth throwing away her life?

She couldn't stand in this hallway forever. She considered going to Nate's room, but her troubles were too large. She could not explain the feeling of the world being swept away. She put one leaden foot in front of the other to get back to the stairs, half wishing she tumbled down them in the dark and broke her noncompliant legs and knocked herself out. But she didn't really want that, because she held the rail and the wall and took the steps with care.

Maybe David would come out of his room and stand at the top of these steps, looking down at her, eyes soft and contrite. His hair would be standing up a bit from where he'd run his hands through it in despair at what he had just said. He would say something like, "Hey, why don't you come back up." And she would pause like she was considering it and then say . . .

Maybe the sun would get around to it and finally swallow the world.

Now she was standing in her own dark hallway, which felt even bleaker. She was too confused to cry, too broken to sleep, too lost to move. But there was a light on in the common room. Someone was awake. Stevie didn't want to see anyone, but she also didn't want to be alone. She was trapped in the hall, stuck in every space in between where she needed to be.

But you can't stay in the hall forever. That's not what halls are for. She made her way to the end and peered around the doorway and caught sight of the inhabitant. It was Hunter, wearing the fleece she had gotten for him that day in Burlington, huddled on the sofa, bent over a tablet. The room still smelled of old smoke, but the fire was out in the fireplace. He didn't see her, and she considered backing away, but she couldn't make up her mind about going forward or backward. She must have made a noise by accident, because Hunter looked up and jolted.

"Jesus!" he said, almost dropping the tablet.

It was a good look, probably, just her head poking around the corner, like a ghoul.

"Sorry! Sorry. Sorry, I . . ."

"It's fine," he said, recovering himself. "I'm not used to this place. Are you . . . okay?"

Stevie would sooner have dropped into the molten core of an erupting volcano more willingly than she would tell someone she was not okay. She nodded briskly.

"Can't sleep," she said.

She strode across the room like she had meant to be here all along and busied herself in the kitchen for a moment, filling the electric kettle to make herself a hot chocolate. She dumped two packages into a mug and looked at the pile of chocolate dust she intended to consume. Was this supposed to make up for something, this dust? Was it supposed to repair whatever in her that had ripped in two?

That was a lot to ask of a mug of cocoa dust.

"Do you want something?" she said to Hunter, leaning out of the kitchen. "To drink? I'm . . ."

She jabbed her hand in the direction of the kettle to indicate *"I am bringing water to the boiling point in order to make hot beverages of all kinds."*

"Sure," he said. "Some tea or something?"

Stevie stuck a tea bag in another mug and brought both drinks out. Hunter had chosen one of the coldest spots in the room to sit. There was frigid air coming down from the chimney, as well as slipping in from the front door.

"Find anything good?" she asked, setting down the mug on the brick edge of the fireplace.

"I don't know what I'm looking at," he said. "We got a drive each to read. I read about a thousand emails about campaign strategy and dozens of spreadsheets of financial transactions. The emails show that everyone in this campaign is an asshole. No surprises there. I don't know what the spreadsheets mean. Someone is paying a lot of money for something, but I have no idea what it is or what it's for. This is a weird way to spend a night."

He shoved the tablet between the sofa cushions and picked up the mug.

"Thanks," he said. "I didn't think my aunt's house was going to burn down. I didn't think I'd be up here, in a blizzard, reading emails from inside the Edward King campaign."

It was a good reminder that someone had bigger problems than she did.

"Can I ask you something?" he said. "David? Is he . . ."

Stevie waited for the end of the question, because questions about David could go a lot of ways. Everything inside her coiled up like a defensive snake.

"I mean, the first time I saw him was when he was getting beaten up. And he's King's son. And getting this stuff? I mean, stealing it . . . it's pretty hardcore. It's good? I think? I don't know what to think."

"Me either," Stevie said.

"You and he . . ." Hunter let the words linger. "There's something. There's obviously something."

"No," she said, looking into the sludge of chocolate she was drinking, with gray, scummy lumps of undissolved cocoa floating on top.

"Oh," he said. "Sorry."

Hunter was perceptive enough to know that *sorry* was probably the right word. She felt her shoulders relax a bit but kept her gaze deep into the murk of her drink. They settled into an uncomfortable silence for a moment. Hunter was an easy person to look at—not in the sense that he was stunningly handsome, like some kind of consumable. He was easy in his manner. Unlike David, he didn't appear to be sizing you up. The spray of freckles across his face was like a starry sky. He had a strong build. He was solid and real. He could be trusted.

"Can I talk to you about your aunt a little?" Stevie asked.

He nodded.

"On the night—the other night—I called her," Stevie said.

"She seemed busy. She said she couldn't talk. It seemed like someone was there. Did you see anyone?"

"No," he said. "I had my headphones on. You know she used to play her music really loud, and the downstairs smelled a lot, so I stayed upstairs most of the time. I was working on my end-of-semester paper. I was way into all the plastics we find in the ocean."

"So the first thing you noticed . . ."

"Was smoke," he said. Something passed across his face as he said the word. His gaze turned away from her and went up and over, which, according to the books Stevie had read about profiling, meant someone was remembering. "I smelled it. I've smelled smoke before, but this was a lot of smoke, and it had this really harsh smell. Not like woodsmoke. Like things were burning that shouldn't be burning. You know when you smell something like that that something is wrong. I pulled off my headphones and then there was this sound, like cracking. Imagine a tray of glasses falling over and over. By the time I got to the door and to the stairs, it all happened really fast. There was smoke, fumes. I had trouble seeing getting down the stairs; it was burning my eyes . . ."

He was shaking his head as he spoke, as if he couldn't believe what he had seen.

"The kitchen, where she was, must have gone up quickly. I guess the gas had been going for a while. It spread into the living room. There was so much flammable stuff everywhere—books and papers and trash. All that furniture was old, and the carpets were too. By the time I got to the bottom of the stairs . . . I saw fire pretty much everywhere leading to the kitchen. I called to her. I think I tried to get to her office to see if she was in there, then I was going to try to run through to the kitchen. Somewhere in there I passed out."

Stevie had no idea what to do for a moment. Her thoughts of David were temporarily suspended. Hunter lingered in his memory for a moment, then let out a loud sigh and rubbed his face.

"Maybe I'm more freaked than I realized. I'm fine, but it's . . . it was a lot of fire."

Stevie looked back down into her drink.

"What are you going to do?" she said.

"Go to therapy," he replied, dealing the cards. "I was just in a house fire that killed my aunt. I'm calm *now*, but I don't think that's going to last forever."

"That seems really smart," Stevie said.

"It is smart. I'm a smart guy."

He went silent for a moment, and Stevie felt a burble of anxiety putter up to the surface.

"Was that your question?" he said. "Or was there something else?"

Everything in his tone said, "I too am fine and am ready to move on with the conversation."

"She said something really weird on the phone," Stevie said. "'The kid is there.' Do you know what she was talking about?"

"'The kid is there'?" he repeated, shaking his head. "I have no idea what that means. You don't think . . . Alice?"

"Alice wouldn't be here," Stevie said. "It makes no sense."

"Maybe she didn't say kid? Maybe she said . . ." He searched for something that sounded like *kid*, then shook his head. "Look, my aunt was drunk that night. Really drunk. So drunk she burned the house down."

"She said *kid*," Stevie replied.

Hunter shook his head in confusion.

"Then I have no idea what she meant. But she was really hung up on the codicil for those last few days. She was talking about it more and more. She said Mackenzie told her. There was a document. He hid it so that the place wouldn't be over-run with fake Alices. She said the school knew all about it and was banking on it, because when it expired, they would get the money."

"She said the school knew about it?" Stevie said, leaning forward.

"Yeah. Look, I know how she seemed. I know she could be . . . she had some issues. I know what I just said about the fire. But she knew what she was talking about when it came to this stuff. And when she got into this stuff with the will, she changed. She didn't seem as interested in the case as she did with this idea that there was, like, a *prize* out there. A really, really big prize."

"I asked about it," Stevie said. "I asked Call Me Charles."

"Call Me . . ."

"It's what we call Dr. Scott."

Hunter nodded, understanding the nickname at once.

Neither of them seemed to know what to say next. Stevie

cycled through many possible things—like telling him about her solution to the Ellingham case or asking him if he really thought his house burned down by accident. But both of those things were too much.

"Nate said something about a board game earlier," Hunter said. "Do you want to play one, maybe?"

Stevie was caught completely off guard by this. It was too normal.

"There are games," she said. "Around here. Somewhere . . ."

"There's nothing as serious as a game" was one of Albert Ellingham's mottos, and since the school opened, there were always board games around. Back then, it was mostly Monopoly, but since there were so many games around now, the collections had grown. There was a whole pile of games in a corner of the common room. Stevie had never really paid them much attention except when Nate pulled one out and persuaded her to play.

It was something to do now, on this strange night.

She found the game pile, four in all, in the cabinet along with the cleaning and fireplace supplies. She set them down on the farm table like an offering. Hunter examined them expertly.

"This one is better with more people," he said, pushing one aside. "I don't know this one, but it looks complicated. This one, though . . ."

He held up a small box that contained a card game called Zombie Picnic.

"I played that one with Nate," Stevie said. "It's pretty good. You try to have a picnic while zombies attack you."

"I know this one too. Come on. Sitting here like this sucks. Let's play."

Had you asked her a half hour before, Stevie would not have believed that she would be playing a card game instead of, say, crying in the corner of her room or making plans to fake her own death. Life went on, in the form of cards showing pictures of sandwiches and potato salad and zombies chewing people's heads off. She was still here. David was still upstairs. Things could be fixed.

For an hour or two, there were no murders. There was no case. She looked at her phone at one point and saw it was after midnight. Then it was two in the morning. She became giddy on sleeplessness and adrenaline and whatever comes after sadness. Hunter was good company, and the game was ridiculous. Maybe Albert Ellingham had been on to something with this game thing.

Once they had passed the three or four o'clock mark, then it seemed only reasonable to go on until the sky lightened, which it finally did. It turned from night pink and black to day pink and white, then pure white. She and Hunter were now night companions, linked in some way she could not define. All felt good for a while. They would get up and start laughing at nothing. They made popcorn. They stuck their heads out the window and let snow fall on their faces, waking them up.

It continued like this until sometime around dawn, when there was a creak on the stair. David emerged from the hallway.

"Game, huh?" he said.

"Yeah, well . . ." Hunter arranged the cards in his hand. "We're just taking a break."

David made a *hmmmm* noise and disappeared into the kitchen, reappearing a moment later with an untoasted Pop-Tart sticking out of his mouth. He sat in the hammock chair and spun, causing the rope to twist audibly.

"I was up half the night reading your stuff," Hunter said. "Do you have *any* idea what we're supposed to be looking for?"

"Nope," David said, using his feet to stop the spinning. "Just that it's important."

"So if I was looking at a bunch of spreadsheets, banking records . . ."

David stuck the last piece of the Pop-Tart in his mouth and shrugged.

"Helpful," Hunter said. "So how do you know it's important?"

"Because my dad is trying to hide it," David said. "Because of the way he's been acting. Because of stuff he's said or hasn't said. I know when my dad is up to some shady shit."

"Isn't that always?" Hunter asked.

"He's always up to *some* shit," David clarified. "It's not always shady. This is shady. And whatever is on those drives, he was keeping it off the server."

"A lot of the stuff seems routine," Hunter said.

"Some of it may be. I think some of those drives are back-ups, which means we have to find the interesting thing. It's fun."

"Fun," Hunter said.

"Like what you're having. Oh, morning, Stevie."

Stevie tried not to twitch. Everything about David was deliberate.

Hunter gathered up the cards and stacked them into a pile, tapping them neatly on the table surface before putting them back in the box. "You've set up some kind of fake identity in your dad's campaign, right?" he said.

"You mean Jim?" David said.

"Yeah. Jim. Can Jim do something?"

"Like what?"

"Like send an email to the school asking to see the codicil."

David eyed Hunter, somehow making sure to shut Stevie out of the look. Stevie, for her part, almost got whiplash from the turn in the conversation.

"What codicil?" he asked.

"The one that says that the person who finds Alice Ellingham gets a fortune," Hunter replied. "The one the school doesn't show anyone."

David tilted his head in interest.

"Why would Jim do that? Jim is a busy guy."

"I'm helping you with your stuff," Hunter said. "You could do me a favor too."

"A favor for *you*?"

"A favor," Hunter replied, ignoring any implied question. "An exchange of labor."

"And this favor is for you?" David asked again.

"It's something my aunt believed in," Hunter replied. "I want to know. I'll help you; you help me."

David waited a long beat, then spun in the chair again, twisting the rope. Stevie suddenly found that she was wide awake, and maybe about to throw up.

"Well, the Wi-Fi is out," David said. "If Jim wrote such a note, I don't know when it would send. But why would the school share it with Jim if they don't show anyone?"

"It's not that they don't share it with anyone," Hunter replied. "It's probably more that they don't share it with *just* anyone."

It took Stevie's foggy mind a moment to absorb the difference.

"Board members," she said. "Legally, there must be people who would know."

"Right," Hunter said. "And maybe there's a reason that Senator King would want to know about it because his son goes here. Maybe we could come up with a reason . . ."

Hunter was on to something. Stevie's brain switched back on for one last burst of activity for the night.

"He would want to know because of news stories," she said. "Because of the deaths. You don't have to explain that much."

"My parents are both lawyers," Hunter said. "You write short, terse notes and make it sound like people have to do what you want. Only say what you need to. I think it might work."

David scratched at his eyebrow and then rubbed the stubble on his chin. Chin stubble. Stevie had to tell herself not to look at it, or the way he stretched out his legs. Human sexuality was amazing and confusing and horrible, and messed up all her thoughts just as she got them in order. *Focus.*

"Will you write it?" she asked David. She looked right at him, challenging him.

"Again, I need a reason."

"I'll owe you."

He laughed out loud at that.

"And it dicks around with your dad a little more," Hunter added. "If you made a guy, why not use him?"

Stevie could almost see the calculations going on behind David's eyes.

"Fine," he said. "You tell me what to say and I'll send it, and you keep reading. We don't have a lot of time."

It took only a few minutes to come up with Jim's wording:

I am writing on behalf of Senator King. The senator would like to see a copy of any legal documents that state that there is some kind of financial benefit for anyone who produces Alice Ellingham. This document has been long rumored to exist. The senator would like to know about any potential legalities or news stories that might involve the school, and obviously, any kind of

**windfall would be rich fodder for the press. Thank
you for your attention to this matter.**

"It's short," Hunter said. "Keep it brief. Sounds more important, like you're entitled."

"Relatable," David said as he finished typing. "Fine. I'll send it off as soon as I have a signal again. Are you going to read the stuff I gave you now?"

Hunter got up without a word, sat back on the sofa, and picked up the tablet.

Exhaustion dropped on to Stevie. The bubble burst, and the air was sucked back out of the room. David was twisting in the chair and the wind was howling. She was not needed.

"I'm going to bed," she said.

As she got up to go, David trailed her loosely in the hall.

"Are you following me?" she said.

"I'm going to my room to get a power cord," he replied. "Like I said, I was reading all night. Looks like you had fun, though."

Stevie gripped her doorknob so hard she thought she might rip it off.

"Not everything is about you," she said.

Then she went into her room and shut the door in his face.

15

THE WHOLE HOUSE WAS SHAKING.

Stevie opened her eyes. The light in the room was dim. She blinked a few times and reached for her phone. It was almost three in the afternoon. There were no texts or calls from her parents, which suggested that there had been no signal.

She found she had made a nest for herself to keep warm—all the blankets, her robe, her fleece, even a few towels. At one point, she remembered she had considered tipping out her bag of dirty laundry on top of herself. She pieced together the events that had gotten her here. She had been with Hunter and David in the common room until early in the morning, then the exhaustion had come down on her and she had gone into her room to rest for a minute. The minute had turned to hours, and the day had vanished.

She slithered out of bed and went to the window. Outside, the snow was coming down sideways, even blowing back *up*. It had so coated the trees and ground that it was hard to figure out what was outside at all. It was impossible to calculate how much snow had collected on the ground, but it looked like it was now a few inches below the window. So, two feet? Three feet?

What to do now? She returned to her bed and sat on the edge. There was no going outside—not outside-outside and possibly not outside this room. She looked at the wall, the gently lumpy, overpainted surface where the message had appeared all those weeks ago. Between the cottony view out the window and the post-nap fuzz in her head, reality distorted and a ball of adrenaline shot through her system. This place was dangerous. She should have heeded the warning on the wall. She kept brushing up against death's sleeve, avoiding it by inches and moments. It was at the end of a tunnel, under the floor, at the other end of the phone. She should have gone home, left this terrible place, because her luck suddenly felt fleeting. Now there was no escape.

Just as she felt the first ramp up into an anxiety attack, there was a gentle rapping on her door, and Janelle poked her head in. She had her comforter wrapped around her like a regal cape. It dragged along behind her as she came in.

"I thought I heard you," she said. "You're up."

The mental monsters ran away in Janelle's presence. She had that effect, and Stevie almost welled up with appreciation.

"Where's Vi?" Stevie asked, casually wiping at her eye.

"Up in David's room. They're reading. David, Hunter, Vi."

"Nate?"

"He's writing?" Janelle said. "I think? At least he has some sense. I'm surprised you're not up there."

"Yeah." Stevie smoothed out her blanket. "I'm still not welcome."

"Don't worry about that," Janelle said. "Forget him."

There was an extra edge in her voice now, and a bit of a rasp. Stevie wondered if she had been crying this morning.

"Are you two fighting?" Stevie said. "You and Vi?"

Janelle sat on the bed and tightened the comforter cloak around herself.

"It's not a fight," Janelle said. "It's a disagreement. Vi is an activist. I know this about them. They have strong opinions and want to do good in the world. That's what I love about them. But I don't think they should be . . . David's ideas aren't good. This isn't good. Well, maybe the part where we all stayed. But . . . I mean. Yeah. We're fighting."

She put her head in her hands for a moment, groaned, then looked up.

"What are you doing?"

"Looking at the wall," Stevie replied honestly.

"Guess it's as good as anything else," Janelle said.

"Walls are more interesting than you think," Stevie said, realizing that she may have just uttered the most boring statement anyone had ever uttered. "In mystery stories, a lot of things are behind or inside of walls," she said. "But it's true in life too. People find stuff in walls all the time. Letters. Money. Witches' bottles. Razors. Mummified cats . . ."

"Wait, what?"

"It's a thing that used to happen," Stevie said. "Bodies

have been found. There are stories of people who lived in walls—well, that happens in books more. People tend to live in attics, like this guy Otto who lived in his lover's attic for years and used to sneak down when they were out, and eventually he murdered the husband. Or this guy they call the Spiderman of Denver who lived in these people's house and murdered the owner one night and then kept living in the house for a while. You can usually tell when you hear strange noises at night and food goes missing. . . ."

"Oh," Janelle said.

"I mean," Stevie said. "Cases get solved because of walls. For instance, there was a case in England of a man who was accused of sexually assaulting lots of teenagers in the 1970s. They all talked about the fact that he had a wall in his house where victims wrote their names and phone numbers. So the police went to that house, in the present day, and they brought in some decorators to strip the wall, because decorators have the equipment to do that. They took off layer after layer of paint until they literally uncovered the 1970s, and there was the wall with all the names and numbers and dates, just like everyone said. The evidence was all there. They peeled back the past. I was thinking about it because this friend of Ellie's in Burlington said that Ellie talked about stuff being in the walls here."

Janelle considered the blank space of wall for a moment. Then she dropped the comforter and stood up.

"Wait here," she said. "I'll be back. I have to do something."

Stevie waited in the same position for several minutes.

Ten, fifteen. Stevie didn't hear her upstairs, or even in her room. Stevie listened to the house groan and move. She leaned back against her pillows and pulled both her own and Janelle's comforter over her. Finally, there was a noise in Janelle's room. Doors opening and closing. Then Janelle cracked open Stevie's door and slipped inside, shutting it tight behind her. She was wearing different clothes than she had been before— she had changed back into her fuzzy cat-head pajamas, furry slippers, and a robe. She was flushed, her body damp from snow and exertion, the freezing chill still on her body. She had snow in her hair, on her eyelashes. She had a small object in her hand. It looked a bit like an oversized phone.

"What did you do?" Stevie said. "I thought you were on your computer or something."

"You wanted to look in the walls," she said. "I went to the maintenance shed and I got the wall scanner."

"You went out?"

"You don't have a monopoly on busting rules," Janelle said, shaking out her legs to warm them and restore circulation. "You want to have a look and see what's under there? Let's look."

The wall scanner was a simple device, with a small screen. Janelle tried to look up a video on how to use it, but the Wi-Fi didn't cooperate. She worked it out on her own without too much difficulty.

"Okay," she said. "The idea behind these is to look for things like pipes, wires, studs, stuff like that. So let's try this wall."

She went over to the wall that Stevie had been staring at, then slowly ran the device over it.

"See here?" She ran it back and forth near a light switch. "Wires."

She ran it along another strip of wall.

"Studs," she said. "Lots of pockets of space. See? We can look for things too, just like they are. Except this is legal and constructive."

She surveyed the room. "Can you take everything off your nightstand? I'll use that to stand on. And we need to move all the furniture away from the walls."

The room, which had been so gloomy a short while ago, was a sudden hub of activity. It turned out, shoving furniture around was a pretty good way to clear your head. Janelle was so focused that she didn't even mention the large dust clumps behind the bureau and under the bed. Once they'd moved everything aside, Janelle began a sweeping scan. Along the outside wall, it was all structural materials. When Janelle moved in, she found more wires, voids, a pipe or two. Aside from something that might have been another dead mouse, there was nothing of note.

"Okay," Janelle said when they had done all four walls. "We have a sense of how this thing works. Now we try in Ellie's room. Do you think Hunter would let us?"

"There's a bit more wall to do," Stevie said, pointing at the closet.

"Good point."

It took only a minute or two to dump out the contents

of Stevie's closet onto the bed. Her room was completely in shambles. Janelle climbed into the closet and began running the machine over the walls.

"Oh," she said. "I think we have a bunch more dead mice in here."

"Cool," Stevie said. "That's fun to know."

"When you open the door to knowledge, you have to take what you get— Wait."

Janelle was down low, running the machine along the seam of the wall and the floor.

"There's something there," she said. "Not metal. It's sort of . . ."

Janelle set down the scanner and felt around the base of the wall, around the molding.

"There's a lot of paint on this," she said. "We're going to need to get through it. Hang on."

She went to her room and returned a moment later with her crafting tool belt. She started with a utility knife, working the edges. She moved from there to a screwdriver, working slowly and methodically to pry the board loose. Stevie heard a few promising pops and cracks. Out came a larger flathead screwdriver. More pushing and tapping and wedging, then . . .

Pop. The molding cracked as it came off.

"Whoops," Janelle said. "Oh well. It's in the closet. Who cares. I need a . . ."

She made a pinchy-pinchy motion with her fingers.

"A crab?" Stevie said.

Janelle looked up and around, then stood and grabbed

two empty hangers from the closet bar.

"Get the flashlight and hold it in there," she said.

Stevie snagged her flashlight and shone it into the space Janelle was working in. Janelle delicately pushed the ends of two of the hangers inside and pressed them together, creating a claw. It took her a few tries, but she eventually fished out a small, crumpled paper. She pulled on it. It was a degraded pack of Chesterfield cigarettes. The pack still contained several cigarettes, which looked extremely fragile.

"These look old," Janelle said. "Someone was using this to hide their stuff."

She picked up the scanner again and ran it back over the spot.

"There's still something else," she said. "Higher up. About eight inches high, maybe five across? Perfectly rectangular."

"Like the size of a book?" Stevie said.

Janelle craned her arm up into the space as well, but soon pulled back and dusted herself off.

"I don't think we're going to get at it that way," she said. "I think we're going to have to go through."

"Through?"

Janelle got up and returned a moment later with a mallet and a large, heavy knitting needle.

"What don't you have in your room?" Stevie asked admiringly.

"A circular saw. And I tried. Turn up some music. This may be loud."

Stevie went over to her computer and looked around for

something that seemed like passable music, pushing the volume as high as her laptop could manage. It rattled through the bass speakers. Janelle shrugged, as if to say that the poor sound would have to do. She tested the wall again, tapping until she found the spot she wanted. Then she set the knitting needle against it and gave it a hard whack with the hammer. This made a small pockmark. She did it again, and again, until a small hole appeared. She worked around the small hole, creating a series of small holes until there was a small honeycombed pattern. From there, it took only a few taps with the mallet before the patch dented, and one more before a hole about six inches across opened up.

"Flashlight," Janelle said. "The good one, not a phone."

Stevie scrambled over to her set of drawers and retrieved the high-powered flashlight the school provided for emergencies. Janelle shone this into the wall, revealing a small cavern of dust and dark. She reached her hand inside. This time, it took very little effort.

"Got it," she said to Stevie.

After a minute of maneuvering, plus a few more taps of the mallet, Janelle pulled a small red book out of the opening.

The wonderful thing about reality is that it is highly flexible. One minute, all is doom; the next, everything is abloom with possibility. The terrible feelings of the night before were replaced with a glow, a heartbeat that shook her arm and hand as she took up the book. It was bound in red leather, which had probably been bright originally and now was a bit blackened with grime, but not so much as to mar its appearance too badly. The corners of the book were rounded, and the word *DIARY* was written on the front in gold lettering. The paper edges were also gold in color. Seeing it come out of the wall filled her with a sensation she had no words for. It was a kind of wild, high focus, a feeling that time was collapsing and the past was popping out to say hello.

"Open it!" Janelle said. "Open it!"

The book made a gentle cracking sound as the brittle binding and leather gave way for the first time in decades. Directly inside were several black-and-white photos. It was instantly clear that these were part of the set she had found in the tin. Francis and Eddie. Eddie was stretched out on the grass, looking into the camera, a naughty smile on his lips. There was another of Francis in her Bonnie Parker outfit. There were other scenes as well. Whoever took the photos was making an attempt at art. There was a dramatic photo of the Great House, another of the fountain splashing, Leonard Holmes Nair painting on the lawn. The book was thick with clippings, with writing.

"Holy shit," Stevie said.

"See?" Janelle said. "You come to me for results."

There was a quick knock on the door, and Pix peeped in. "Dinner!" she said.

February 25, 1937

THE DRIVE LASTED ALL NIGHT—A WINDING PATH THROUGH THE Adirondack Mountains, past lakes, down roads that were thin paths through ice and snow.

As George suspected, Jerry knew where to go, generally speaking. He knew the town—Saranac Lake—and had a rough set of directions beyond that. Jerry was not bright, but even he wouldn't completely misplace the most valuable kidnapped person on the planet.

The car struggled, and had the weather been a bit less temperate, there was no way they would have made it. As dawn approached, they were on the outskirts of Saranac Lake, and he seemed surer that this was the right area. He guided George to a series of small roads outside town.

"Tell me about Iris," George said.

Jerry was in a stupor from exhaustion and fear. He lifted his head and lolled it toward the window.

"Andy thought we were being suckered," he said tiredly. "That's how it started. He said you got a big head since you'd been living with Ellingham. He showed me all the papers, all the stories about Ellingham. He said that he was one of the richest guys in the world and that a couple of thousand was nothing. He said this was the big score. This one-and-done. It was coming to us on a plate. We would take the woman and use you to get us more money. But then, we stopped the car, and there was a kid in there. It all went wrong right at the start."

"You could have left the kid on the road."

"I said that! But Andy said we had to keep going—that it would be even better with the kid. And it was at first. The woman—she was quiet; she wanted to make sure the kid wasn't hurt. Everyone was behaving real nice. I thought we would let them go after the score we got that night on Rock Point, but Andy thought we could get a million. A million bucks is nothing to a guy like Albert Ellingham. He said we should hold out a little longer. He found this place, some farmhouse out in the middle of nowhere. He said they couldn't look in every farmhouse in the country. I think you turn right up here."

George turned the car, watching Jerry out of the corner of his eye.

"It was a few days in," Jerry said. "We kept them comfortable. I'd talk to them. I even brought in a radio for them to listen to. We kept the woman tied up, but the kid, I would let her play sometimes when Andy was out. As long as"—he couldn't seem to say the name Iris—"*she* could see the kid, she would stay still. She saw I was feeding her. I even brought her a doll. I kept telling her it was all going to be okay. She was quiet for a while. She and the kid would sleep together. It was all going to be all right. But then, that day . . ."

Jerry had to stop for a minute.

"Keep going," George said.

"I let the kid play a bit one day when Andy was out getting food. All of a sudden the woman said, 'Alice, go play!' And that kid *took off running*. I think she had been coaching the kid to do that, like it was a game or something. Before I could run after the kid, the woman jumped at me. She had gotten her hands loose. She was *strong*. You never met a broad so strong. She jumped on top of me, dug her thumbs into my eyes. I dropped my gun. I didn't want to hurt her. I thought, *Just let her go; let her run*. But something in me . . . I don't know, if you fight all the time you can't not fight if you get jumped. She was going for the gun, and I grabbed a shovel or something from the wall and hit her with it, hard. There was blood, but . . . she was still standing. She started running. I can still see her running across that field, screaming for the kid to run. The kid was nowhere. In my head, I'm thinking, *It's over. Good. It's over. We can just go now.* But she was screaming so loud I got scared. I caught up to her when she fell. She had blood on her face, in her eyes. I told her to shut up, *shut up* and everything would be fine. I hit her once or twice, just to try to get her to stop. And she started . . . laughing."

At this, Jerry stopped and seemed genuinely puzzled by the story. George tightened his grip on the steering wheel.

"Andy came back when this was going on. When I saw him, I let her go. Because I knew. I thought, *Give her a chance.*

She got up and started screaming again. And Andy, he just..."

The picture was complete and all too clear to George. Iris was one of the most alive people he had ever met. She loved a dance, a party... she could swim for miles. That moment in the field—she had trained for that her whole life. She was a Valkyrie. She went down fighting.

"... shot her," Jerry said simply. "It all happened so fast."

Jerry fell silent, lost in the moment of Iris's death there in the field.

"Alice," George prompted him.

"It took us an hour to find the kid," Jerry went on quietly. "I told her her mother had gone home. She started crying. We moved to another place. We wrapped the woman's body up and Andy drove back to Lake Champlain and put it there to make it seem like we were closer to Burlington than we were. After that, Andy started getting nuts, talking about the FBI all the time. He never left me alone with the kid again. We'd drive from place to place. We slept in parks, sometimes hotels, but usually out in the open, in the car. Then one day he decided he could leave me with the kid again for a little while. He went out for an hour and came back and said he'd found this place. We were going to leave the kid for a bit and come back when it was less hot for us. This couple would watch her. We told them she was his sister's kid, and that the husband was no good and we wanted to keep the kid safe for a bit while we dealt with it. They seemed to buy it, and they liked the money. We slept in a barn that night. Andy talked about Cuba, that he knew a guy with a boat who would take us there for five hundred. He said we should go there. We'd drive to Boston and get in the boat. When I woke up, Andy was gone. He left a grand in my pocket. I didn't know what to do. I got cousins in New Jersey, so I went there. But I don't know what to do in New Jersey. So I came back to New York. I knew at some point you'd show up."

"So why leave me the card?" George asked.

"I guess I was tired of fighting it. You get tired."

George felt something roiling in his abdomen—coffee and bile. *You get tired.* He was so tired. Once he got Alice, it would be over. Whatever happened to him then, maybe it didn't matter. Get Alice and get Andy. Albert Ellingham knew half the government of Cuba. That would be easily settled. A sweet relief broke with the dawn. So much pain and tension and fear this last year, and for what? Now, there would be some redemption.

"Here," Jerry said. "Turn here."

They turned down something that was barely a road—it was a dirt path cut into the woods, pocked and pitted, full of ice and snow. The car sputtered and at one point almost slid off the road and into a tree. At the end of the road was a house, rough, made of logs and clapboard, with a collapsed-in porch with several deer antlers scattered around. An anemic finger of smoke came from the chimney.

"This is it?" George said.

"This is it. This is the house. These are the people. Nice people."

"So here's what we're going to do," George said. "I untie

you. You walk up to the door in front of me, in case these are the kind of people who say hello with a shotgun. I'm behind you with my gun. Remember, I *want* to shoot you. You do anything funny, I give in to my impulse."

"Nothing funny, nothing funny."

George tugged the ropes loose so that Jerry could get out. The cuffs he left on, covered once again with George's coat. Jerry stumbled ahead as the front door of the house opened and a man walked out. He may have been George's age, or even younger, but time ravaged here. His hair was thinning and greasily patched to his head. He had a gray complexion, the look of someone who hadn't seen the sun or a decent meal in some time. He wore loose overalls and a flannel shirt, but no coat. He did not seem happy to have visitors.

"Morning!" Jerry said with a queasy fake cheerfulness. His New York accent sounded like snapping twigs in the cold morning. "You remember me? With the kid?"

The man regarded them both for a long moment, and George rested his hand on the butt of his handgun tucked into the back of his trousers, just in case. This man had keen eyes and seemed to read the situation well—he took in Jerry, supplicant and bundled, and George, who always looked like a cop, no matter what he did.

"Took you long enough to come back for her," the man said, sounding annoyed. "You said a week. Lot more than a week."

"I know," Jerry said. "I'm sorry. But we're here now."

"Only paid us for the week."

"You'll be paid," George cut in before Jerry could say anything else. "Take this for a starter."

He reached into his pocket and grabbed a handful of bills. He had no idea how many. Could have been two hundred bucks or two thousand. He held them out, and the man stepped down from the porch and took them. His hands were rough and worn from work, but clean. This lightened George's heart somehow. This was a poor house in a rough terrain, but there was nothing wrong with being poor, and people knew how to live here, how to keep warm and fed, even during the depths of an endless winter.

"Thought so," the man said, looking at the fistful of cash. "It's that kid from the papers, isn't it? Has to be. The Ellingham girl."

George tilted his head noncommittally.

"Bet there's more where this came from," the man said, holding up the crumpled notes.

"You'll be paid well."

The man grunted. "You should have come sooner. Been a long time. You said a week or two."

"We're here now," George said.

"She's in the back."

George went to walk up the stone steps, but the man shook his head.

"No, not in the house. She's outside, out back. Come on."

George looked out at the snowy field that stretched behind the house. A good place for a kid. A kid could build a good snowman out there. He could almost see her already, thumping through the snow, laughing. Maybe this had all been for the best. Maybe Alice had had a normal life here, a simple life. Maybe she had swum in a lake in the summer, picked apples in the fall.

"Bess liked having a kid around," the man said, trapping through a half foot of snow.

George looked around at the smooth, pure snow. There were, he noted, no footprints.

"Where?" he said, scanning the area.

"Over there," the man said somewhat impatiently. "By them trees."

George began to walk faster, forgetting Jerry, who stumbled along with his hands bound behind his back, the coat slipping from his shoulders. Alice. Alive. Alice. Alive. Those words were so alike. She was here, playing. She was here, in the snow. She was . . .

There was no one by the tree.

George felt the rise of the panic and his reflexes kicked in. He pulled the gun from his waistband and spun in one move, hampered a bit by the snow packed around his ankles. How had he been so stupid? He had walked into a trap. This was a conspiracy, and George was about to be taken down.

And yet, when he faced the stranger and Jerry, there was no gun pointed at him.

"What's going on?" he yelled. "Where is she?"

"I just told you," the man said. "She's here."

"There is no one here."

"Look down," the man said.

George looked down at snow.

"It happened not two weeks ago," the man said. "She got the measles. Marked her there, where the stone is."

George saw it now—a stone. Not a headstone. Not even a marked stone. Just a rock, covered in snow.

"I told you, you shoulda come sooner," he said. "Can't do nothing with the measles. Kept her in the back. She was never gonna make it, kid like that. Kid was weak."

George stared at the rock that marked his daughter's grave.

"Did you get her a doctor?" he rasped.

"Couldn't get a doctor out for that kid," the man said dismissively. "Once we knew who she was."

Once we knew who she was. George breathed in the freezing air evenly. He felt no cold.

"Get a shovel," he said.

George sent the man back to the house and stood guard as Jerry did the digging. The first layer was quick—all snow. Alice was not buried deep, barely a foot underground, and not even in a coffin. The body had been wrapped up in some sacking.

"Oh God," Jerry said, looking down at the bundle. "I never . . ."

"Put the shovel down and move away from her."

Jerry stumbled back, dropping the shovel. He held up his hands in surrender.

"I'm not going to shoot you, Jerry," George said, tucking

213

his gun into his waistband.

Jerry half collapsed, breathing heavily, heaving, praising George and God in equal measure. He did not see George pick up the shovel, and was shocked by the first blow, which knocked him to his knees. They came fast, a flurry mixed with cries and gulps. The snow splattered with blood.

When it was over, George tossed the shovel down and panted. There was no movement from the direction of the house. They were far enough that nothing may have been seen or heard. The stranger would have been listening for shots, most likely, and there had been none.

Gathering himself, he walked over to the grave. He lifted the little parcel from the hole. It had frozen stiff. He set Alice down carefully on the fresh snow, then used the shovel to enlarge and deepen the hole. He deposited Jerry, facedown.

He carried Alice to the car and put her gently on the back seat, carefully arranging the car rug over her as if warmth could revive her.

After taking a moment to consider what he had done, he removed his gun from his waistband, confirmed that it was loaded, and began the walk back to the house.

16

STEVIE FELT LIKE SHE WAS CONCEALING A BOMB.

It was so weird that it was night now, weird that the group was back together around the big farm table. In the excitement of the search, Stevie had temporarily forgotten everything else that was going on—the snow, David, the files they were reading.

Pix, unaware of all the activity going on around her, had put out bread and sandwich makings, plus some of the salads and odds and ends that the dining hall had left behind. There were cold drinks with snow still on the bottles. Stevie grabbed one of the maple spruce sodas that she thought were disgusting. She didn't care how anything tasted right now. She needed to go through the motions, eat, and go back to her room with the diary that was sitting on her bed. There was a bowl of tuna salad. She grabbed two slices of the closest bread and smacked on a gob, squashing it flat. She sliced it with one long cut and dropped down into a chair at the far end of the table.

David sat at the other end, one of the old tablets next to him, facedown.

"I don't eat tuna salad," he said, grabbing a piece of bread. "It's too *mysterious*. People sneak things into it. It's a sneak food."

"I like it," Hunter said. "We make it at home with sliced-up dill pickle and Old Bay Seasoning."

"Good to know," David said. "Nate, where do you come down on tuna salad?"

Nate was trying to read and eat some cold mac and cheese in peace.

"I don't eat fish," he said. "Fish freak me out."

"Noted. What about you, Janelle?"

Vi kept sneaking looks over at Janelle. Janelle remained polite but resolute. She made herself a plate of cold roasted chicken and salad, then sat next to Stevie. Vi stared into the depths of their mug of tea. "I have better things to think about," she said. "How has your day gone?"

"Slow," David replied. "But, you know."

"I don't, actually," Janelle said.

David kept looking over at Stevie. His expression was impossible to read. It wasn't unfriendly. It was almost . . . pitying? Like he felt *bad* for her?

That was unacceptable. Give her the smirk. Ignore her. But pity didn't sit well on David's sharply angled face. Stevie lifted her chin and stared back as she ate her tuna salad. And when she accidentally dropped some tuna salad on her lap, she brushed it to the floor, refusing to acknowledge that it had happened.

She excused herself as soon as she had cleared away her

plate. Janelle came with her. Back in her room, Stevie knelt next to her bed, like someone praying or bowing before an artifact. Janelle sat on the bed and watched as Stevie opened the book again. The cover made that same creak. It had a very faintly musty odor, and the pages were a milky yellow, but the diary was otherwise in good repair. The handwriting was an ornate cursive, perfectly level, small and exquisitely formed. The ink was smudged in places.

"Let's start with the pictures." Stevie held up the photo of the girl in the slinky knit dress, her hand on her hip, a cigar in her teeth. "This is Francis. This has to be her diary. She lived here."

Francis Josephine Crane and Edward Pierce Davenport were both students in the first Ellingham class of 1935–36, the class that had to go home early in April when the kidnappings happened. Francis lived in Minerva; this had been her room. Her family owned Crane Flour ("America's favorite! Baking's never a pain when you're baking with Crane!" had apparently been their slogan). They were a massively wealthy family, friends of the Ellinghams in New York City; they had adjacent town houses on Fifth Avenue. She was only sixteen when she was at Ellingham, but her life was full of travel, tutors, summers in Newport, winters in Miami, trips to Europe, balls and parties, everything afforded to the rich during the Depression while the country starved. Her life after Ellingham was a bit of a mystery. She had a coming-out ball at the Ritz when she was eighteen, but there was very little after that.

Edward, or Eddie, came from a similar background. He

was a rich kid who had burned his way through schools and tutors. Eddie wanted to be a poet. His fate was known. After Ellingham, he went to college, then dropped out and went to Paris to be a poet. On the day the Nazis took over the city, he got drunk on champagne and leaped off the top of a building and onto a Nazi vehicle, a fall that killed him.

In these photos, they were alive again, and wild. Stevie turned the pages carefully, first examining the clippings. Many were from newspapers—stories of John Dillinger, Ma Barker, Pretty Boy Floyd. All bank robbers. Outlaws. There were other things too—pages torn out of science textbooks. Formulas.

"These mean anything to you?" Stevie said to Janelle.

"Only that most of these things are explosive," Janelle replied.

In the margin of one of the pages was a note: *Fingerprints: H2SO4 NaOH*

"What's this?" Stevie asked.

"Sulfuric acid and sodium hydroxide. Common acids. I don't know what the fingerprints means."

"I think it means burning off fingerprints," Stevie said. "Gangsters and bank robbers did that. Burned them off with acid."

The next few pages were full of hand-drawn maps, very detailed and finely done in pencil, hearkening from a time before Google, when you had to find physical copies to plan your route. Whoever had drawn this was competent at sketching, with a steady, precise hand. There were more pages, both handwritten and torn out of other sources, about guns and ammunition.

"This is some scary stuff," Janelle said. "Like someone preparing for a school shooting."

"I don't think that's it," Stevie replied. "I think this is a self-written guidebook. This is about becoming a gangster or a bank robber. There was no internet, so she made herself a textbook."

A ribbon divided the book in two. Stevie opened to this dividing point. Here, it was less clippings and more handwriting. These were diary entries. Stevie scanned the first few:

9/12/35
Everything was supposed to be different here, but it looks to me to be a lot of the same crummy stuff that happens at home. I have to look at Gertrude van Coevorden every day, and sometimes I think if she says one more inane thing I will have to set her hair on fire. She's an unbelievable snob. She's really mean to Dottie, who seems to be the only one around here with any brains at all. It's a shame she's so miserably poor.

9/20/35
A bright spark. His name is Eddie, and he's a very interesting boy. If he's the same Eddie I'm thinking of, the stories about him are something else. They say he fathered

*a baby once and the girl had to be sent away somewhere
outside of Boston to give birth in private. He looks capable
of it. I intend to find out more.*

9/21/35
*I asked Eddie about the baby. He smiled and asked me if I'd
like to find out about it, that he'd be willing to show me. I
told him if he said anything like that to me again I'd put out
a cigarette in his eye. We're going to meet tonight after dark.*

9/22/35
*Eddie gave me some lessons. This place will not be so bad
after all.*

9/25/35
*Quite intensive studying with my new professor. Oh,
Daddy. Oh, Mother. If you only knew. Bless you and your
devotion to your friends. Thank you for sending me here.*

"Get yours, girl," Janelle said.

Stevie flipped around, scanning the entries. As the book
went on, there were some poems.

OUR TREASURE
All that I care about starts at nine
Dance twelve hundred steps on the northern line
To the left bank three hundred times
E+A

Line flag
Tiptoe

This one stumped Stevie a bit more. E suggested Eddie, but who was A?

Then she got to the page that almost stopped her heart. Here, in black and white, was the draft of Truly Devious. Stevie could see them working out the wording.

Riddle, riddle time for fun
Should we use a rope or gun?
~~Matches burn, scissors slash~~
~~Knives slice, matches burn~~
~~Knives cut~~
Knives are sharp
And gleam so pretty
~~Bombs are~~
~~Poison's bitter~~
Poison's slow

There were three pages of this before they got to the final version.

Stevie had to walk around the room several times.

"You know what this is?" Stevie said.

"Proof," Janelle replied.

"More proof. Of something. At least that Truly Devious is—"

Then the power went out.

17

"FUN FACT," STEVIE SAID, TRYING TO LIGHTEN THE MOOD IN THE VAST, gloomy space. "This fireplace? Henry the Eighth had one just like it, in Hampton Court. Albert Ellingham had an exact copy made."

"Fun fact," Nate replied, "Henry the Eighth killed two of his wives. Who wants a murderer's fireplace?"

"I'm not sure, but that's the name of my new game show."

Nate and Stevie were the first to make it over to the Great House, which was where all the residents of Minerva were to be moved after the loss of power; the Great House had its own generator. The distance from Minerva to the Great House was only a few hundred yards, but conditions outside had become too dangerous for walking. Mark Parsons drove over in the snowcat, which he had parked under the portico in preparation for the storm. The cab of the snowcat could hold only two of them at a time, along with Mark. There was a lot of confusion while everyone worked out who would go with who, and in what order. Janelle and Vi edged around each other uncertainly. Hunter looked deeply uncomfortable with everything that had happened in this confusing universe he had just landed in. David was giving dark, baffling looks.

"I'll go with Stevie," Nate said, cutting through the nonsense.

In the few seconds she was outside, the wind almost blew Stevie over sideways. Luckily, the snow kept her upright. It was now to her knees. The snowcat wound its way back through the paths, its lights the only thing in the world aside from the swirling snow. Mark didn't look thrilled about having to come out of a warm building to ferry a bunch of idiot students around in a blizzard, but he said nothing about it. He had probably seen a lot of idiot student behavior over the years.

Charles and Dr. Quinn were waiting for them. Charles was dressed more casually than normal, in a heavy fleece and sweatpants. Dr. Quinn rose to the occasion in a rose-gray cashmere sweater, a sweeping wool skirt, black cashmere tights, and tall black boots. No amount of cold was going to rob her of her queenly graces. Charles had a look on his face that said, *"I'm not angry, but I am disappointed."* Dr. Quinn's expression said, *"He's passive-aggressive. I'm not. I am aggressive. I have killed before."*

"We'll speak to you all when the others are here," Charles said. "For now, sit over by the fire."

Nate and Stevie sat, side by side, warming themselves. The fires were nice at the beginning of the storm, but the appeal was waning. You were either too close or not close enough. One side of you would cook while the other would freeze. There was a lot of moving around, approaching, retreating, sweating, shivering.

Inside, the massive hall was in brownish shadow. There were some lights on, but the power was clearly being conserved. The Great House, which had been built to withstand Vermont blizzards, creaked as the winds smacked up against it. Cold air crept through the chimneys, under the massive door. It circled and spun in the great hall, sliding up and down the grand staircase and whispering along the balconies above.

As she sat there, Stevie noticed how the Great House changed its personality in different kinds of light. When she had first walked into it on a brilliant late-summer day, it was cool and vast like a museum, its opulence muted by the bright sun. During the night of the Silent Party, it had sparkled, light dancing off the crystal in the chandeliers and the doorknobs. This was another personality, the stoic one, full of shadows and nooks. A place of hiding from the storm. It never failed to amaze her that this palace of marble and art and glass was built to house three people, really. Three people, their staff, and their guests—but three people. At the height of the Depression, when people were sleeping in boxes in parks. Money lets some people live like kings while other people starve.

"Sometimes I don't know why I'm here," she heard herself saying. "What am I doing? No one can help the Ellinghams. They're gone. No one is ever going to find Alice."

"They might," he said. "She could still be alive, right? And people—things—turn up all the time. Like in a DNA database or something."

"But finding her wouldn't *help* her," Stevie said. "She was kidnapped in 1936. Nothing I'm doing helps anyone."

Nate eyed her wearily.

"I think you're working out your business," he said. "We all have business. Like, I know I can write because I wrote something one time. But I think I can't write again because I'm scared. I'm scared that what I write down won't be as good as what's in my head. Because I don't know how I do it, only that it happens. And because I'm lazy. We've all got doubts. But you've done something huge. You figured out so much of this case. *Tell someone.*"

Stevie chewed on a nail for a moment.

"What if I'm wrong?" she said.

"So you're wrong. They're dead. They can't get more dead. And you have . . . stuff. You have clues. Show your work to someone."

"But then it's over," she said.

"Well, didn't you want it to be?"

Stevie had no idea how to answer. Luckily, Vi and Janelle came in next, interrupting this conversation. The two of them were similarly bundled—Vi was wearing some of Janelle's clothes, because, of course, Vi had never had a chance to go back to their house after breakfast. Even though there was a chill between them, Janelle was not going to deny Vi a sweater and scarves and a hat.

They were followed by Hunter and David. Pix brought

up the rear. Once everyone was in place, Call Me Charles and Dr. Quinn started their rant—how they *were* disappointed, and yes Charles understood (Dr. Quinn was silent on this) that it was hard to leave school. But the students put themselves and others at risk, like Mark, who shouldn't have had to go out in the snowcat tonight. He was red and shivering from his many trips in the snowcat.

"It's too cold upstairs," Mark said. "We need to conserve the heat. If they sleep in the morning room, I can get that up to a decent temperature."

"Fine," Charles said. "I'll help you get the blankets and pillows from upstairs."

"We can *all* help," Pix said.

"No. Everyone stay down here. I'm not taking any chances on anyone falling in the dark."

So everyone sat by the fire, cowed and quiet. All except for David, who got out a tablet and continued reading as if nothing was wrong at all. Mark and Charles tossed blankets and pillows from the upper balconies to save the trips down. All of these things were dragged into the morning room, which was colder than any room had a right to be.

"We don't have any cots," Charles said. "There are some rubberized floor covers that we use in the ballroom. That will take off the chill and make it a little less hard. But you will have to sleep on the floor. One or two of you can use the sofas and chairs. You all have to stay in this room or the main hall. No upstairs. No outside, obviously. I'm sorry for this, but it's what we have to do. There's food and drinks back in the faculty kitchen."

They headed out of the room to let the group settle. The wall sconces were on halfway, bathing the room in soft light, just enough to see the way around the delicate French furniture.

"Everyone find a spot," Pix said. "Make yourself comfortable. We're going to be here for a while."

Everyone began to pick through the pile of random bedding. There were enough blankets for everyone to have two each, but two wasn't going to cut it, especially sleeping on the floor.

"Funnnnn," Nate said in a low voice, picking up a pillow. "This is like being on one of those trips to Mount Everest. You know, the ones with the ten percent death rate and half the landmarks are frozen bodies."

"There's Wi-Fi," Vi said. "That's something."

"Is it?" Nate asked.

David grabbed a blanket and set himself up on two chairs, pulled his blankets over himself, and kept reading. It wasn't as dickish as taking the sofa. And yet, somehow, taking the slightly less dickish path felt even more dickish. Janelle and Vi once again looked at each other, then looked away, each setting up their nests in a different little nook around the low, ornamental tables full of Ellingham brochures.

"What is going on with those two?" Pix asked Stevie in a low voice.

"Nothing," Stevie said. "I don't know."

Stevie opted for the floor behind the sofa. There was carpet there, and the sofa felt like a windbreak. Nate curled up in the corner. Hunter was left with the sofa, as being on the cold, hard floor would have been difficult on him.

Once the blankets were down, the room quickly divided into two camps: the people with the tablets and the people without them. Vi, Hunter, and David sat in proximity to each other and read, occasionally comparing notes. On the other side of the room, Stevie, Janelle, and Nate sat together and separate, each zoning into their own world. Janelle had her headphones on and was listening to something loud enough that the sound was seeping out. She was reading a book with a lot of mechanical diagrams in it. Everything in her manner said she was trying to block out what Vi was doing. Nate flicked between his book and his computer. Stevie even thought she saw him open up a file that looked like his book. She saw the word *chapter* at the top of a few pages as he scrolled down. Since Nate only wrote when forced to, this indicated pretty clearly what he thought of the situation.

Stevie was left to marinate in confusion and a light, undefined panic. If she could, she would have done nothing but stare at David. Her fingertips could still feel his hair, the muscles in his shoulders. Her lips remembered all the kisses. And the warmth—being next to someone like that.

He might as well have been across the ocean, not ten or fifteen feet away, behind a gilt-legged table and a rose-colored sofa.

As for working on the situation at hand, well, she had no privacy, and she needed privacy to think. She needed to pace and put stickies on walls and mumble to herself.

Maybe nothing was going on. Maybe Hayes and Ellie and Fenton had died in exactly the ways that everyone else thought. Accidents do happen, especially if you take bad chances. They were living proof of it right now. They had gambled with the weather and broken the rules, and now they were trapped here together.

She had to move around. The bathroom. She could go there.

Stevie got up, grabbed her backpack, and headed out into the hall. The bathrooms were behind the stairs, past the ballroom and Albert Ellingham's office. Both of those grand doors were closed. She killed time brushing her teeth and washing her face, staring at herself in the mirror—her blond hair was overgrown now. The brown roots were showing. Her skin was chapped from the cold, and her lips were dry. She leaned into the sink, the same sink where the glitterati had come to touch up their lipstick and dry-heave all those years ago.

Maybe it was over. She had solved the case—in her mind—but her evidence was thin. She could go home, write it all up. Maybe post it online, see if it got traction on the boards. Show her work.

And it would all be over. What then?

She blew out a long exhale, picked up her things, and went back out.

David was waiting for her, sitting on one of the leather chairs out in the hall.

"Remember that favor I did for you?" he said. "I have something, if you want to see it."

He held up his phone.

> TO: jimmalloy@electedwardking.com
> Today at 9:18 a.m.
> FROM: jquinn@ellingham.edu
> CC: cscott@ellingham.edu
>
> Mr. Malloy,
> I don't see how that document is any of the senator's business.
> Regards,
> Dr. J. Quinn

"She shut that down," David said. "It's kind of hot."

"But!" Stevie said, her face flushed with blood. "She said *that document*. Which means there is a document. *There is a document.*"

"Sounds like it," he said.

"Which means we need to see it. We can reply. I mean, Jim can reply. Jim should reply."

"Jim is busy," David replied. "Jim isn't here to do your bidding."

"David," she said, wheeling around in front of him.

"Please. Look. I know. You're pissed at me. But this is important."

"Why?"

"Because if there is a codicil, it means there is a motive. It means there is money. I need to see it."

"I mean, why is this important to me," he clarified. "I know you said not everything is about me, but . . ."

"Seriously?" Stevie replied.

"And if I find something? What if I said I would do it for you if you left me alone?"

"What?"

"I'll do what you want," he said. "I'll reply. I'll help you get your information. But you and I, that's it. We don't talk anymore."

"What kind of a weird request is that?" she said, her throat tightening.

"It's not weird. It's really straightforward. My dad gave you something you wanted in order for you to come back and watch over me. So I'm giving you something similar. I want to know which is more important. Me, or what I can do for you?"

It felt like the Great House was tilting to the side.

"Taking a long time to decide," he said.

"I don't think it's fair."

"Fair?" he replied.

"You're saying this while you are, right now, having other people go through your dad's stuff. Which you stole."

"To stop him from getting more powerful."

"And I'm trying to find out what happened to Hayes, to Ellie, to Fenton."

"Is *that* what you're doing?"

"Yes," Stevie snapped. "It is."

"Because it sort of looks like you want more dirt for your pet project."

It was the words *pet project* that did it. A kind of blue-white rage came up behind her eyes.

"I want the information," she said.

David smiled that long, slow smile—the smile that said, "I told you this is how the world works."

"Okay," he said chirpily. "Let's write a nice note."

The note poured forth with surprising speed. David spoke under his breath as he typed. Perhaps this was what it had been like when Francis and Eddie composed their Truly Devious note, head to head:

The senator regards anything involving his son as his business. This is why the senator donated a private security system to assist you after your recent issues. I need not remind you that two students have died at the school and the senator's son ran off while under your supervision. The senator would like to know of any potential issues that may arise due to your negligence; this includes any publicity having to

do with the historical issues of the school. We felt this was a polite way of getting information, but if you wish for us to take more legal action, we will do so.

Regards,

J. Malloy

"There," he said. "I knew all the years I spent around these choads would pay off. Your note. And now, we're done."

He hit send, then he turned and walked back toward their camping room.

April 13, 1937

Montgomery, the butler, presided over the morning's side-board with his usual taciturn efficiency. The house still turned out a good and ample breakfast, with great lashings of the famous Vermont syrup gently warmed by a spirit lamp. There was enough food to feed twenty guests, but the four people at the table wanted very little of it. Flora Robinson sipped at a cup of coffee from the delicate fairy rose pattern that Iris had chosen. Robert Mackenzie was going through the morning mail. George Marsh hid behind a newspaper. Leonard Holmes Nair made a few stabs at his half of a grape-fruit, none of them fatal.

"Do you think he'll come down this morning?" he asked the group.

"I think so," Flora replied. "We need to act as normal as possible."

Leo was polite enough not to laugh at this suggestion.

It had been exactly one year since the kidnapping. One year of searching and waiting and pain . . . one year of denial, violence, and some acceptance. There was an unspoken agreement that the word *anniversary* would never be spoken.

The door to the breakfast room swung open, and Albert Ellingham came in, dressed in a light gray suit, looking strangely well rested.

"Good morning," he said. "I apologize for my lateness. I was on the telephone. I thought we might . . ."

He eyed the breakfast suspiciously, as if he had forgotten what food was for. He often had to be reminded to eat.

". . . I thought we might all go for a trip today."

"A trip?" Flora said. "Where?"

"To Burlington. We'll take the boat out. We'll stay in Burlington for the night. I've had the house there made ready. Could you be ready to go in an hour?"

There was only one answer to give.

As they stepped out to the waiting car, Leo saw four trucks rumbling up the drive, two full of men, and two full of dirt and rocks.

"What's going on, Albert?" Flora asked.

"Just a bit of work," Albert said. "The tunnel under the lake is . . . unnecessary. There is no lake. Best to have it filled in."

The tunnel. The one that had betrayed Albert, letting the enemy in. It would now be smothered, buried. The sight of the rocks and dirt seemed to trigger something in George Marsh, who set down his bag.

"You know," he said, "it might be better if I stayed here to keep an eye on things."

"The foreman can handle anything that comes up," Albert replied.

"It may be better," George Marsh said again. "In case any reporters or sightseers try to get in."

"If you think it's best," Albert replied.

Leo took a better look at George Marsh, and the strange, fascinated way he was watching the wheelbarrows full of dirt and rocks that were heading to the back garden. There was something there, on George's face—something Leo couldn't quite identify. Something that intrigued him.

Leo had been watching George Marsh since he had learned the truth from Flora, that Marsh was Alice's biological father—the great, brave George Marsh who had once saved Albert Ellingham from a bomb, who followed the family everywhere, providing reassurance and protection.

Of course, he had not protected Iris and Alice that fateful day, but he could not be blamed for that. Iris liked to go out on her own. He couldn't be faulted for not retrieving them that night—he had gone to meet the kidnappers and gotten himself beaten to a pulp in the process. He wasn't a great brain, a Hercule Poirot, who solved crimes in his head while tapping on his boiled egg with a spoon at breakfast. He was a friend, muscle, a good person for someone like Albert Ellingham to have around. And yes, he was with the FBI, but he never seemed to do much for them. Albert had made sure he was made an agent, and there were vague notions about him looking for drug smugglers coming down from Canada, but he'd never seemed to notice the ones Leo met regularly, the ones who supplied Iris with her powders and potions of choice.

Or maybe he had and had looked away.

Right now, George Marsh was lying about why he wanted to stay. Of that, Leo was certain. That people lie was nothing of particular interest. It's not the lie itself that matters—it's why the lie happened. Some, like Leo, lied for fun. You could have some excellent evenings with a good lie. But most people lied to hide things. If it was as simple as a love affair—well, no one would have minded that. Whatever it was was *secret*, not just private.

George Marsh, Leo could see very clearly, had a secret.

"All right, then," Albert said, ushering Leo, Flora, and Robert toward the waiting car.

George Marsh stood by the front door and watched the car drive off. Once he was sure that the group was a decent distance away, he got in his own car and left the property.

He was gone for several hours, returning near nightfall. He parked on the dirt road, far back from the house. He returned to the house and made note of who remained. The work crews had gone, as had the day servants. Montgomery had retired to his rooms and the other servants to theirs. He checked in with the security men, sending them out to patrol the edges of the property. Once all of this was done, he changed his clothes, putting on work pants and a simple undershirt. Then he took a lantern and walked out into the back of the house, grabbing a shovel as he went. He slid down the muddy ground, into the marshy pit where the lake had been, then he walked to the mound in the middle where the glass dome reflected the early moonlight.

It was unpleasant to go back into the dome now. It smelled of dirt and neglect and was full of footprints from where the workmen had been. There were no rugs or cushions now. He sat down on the bench on the side, exactly where he had been when he faced Dottie Epstein. She had tried to hide under a rug on the floor, but fear and curiosity got the better of her . . .

"Don't be afraid. You can come out."

Dottie looked at the things he had put on the floor—the rope, the binoculars, the handcuffs.

"Those are for the game," he had said.

"What kind of game?"

"It's very complicated, but it's going to be a lot of fun. I have to hide. Were you hiding in here too?"

He had started sweating profusely at that part of the conversation, as he felt it all unraveling. How had he sounded so calm?

"To read," she had replied.

The kid had a book with her. She was clutching it like it was a shield.

"Sherlock Holmes? I love Sherlock Holmes. Which story are you reading?"

"*A Study in Scarlet.*"

"That's a good one. Go ahead. Read. Don't let me stop you."

At that point, he had decided nothing. His brain was

spinning. What to do with her? Dottie had looked at him, and he could see it in her eyes—she knew. Somehow, she *knew*.

"I need to get this back to the library. I won't tell anyone you're here. I hate it when people tell on me. I have to go."

"You know I can't let you leave," he had replied. "I wish I could."

The words came out of his mouth, but he had had no idea what they meant.

"You can. I'm good at keeping secrets. Please."

She had hugged the book.

"I'm so sorry," he said.

George Marsh put his head in his hands for a moment. He couldn't play the rest in his mind, the part where Dottie dropped the book and made her heroic, doomed leap toward the hole. The sound she made when she hit the ground below. Scrabbling down the ladder—all the blood. The way she moaned and dragged herself along the ground.

He blinked, stood, and shook it off. He lowered his lantern with a rope, then dropped the shovel and climbed down. The shelves had been emptied of liquor bottles. The little space was empty, cold. He pushed on, through the door, into the tunnel. The crew had started filling in the tunnel in the middle, so that is where he would go. He walked into the pitch-black, his little halo of light barely cutting into the shade.

It was like he was going to the underworld. To hell. To the place of no return.

The smell of earth was getting stronger, and soon some

was underfoot. He stopped, set the lantern down, and tested the space with the shovel. Then he began to dig, shoving the earth to the sides, creating an opening. When the space met his satisfaction, he picked up the lantern and returned the way he had come, back into the world of the living. He walked out of the dome, back through the sunken pit, all the way to his car. He opened the back door.

There was a small trunk inside. He opened that as well.

There were ice cellars in Vermont, packed with ice and snow and hay. That was where he had been keeping Alice. She was not frozen solid, but she was stiff.

"Come on," he said to her quietly. "I'm taking you home. It's okay."

He closed the trunk and removed it from the car. George bore his sad burden back the same way, moving carefully so as not to drop it as he made his way down the slippery side of the once-lake. He lowered the trunk with a rope, taking care to put her on the ground as delicately as possible. Then he carried her into the tunnel and into the space he had excavated. He packed the earth around her by hand. Once she was mostly covered, he began to fill with the shovel, until he had put several feet of dirt between her and the world.

It was nearly midnight when he emerged, his face slick with cold sweat. He moved silently toward the house, taking a route where he would not be seen from Montgomery's window.

As soon as he was inside, there was a movement from behind a tree at the edge of the garden patio, the sound of a striking match, and the small glow of the tip of a cigarette.

Leonard Holmes Nair emerged and watched as George Marsh walked out of sight.

"What have you been doing?" he said to himself as the door closed.

Then he moved silently through the garden, tracing the path that Marsh had just come.

18

It was morning, not that you'd know it.

The snow obliterated the horizon. There was no sense of where the sky ended and the world began. There were hints of trees, but they were shortened in perspective by the depth of the snow, and their spindly, bare branches wore white gloves. Only the dome on the little mound seemed to be in the right place. The sunken garden was being refilled. The world was being erased and reset.

The morning room, where everyone was camped, managed to be both cold and stuffy at the same time. Stevie woke, stiff and still tired, and stared out from her sleeping place. The rubber mat and blankets didn't do much to keep out the hard chill of the floor. She had a limited view under the sofa and could see Janelle's extended arm reaching in Vi's general direction, though Vi was several feet away, sleeping upright, tablet still in hand. Nate was curled into his blankets, which he had pulled over his head. There was a gentle, soft snoring coming from someone.

Stevie wiped away some drool and pushed herself up

quietly to a standing position. Even David was asleep, draped over the chair, legs hanging off the side, a tablet next to him. Hunter, the lightly snoring one, was flat on his back on the sofa, his knit hat pulled over his eyes like a sleeping mask. There was something odd and intimate the way the soft light fell on her sleeping friends; it was almost as if the Ellinghams had even planned a room where the light would come down gently on any revelers sleeping off a party.

She tiptoed out into the main hall, where Call Me Charles was by the fire with his computer and a stack of folders. Call Me Charles was a lot to take at what her phone informed her was six in the morning, but there was no avoiding it.

"I don't know about you," he said, waving her over, "but I didn't sleep much. I caught up on some work. Reading applications for next year's class."

Applications. More people would be coming, taking the same chance Stevie had—writing to Ellingham about their passions, hoping someone would see a spark and admit them. It was so weird to think of people coming after her.

"I hope we have a school then," he said.

"You think the school won't reopen?" Stevie said.

Charles sighed and shut his computer.

"The cat only has so many lives," he said. "We'll do our best. We could live to fight another day. We have to be hopeful."

He sipped his coffee and gazed into the fire for a moment.

"Let me ask *you* something," he said. "The Ellingham case. Do you think you understand it any better since being here?"

Stevie could have said, *I solved it. So, yeah, kind of better.* But it wasn't time, and Charles was not going to be her official way of getting this out into the world.

"I think so," she said noncommittally. "Why?"

"Because," he said. "That's why you were admitted."

"Did you really think I could solve it?" she said.

"What I thought and what I still think," he replied, "is that I saw someone with a passionate interest. In fact, I thought you might be bored here, so I went up to the attic last night and got you something."

He indicated the small table next to him, where four large green volumes sat. She recognized them at once, with their gold lettering on the side, indicating years and months.

"The house records," she said.

"I thought you might like to go through them," he said. "Only if you want."

Stevie had read through these records before. They had been kept by the butler, Montgomery. They listed the comings and goings in the house—what meals were served, what occasions were held, which guests were in attendance.

"Thanks," Stevie said, accepting them.

Above, Dr. Quinn came out of one of the offices. She was dressed in a cashmere sweater and a pair of elegant yoga pants with flowers twining up the sides. Ellingham was still ticking away.

"Can I sit in the ballroom and read?" Stevie said.

"I don't see why not," Charles said. "It's cold in there."

"I don't care."

He got up and unlocked the room for her.

The Ellingham ballroom was a magnificent hall of mirrors, and as such, it was very cold and empty. She sat in the middle of the wooden floor, surrounded by a thousand other Stevies. She set down the pile of house records and reached into her bag for the red diary. She felt the pages, which were surprisingly smooth given their age. Expensive paper in a well-made book, the penmanship formal and exquisite, with occasional drips of ink on the page. Francis Josephine Crane, baking flour heiress, had a lot to say about the school and the people who lived there. For starters, she didn't have a lot of good things to say about the school's benefactor.

11/13/35

Albert, Lord Albert, the man must think he's a god.
After all, he's built himself his own little Olympus and
furnished it with Greek deities. And he can say all he
likes about his great experiment, but what he wants
is to make a whole group of little Alberts, or what he
believes himself to be. Luckily, he has rich friends who
will give him their children (my parents couldn't say yes
fast enough) for the purpose. And poor people? Well, who
wouldn't entrust their son or daughter to the great Albert
Ellingham? The talk of games is especially tiring. I think
his wife may be all right. I've seen her around and about,
speeding off in her car. (A very attractive one. Cherry

*red. I'd like one like that.) I think she skis and drinks, and
she's friends with Leonard Holmes Nair, who comes here
to paint and visit.*

11/16/35
*The great Albert Ellingham took me around the campus
today, the sanctimonious prick. I had to pretend to be
impressed with everything he's done in order to get him
to show me anything interesting. He laughed at me.
Something will have to be done about that.*

She also had things to say about Iris that were surprising.

12/1/35
*Amazing discovery. Eddie and I slipped into the back
garden today, where the Ellinghams have a private lake.
Iris and her friend were sitting out there in the cold,
wrapped up in furs, giggling about something. We watched
as Iris took a small compact from her purse, scooped
something out of it with a small silver object, and snorted
whatever was in it right up her nose! Her friend then
took some. Our dear Madame Ellingham has a taste for
cocaine! Eddie was delighted and said we needed to go over
and ask for some—he loves the stuff. I've never had it, but
he said it makes you see galaxies. In any case, we didn't, but
it's a very good fact to put away. You never know when
that one will come in handy.*

There were always hints that Iris Ellingham liked a good party, but nothing about cocaine. There were observations about Francis's housemates and housemistress as well.

12/3/35
Gertie van Coevorden made a cutting remark about the time I spend with Eddie. She said, "Whatever do you spend all that time doing?" I told her we do the same thing her father does with the downstairs maid. She did not understand. She is genuinely that thick.

12/6/35
The only one around here worth a damn aside from me and Eddie is Dottie Epstein, and that is mostly because she is a sneak.

12/8/35
Nelson is a drip. She swans around the house in her one good skirt and sweater, telling us all when we must retire for the evening, when we must study. Eddie tells me the boys' houses have no such rules. Nelson has a secret. I don't know what it is, but I will work it out.

1/16/36
Gertie van Coevorden drinks so much gin that if you set her on fire she would burn for a week.

As the entries went on and became more about cars, guns, open safes, and routes to the West, there were a few entries about Eddie that had a different tone than the rapturous ones at the start of the diary.

2/5/36

I wonder if Eddie is strong enough to do what we mean to do. I know I am. He likes to talk about poetry and the dark star and living a perfectly reckless life, outside of morality, but does he know what it means? What if he turns out to be like the others? I can't bear it.

2/9/36

I have always felt that boys are weak-minded. I don't think they can help themselves most of the time. I believed Eddie was different. What he is is drunk and debauched. Those are virtues, to some extent, but I thought there was more. What if there isn't?

2/18/36

He's such a spoiled boy. I'm spoiled too, but it didn't rot me in the way it rotted him. The money corroded him. What is it about me that loves the decay?

And there was this entry, which Stevie kept coming back to.

OUR TREASURE
All that I care about starts at nine
Dance twelve hundred steps on the northern line
To the left bank three hundred times
E+A
Line flag
Tiptoe

Stevie set the diary down on her lap.

She was tired of people not saying what they meant. This, of course, was going to be a big part of her job as a detective. People would lie to her or talk around things. It was something she would have to get used to.

But David . . . he couldn't have meant what he'd said last night, about ignoring each other forever. That was one of his games. A test.

Why had David even come back?

By midmorning, she had grown weary of staring at the diary and the house records. There was only so much energy she could spend on lists of routes and menus from 1935. She got up and rejoined her friends.

The morning room door was mostly closed, and there was a low hum of conversation. When Stevie stepped in, Janelle and Nate were watching the goings-on across the room like they were spectators at a major sporting event.

"What are you doing?" Stevie asked.

Nobody on that side of the room answered, or even looked up. Stevie turned to Nate and Janelle. Janelle beckoned her over.

"Something's going on over there," Janelle said, in a low voice. "They got really excited about an hour ago."

David was comparing the screens on two of the tablets. Stevie went over and sat on the arm of the sofa and looked down at them.

"Is there something going on?" she asked.

Vi shushed her, which is not the kind of thing they would usually do.

"So all these payments here," David said to Hunter.

" . . . match the payments here. And the dates."

"Plus the email records on the third one," Vi added. "All the donors have been doing it. This guy, the private investigator, is always listed on the ones with an asterisk."

Stevie tried to piece this all together. Payments. Private investigators.

"Are you guys talking about blackmail?" she said.

Three faces tipped up to look at her.

"Something like that," Hunter said, smiling.

"Who's being blackmailed?" Stevie asked. No matter what was going on, talk of private investigators and blackmail was going to interest her. She addressed most of this to Hunter and Vi, trying not to make eye contact with David after the events of last night.

"What seems to be happening," Vi said, "is that whenever this person, who we found out is a private investigator, shows up in the files regarding these major donors to the King campaign, these donors suddenly give a lot more money, and on a regular schedule. They formed organizations to raise even more."

"What is the private investigator doing?" Stevie asked.

"Something with financial documents," David said, not looking up. "He delivers loads and loads of these spreadsheets. We can't work out what they mean exactly, because we don't have enough information, but it definitely seems like this is information about activities these people want hidden. Maybe it's tax fraud or something. Whatever the case, my dad has this information on them, and then his campaign gets a ton of money. That's blackmail."

"And these people?" Vi said, breathless. "They're the worst people you can imagine. This guy here"—she pointed at a line on the spreadsheet—"is almost singlehandedly responsible for the cover-up of a major oil spill."

"Major, *major* oil spill," said Hunter.

"This is how he did it," David said, almost to himself. "He never had enough money to start his presidential campaign, and then it all comes rolling in as soon as he gets this material. And there's no way this stuff was obtained legally. He's getting information about things that are probably crimes, and he's using it to power his campaign. Crimes to power crimes."

"This is a treasure trove," Vi said. "If you sent this stuff to a Dropbox for any media outlet, you could blow this all wide open. If we release this stuff, we could take down some of the worst people out there today."

"Or you could destroy it," Janelle said. She and Nate had come over to listen to this conversion. Janelle sat primly on the sofa. Even wearing cat-head pajamas, she looked serious.

"Destroy it?" Vi repeated.

"If the goal is to take down Edward King," Janelle said, "you take away the thing he's using to get his money. Once you destroy it, he has no leverage against these people."

"And we have nothing on him," Vi said. "Or them."

"But you've completed your objective," Janelle said. "If this material was obtained illegally, then destroy it. End the crime. Don't go any farther down this path. If you want to do good, do it the right way."

"But all these people . . . ," Vi said.

"If the stuff was stolen," Janelle said, "destroy it."

"This is tough," Hunter said. "Not sure what I would do."

David leaned back against the wall and stared at the tablets.

"Honestly," he said, "if this stops my dad, I don't care how we do it. Vi, it's your call."

This left Vi, who gazed at the tablets and the bag of flash drives.

"There's so much here," they said.

"And these people will go down," Janelle said. "But there are right ways and wrong ways."

Vi looked to Janelle. Stevie could feel something pass between them, something palpable in the air. Vi got up and gathered all the tablets. They put them in the cold fireplace, then grabbed the poker and began to smash them. As they did so, Janelle sat up straighter, her eyes brimming with tears.

"I'll flush these," David said, picking up the flash drives and gathering the remains of the tablets.

Everyone in the room moved away to give Vi and Janelle a little space as Vi sat next to Janelle and took her by both hands.

As David left the room, Stevie almost thought she felt him give her a look as well. At least, someone was watching her. She could feel it.

19

Being stuck in a mountaintop retreat during a blizzard sounds fun and romantic, especially if you are talking about a place like Ellingham Academy, which was entirely made of nooks and views. It had ample firewood and food. It was big enough for everyone. It should have been pleasant, at least.

But snow does funny things to the mind. Everything felt close and airless. Time started to have no meaning. Now that the task many people in this particular group had stayed to perform was complete, there was a baggy confusion to what was supposed to happen next. At least Vi and Janelle were back together, sitting pressed up so close to each other that Stevie thought they might actually overlap. Hunter was napping. Nate was trying to sink into the sofa and be left alone.

And David? Well, he sat on his chair and played a game on his computer, looking at Stevie over the top occasionally.

She got up and left the room, taking her bag with her.

They weren't supposed to go upstairs, but nobody had said they couldn't sit *on* the stairs, so that's where she sat, alone and in public, on the grand staircase. *Where do you look for someone who's never really there? Always on a staircase, but . . .*

"We'll probably be able to get out in about twenty-four hours," she heard Mark Parsons saying. He was up on the balcony walkway above with Dr. Quinn and Call Me Charles. Plans were being made. They would all leave this place, to go to an uncertain future.

She sat on the landing, wrapped in a blanket, and stared at the portrait of the Ellingham family. This would be her anchor. It made as much sense as anything else. The swirling colors, the distortion of the moon, the dark sky, the dome looming in the background. Her pulse surged and the world swam, so she dove into the painting. She was there, standing alongside the Ellinghams in their kaleidoscopic world. The doomed Ellinghams.

The painting. That photo of Leonard Holmes Nair painting on the lawn . . .

She pulled her bag over and removed the diary. She blinked away some of the spots from in front of her eyes and flipped it open, grabbing for the photos inside, flipping through the shots of Francis and Eddie in their poses, in the trees, and there . . .

There it was. The photo of Leonard Holmes Nair on the lawn. She looked at the photo and up at the painting several times. Then she got up and went over to the painting, examining it closely. She looked at the sky, specifically, the shape of it around the Ellinghams. The placement of the moon.

It was the same painting. The figures were precisely the same. The moon in this painting was in the same position as the sun in the one in the photograph. Where the Great House had been in the photograph painting, the scene had been converted into the background of the dome, into a halo of light.

Same painting. Different setting. Why had he repainted it like this? The moon was high in the painting, and the moonbeams dipped down around the dome, landing on a spot off to the side, right about where the tunnel was. And the pool of light . . .

There was something there, something she couldn't put her finger on.

She turned away from the painting and opened the diary again, flipping through the now-familiar entries. Francis in love. Francis in misery. Francis bored. Francis making charts of ammunition and explosives. She glanced through the poems but kept coming back to the one that stood out from the others.

OUR TREASURE
All that I care about starts at nine
Dance twelve hundred steps on the northern line
To the left bank three hundred times
E+A
Line flag
Tiptoe

Was this about places she had been? Dancing at balls? The Northern Line in London? The Left Bank of Paris?

Something was eating at Stevie. She knew what this was. She had *seen* this. She just couldn't place it.

She rubbed her eyes and looked back up at the painting, the dome in the moonlight.

The dome.

This wasn't a poem. These were *instructions*. And she knew exactly what Francis was talking about.

No one paid any attention as she walked casually back into the morning room and slipped one of the brochures from the table by the door. She retreated to the steps again for privacy and sat on the floor, opening the diary to the poem page and the brochure booklet to the map of Ellingham, the idealized one drawn by the artist who drew books for children.

All that I care about starts at nine. Nine was Minerva House on the map—the house where Francis lived.

Dance twelve hundred steps on the northern line. This was fairly direct. Twelve hundred steps to the north. Stevie couldn't take twelve hundred steps, but the instructions hinted at where to go. To the left bank three hundred times . . . that was a quarter of the distance of the first instruction. If you roughed this out in your mind, it would land you at . . .

The top of the map, to the initials *E* and *A* for *Ellingham Academy*, in the circle that read, FOUNDED 1935.

Line flag. There was a flag on the top of the dome, and in this picture, it pointed right toward the *E* and *A*.

There was something there, something Francis was calling a treasure. Which meant Stevie was going to go and find it.

There was the small matter of the blizzard and not being allowed out. The second part didn't concern her much. When you are already in a lot of trouble, getting in more trouble isn't that big of a deal. David had said earlier that the security system was run over Wi-Fi. While the Wi-Fi was up in the house, it wasn't around campus, so no one would necessarily know she was out there. What she needed were her coat and boots from the security office because they were soaking wet. All she needed to do was go in there, get them, and slip quietly outside. Get some air. Nothing wrong with taking a little walk.

Stevie put her backpack on and descended the stairs casually. She went to the bathroom first and left her bag on the floor. The bathroom windows were large enough to climb through and led out to the far side of the stone promenade that ran around the side and back of the house. She stepped out. Charles and Dr. Quinn were nowhere in sight, but it sounded like they were in one of the offices in the second floor. Mark Parsons had been going in and out and was probably out front with the snowcat. Pix, however, was sitting by the big fireplace in the hall, reading. She would need a way past her.

The best ways, she had noted from her research, were simple ways. She needed only a minute.

Stevie walked up to Pix.

"Um," she said, "I think Janelle and Vi . . . I think they want to talk to you?"

"About what?" Pix asked.

"Not sure. You asked about them earlier . . ." That was good, because it was true. Always put truth in there. "I think they . . ."

She left it hanging and vague, then shrugged. Pix nodded and got up to go into the morning room. Stevie did not hesitate. That was another thing—once you set the plan in motion, keep moving. Don't turn around. She grabbed her coat and boots and walked slowly back toward the bathroom. Never run.

The rest was easy. Coat on. Boots on. Bag on back. She boosted herself onto the sink and got through the window without too much difficulty.

The difficulties began when she dropped herself into three feet of snow. She considered climbing back in the window immediately, but this was it. Now or never.

So she began. First, to Minerva.

That journey, which had to go through the back garden and out of view of the house, took about a half hour, instead of the five minutes it would normally have taken. The snow was heavy, sticky stuff that clung to her boots and legs. The cold air dried out her windpipe and made every breath burn, so she pulled her scarf over her face. Once there, she stopped inside to warm herself and heave for a few minutes. She added a layer of clothing and ran her hands under warm water.

Back out into the snow.

Twelve hundred steps north. Stevie pulled out her phone and let the compass spin. She began to walk, counting the steps.

Twelve hundred steps would normally have been a straightforward thing. Twelve hundred steps in this snow was like ten miles. She was winded after the first two hundred steps, and by four hundred, she was drenched in cold sweat. She had to work her way around the yurt and try to calculate for that, and again at the art barn, she had to make a few guesses.

Snowblind and exhausted, she stopped at the point that was likely around twelve hundred paces. This was starting to feel very stupid, and the desire to go back to the Great House was strong, but the way back was about as far as she had to go now anyway. Three hundred paces.

There, back in the snowy trees, back where no one ever went, in a place she had never noticed, was a statue. This was nothing new at Ellingham Academy; the place was littered with them, like someone had gone a little crazy at Statue Target. Statues were like trash cans or lights—just part of the landscape. This one was of a Greek or Roman man, standing tall in his toga, his head covered in snow. He stood on his pedestal, looking bored.

"Okay," Stevie said. "Tiptoe."

Tiptoe? How the hell did she tiptoe in this snow? She stood on her toes and looked at the statue's knees.

Not that.

She turned toward the house and school and stood on her toes. The view did not change.

Maybe it would require more. She jumped a few times. She kicked the base of the statue, sending up a small cloud of snow.

"Come *on*," she hissed, turning around and looking at the dimming sky. "Something's here. Tiptoe. Tiptoe . . ."

When she said it out loud, she got it. It was a very Albert Ellingham thing Francis had done. Tiptoe. Break the word. Tip. Toe.

She brushed the snow off the base of the statue, revealing its bare feet. Sure enough, the big toe of the left foot was slightly raised, as if the figure was about to take a step. Stevie leaned in to look at it and could make out, very faintly, a crack—a joint where the stone was split. She pulled off her glove, ignoring the pain the cold caused, and grabbed the toe, pulling, pushing, pulling again until it gave. It hinged back a bit.

She had no time to express her excitement. This was because she was falling into the earth.

April 13, 1937

A SOFT NIGHT RAIN WAS FALLING ON THE ELLINGHAM GREAT HOUSE. Leonard Holmes Nair stood on the flagstone patio in the mist. His feet and hands were covered in dirt; his trouser cuffs would likely never recover. He was trying to let the rain wash away what he had seen down there in the tunnel.

Leo had been in the house all day; he had never left the property. On impulse, when the car was halfway down the drive, Leo said, "You know, if you don't mind stopping, I feel a bit unwell. I think I may have to go back to bed for the afternoon, if that's all right. The walk back up will help, I think." He got out of the car and returned to the house.

One very good thing about Albert's house was that if you didn't want to be seen, you did not have to be. The size alone made this possible, but the various little passages and nooks made it simple. He watched George Marsh send the security guards to the four winds, he watched Montgomery cleaning things away while he listened to the radio. George Marsh had meandered around all day, slept a bit, and generally done nothing at all until nightfall, when he made his curious journey into the garden. Leo didn't dare follow him down into the dome, but he watched him come back up covered in dirt, go to his car, and retrieve a bundle. The bundle did not come back up again. So when George Marsh went inside the house, Leo went down under the dome to see what had been put there.

Now he was aboveground again, queasy, and in shock. The shock made everything mild, almost reasonable. He had just watched George Marsh bury Alice's body. Leo had seen dead bodies before; in his art-student days he did medical illustrations for money. He had seen human parts in basins and pans and attended autopsies. After the war, he had been unfortunate enough to be present at two suicides. This, however, was something entirely different and new and numbing. It made no sense, and it demanded to be understood.

Which was why Leo was standing on the patio, shivering and wet under a sliver of a moon, planning his next move. What did you do when you were in a remote location with someone you suspected of murder? There were security men about, but they were far. Montgomery was in the house, but he was asleep and not physically robust enough to take on someone like Marsh.

The sensible thing would be to slip inside Albert's office now and call the police. A hundred men would descend on the house within the hour. He could tuck himself away until then.

That was the obvious course of action. Call the police. Do it now. Stay out of sight and wait.

But Leonard Holmes Nair was not a man known for doing the obvious and sensible thing. He was not foolhardy, but he often took the other path, the one less traveled. Whatever was going on with George Marsh—there was a *story* there, a story he might never know if the police raided the house and took him away. This story that was clearly fairly complicated, because if George had killed Alice, why had he brought her back? Questions would linger for the rest of his life, and that was a prospect that troubled Leo quite a bit.

Then again, confronting a man who was used to physical fighting and was probably a bit on the nervous side also didn't seem like a good option.

So what was it to be?

Leo looked to the moon to help, but it simply hung in the sky and told him nothing. The cold was penetrating his clothes. At least the smell was starting to leave his nose. He would never feel the same way about the scent of fresh earth again. He had gone to the underworld and returned, changed.

He opened the door to Albert's office and switched on a small, green-shaded light at the desk by the door. He was fairly certain that Albert kept a revolver in the desk. He tried all the drawers but found them locked. He searched the top of the desk for a key, rummaging through papers, telegraph slips, pen and pencil containers, looked under the phone. He did the same to Mackenzie's much neater desk on the opposite side of the room. He spent a fruitless hour delicately ransacking the room before pausing to lean against the cold fireplace. The French clock ticked away the midnight hours.

The clock. This chunk of green marble, fabled to have been among Marie Antoinette's possessions. Leo picked it up. It was a heavy piece, weighing twenty pounds or more. He lifted it over to one of the reading chairs and set it down, flipping it on its head. He felt around for the catch that Albert had shown him those years before, that snowy day in Switzerland. His long fingers worked the base of the clock until he felt the small indentation, barely noticeable. He pressed on it and felt something give—the little drawer in the base. He flipped the clock upright and pulled it open, revealing a small collection of loose keys.

"Albert, you maniac," Leo said, snatching them up. A few tries revealed which ones opened which drawers, and a bit more poking turned up a small but powerful-looking revolver and some ammunition. Leo had never loaded a gun before, but the general mechanics of the thing seemed clear enough.

Five minutes later, he was making his way out into the great open atrium of the house, his steps echoing against the marble and crystal and miles of polished wood, this cathedral of wealth and sadness. It seemed best not to sneak up on Marsh; one doesn't want to creep up on a person who has just buried a body in a tunnel at midnight. Better to make it loud.

"Hello!" he called. "It's me, Leo! George, are you up there?"

George appeared on the landing in seconds, dressed only in the bottom half of some pajamas.

"Leo?" he said. "What are you doing here? How long have you been there?"

His tone gave away nothing, but his question did.

"I came back," Leo said again. "God, it's dismal. Come have a drink."

George hesitated a moment, gripping the rail, then said, "Of course, yeah. A drink." He walked along the balcony rail, looking down as he approached the stairs. "Anyone else come back? I didn't hear you."

"No," Leo said, trying to sound casual. "I felt terrible and came back earlier. I've been in bed all day. I woke up and thought you'd be about."

It was a strange story and a weird way to announce that you'd been around for hours, but it would have to do. The weight of the gun in Leo's pocket seemed to increase. Would it be noticeable? Perhaps. Best to put it down.

"Come to Albert's office," Leo said, hurrying back in that direction. "The good stuff is in here."

He quickly settled himself in the chair by one of the decanter trollies and stuffed the gun behind him, making sure the barrel was pointed downward. Hopefully it wouldn't set itself off. Guns didn't do that, did they?

"Funny I didn't hear you," George said. "When did you get back?"

"Oh . . ." Leo waved his hand airily. "I never went. Turned around on the drive. Couldn't face a day out there on the boat. The whole thing is very . . ."

He shivered a bit to indicate the emotional state of things.

"Yeah," George said, seeming to relax a bit. He came over

and poured himself a bit of the whiskey from the decanter. "It really has been. I could use a drink."

"You were smart to stay as well," Leo said, sipping gingerly. "This nightmare."

The gun made it impossible to lean back, so Leo hunched forward a bit as if the weight of the day sat on his shoulders like a monkey. The two men drank in silence for several minutes, listening to the rain hit the wall of French doors and the wind whistle in the chimney.

It was now or never. He could drink and go to bed, or he could continue.

"George . . . ," Leo said.

"Yeah?"

"You know I . . . well, I'd like to ask you something."

George Marsh's expression didn't change much. A few blinks. A slide or two of the jaw.

"What's that?"

Leo swirled the liquid in his glass with one hand, keeping the other alongside his leg, where he might slide it back if necessary.

"I saw what you did. I thought you might explain."

There was no immediate reply, just the ticking of the clock and the patter of the rain.

"Saw?" George finally said.

"Out under the dome, in the tunnel."

"Oh," George said.

Oh didn't quite cover the situation, Leo felt, but the

conversation had started. George let out a long breath and leaned forward. Leo had a surge of raw panic and almost slid his hand back for the gun, but George was only putting his drink down in order to rest his elbows on his knees and cradle his head in his hands for a moment.

"I found her," George said.

"Clearly," Leo replied. "But where? How?"

George lifted his face.

"I've been doing some digging around in New York," he said. "Working some leads. I got something promising a few weeks ago, couple of hoods started talking about doing the Ellingham job. I went down, did some listening of my own. I finally found one of the guys, grabbed him outside of a restaurant in Little Italy. It didn't take much to make him talk. He gave me a location. I went there. I found her body."

"So why didn't you say something?" Leo said.

"Because the idea of her is keeping Albert alive," George replied, becoming more animated. "He doesn't have Alice, but if he has this idea of Alice—someone to look for and buy toys for—what would he do without that?"

"Move on with his life," Leo said.

"Or end it. That kid is everything to him." George's voice choked a bit as he said this. "I failed him that night. I failed Iris, and I failed Alice. But then I found her. I brought her here because she should be at home, not in the place I found her, some field. Home. She should be buried with some kind of love. Near her father."

"Near her *father*?" Leo asked.

"Albert," George replied. But the little quiver in his voice told Leo what he needed to know.

"So Flora spoke to you," Leo said.

George sagged, his head lolling toward his chest.

"How long is this supposed to be a secret?" Leo asked. "Forever? Until he gives his entire fortune away trying to find her?"

"I don't know," George replied. "I only know this is what's best for now."

"And then at some point you'll say, 'You'll never guess what happened! I found your daughter and buried her out back. Happy birthday!'"

"No," George snapped. "Forever, then. Probably forever. As long as she's alive in his mind, that part of him is alive."

"And the people who did this?"

"Taken care of," George replied. This time, his tone brooked no further comment.

"So," Leo said, tapping his nails on the arm of the chair, "the case is over."

"Yes."

"With Alice buried here behind the house."

"Yes."

"Something only you and I know," Leo said.

"Yes."

"So what you want is for me to enter a pact of silence with you on this matter."

"Yes. It has to be a secret."

"Obviously," Leo replied.

"I mean, just us. No one else. Not Flora. No one."

"Again, that is obvious. I don't want this on her conscience."

"So," George said, "we agree?"

Leo shifted carefully in his seat, the gun still pressing into his spine. On one hand, it was clear what he needed to do—tell someone. Tell everyone. Call the police now.

And yet . . .

He had seen people give up hope before, seen the light leave their eyes. Albert Ellingham could buy almost anything he wanted, but not hope. Hope is not for sale. Hope is a gift.

"I suppose," he said after a moment, "that nothing can be done for Iris or Alice now. So we must look after the living."

"Exactly. We look after the living. I'm glad you know, actually." George rubbed his forehead. "It's been difficult."

"Well, a burden shared . . ."

The two men continued sipping whiskey as the rain fell. Later, when he retired for the night, Leo took the gun with him to his bedroom. He could not articulate the reason why.

20

FALLING DOWN A HOLE IS EASY. EVERYONE SHOULD TRY IT. YOU JUST let the ground go away and allow gravity to do its thing.

There was some good news about this hole. It wasn't terribly deep, only eight feet or so, and there were no stairs, just a dirt slope. Stevie rolled, which was apparently a good thing to happen if you fall. She stopped about twenty feet later and gave herself a moment to let the world stop spinning. Her backpack had absorbed much of the blow and had kept her head from ever hitting the ground, which, again, was dirt. Hard, frozen dirt, but dirt nonetheless. She felt her face and head for blood and found none, which was a positive.

Still, unexpectedly falling eight feet is not ideal.

She got up slowly and leaned over to catch her breath. She was sore but nothing seemed to be broken. She shuffled around to get her flashlight out of her backpack and walked back up the slope. Above her, the open hatch in the ground revealed a rectangle of sky and an edge of snow. It was immediately obvious that she wouldn't be able to reach the hole, but she jumped a few times anyway, almost tumbling back down the slope in the process. She checked her phone and found it undamaged, and, of course, without a signal. If there was no signal aboveground right now, there was definitely not going to be one in a giant hole in the ground.

"Do. Not. Panic." She said it out loud to herself, the words bouncing back at her.

Unlike many of the other hidden spots at Ellingham, this was not a tunnel—it was more of a cavern, a wide, open space underground, with rough rock walls studded with jutting formations. Yes, it was dark. Yes, it was cold. Yes, she was alone in a hole in the ground. But things had been worse than this recently. A big hole in the ground with an open hatch was better than a narrow hole in the ground with a closed one.

You had to do the best with what you had.

One good thing about the flashlights Ellingham provided was that they were powerful enough to signal an airplane at forty thousand feet. Stevie swept the cave with light and saw that it went back a good distance, maybe twenty yards or so, then it bent to the left. She took a few tentative steps and scanned the ground around her. There were a few things: broken shovels, a whiskey bottle from some bygone era, a spoon, a melted-down candle end, a few planks of wood, some beer bottles, and a bag of screws. There were a few balled-up bits of newspaper; these were in a delicate, disgusting state but she could smooth one out enough to see a date: June 3, 1935.

Her confusion at falling into the hole was being replaced with confusion about where it was she had landed. This was a very unnatural natural cave, full of stalagmites and stalactites that seemed to be man-made. The arrangement was weirdly precise and orderly. She stepped carefully, shining her light up and down, making sure the floor and the ceiling were safe. Her light glinted at something on the ground, and she bent to examine it. Shell casings—lots of them. The wall above them was pockmarked. Someone had been doing a little shooting practice around here. The old cigarette pack she found nearby indicated that this had not been anytime recently.

She went all the way to the back of the cavern. Here, at the back, there was a bend and an opening maybe twice the size of a normal doorway. She poked at the dark with her light, paused and considered the risk of going in.

"It would be stupid to go in there," she said out loud.

But, of course, she went.

As she passed through this portal, she entered into a bizarre fantasia.

The majority of the space was taken up by a low ditch, about four feet at its deepest point. On the far side of the ditch was a boat in the shape of a swan, painted gold. It was tipped on its side, the head of the swan dipping into the ditch. The more she shone the light around, the more Stevie saw the half-complete detail—blue tiles, wires that connected to nothing, wooden vines painted a bright green. Along the back wall was a fresco of women—goddesses, dressed in gauzy robes—looking down from rose-gold clouds.

She was walking in the dream of a weird-thinking man from the past, a dream made real in stone.

This was, almost certainly, the treasure. This was where

Francis and Eddie had come. She found evidence of them almost at once—loads of candles in a ring on the ground, in all degrees of melt. She found a big red button torn off some clothes, more cigarettes, several bottles of wine and gin, and more shell casings.

There were a few bags of concrete off to the side and a few busted crates. She tested theses crates to see if they would be stable enough to stand on, but they were broken.

Stevie sat on the ground in the middle of the candles and took it all in. The world of the present drifted away for a moment. She was in 1936. This was where the pair had come to be together. The button had probably torn off Francis's dress or coat. This was the treasure—another underground spot. Another trip to nowhere. It was fantastic, but it told her nothing.

Light. Out of the corner of her eye, she saw it bouncing. Someone was in here with her. Without a moment's hesitation, she moved behind one of the rock formations, her heart pounding. Someone had followed her. Someone was coming up behind her quietly. She snatched a shovel from the ground. It wasn't much of a weapon, but it was something. She held it like a bat, her hands tense.

The light was close now. The person was inside the grotto. She tensed her stance. She was ready. . . .

"Hey! *Hey!* Stevie!"

The voice was David's.

"What the *hell*?" he said, winded. "Were you going to hit me?"

"What are you doing here?" she said, still holding up the shovel.

"What do you think? I saw you go up to a statue, dance around, kick it, and then you fell into a hole in the ground. What the hell did you think I was going to do? Will you put that down?"

She looked at the shovel in her hand as if she had to consult with it first. She set it down slowly.

"Why did you sneak up on me?" she said.

"I didn't. I was yelling your name up there. When you didn't answer I jumped in after you to make sure you weren't hurt."

"I didn't hear anything."

"Do you think I'm lying?" he said. "So am I supposed to be *sorry* for following you into a hole? Thanks a fucking lot."

Stevie didn't know what she thought, except that sound would seem to echo in a grotto underground. It wasn't something someone would lie about, though. Her breathing slowed a bit. She came out from behind the rock formation.

"I thought you wanted to ignore me," she said.

"You vanished from the house."

"And you ran after me?"

"I didn't run," he said. "It's snowing. There was one set of footprints. Even I, with my inferior mystery-solving skills, can work that one out."

"Okay," she said.

"Okay?"

"What do you want me to say?" she replied.

He shook his head.

"Nothing," he said. "Say nothing."

Stevie had just failed some test she had no idea she had to take, on a subject she was not aware of. She had been sitting here in her hole in the ground, minding her own business, and then this. There was no winning.

David shined his light around the room.

"I've seen some crazy shit here, but this may be the winner," he said. "How did you find it?"

"I found a diary," she said. "From a student who was here in the thirties. There were instructions. I followed them. The last thing I had to do was pull the toe of the statue, and I did that. And then I fell in the hole. I guess no one found this before because no one pulls on statue toes that often."

"Just another way our generation is lazy," he said. "So you came out in a storm to pull on a toe."

He stepped down into the ditch to get a closer look at the lopsided swan boat and the fresco.

"We've got some Mad King Ludwig action going on here, huh?"

"What?"

"Trip to Germany with Dad when I was ten," he said. "This, if I am not mistaken, is a replica of something in one of King Ludwig's castles. Underground grotto, big classical painting on the wall, big swan boat. It all checks out. Why *not* have your own underground grotto with a swan boat? What are you, poor?"

As he looked around, Stevie mind continued to reel. He had followed her through the snow, to a place he could not have known she was going. This could not be his plan if she didn't know the plan herself.

"We're going to have to climb back out of here," he said. "Come on."

"Before we do that," she said, "I want to know something."

"What now?"

"I met some of your friends in town," Stevie said. "At the art colony."

This was clearly not what he was expecting. He pulled back his head a bit in surprise.

"Oh, the art house. Fun place. Did you meet Paul? Is he still talking through puppets?"

"I think he is in some kind of silent phase," Stevie said.

"That's better than puppets."

"Bath—Bathsheba—said that Ellie told her something about the message that showed up on my wall that night before Hayes died. . . ."

"I told you before and I'll say it again—I didn't shine any creepy message on your wall."

"Well, Ellie knew about it and thought it was real, and she seemed to know who did it. If you didn't do it and Ellie didn't do it, who did it?"

"I have no idea," he said. "But it's getting late. If we're going to get out of here, we have to go. Come on."

It must have gotten considerably darker outside, because as they approached the entrance there was no patch of light where the hatch was, no dim square of snow sky. As they got closer, the slow and sickening realization entered her bloodstream. She knew it before she saw it for sure.

The hatch had closed above them.

21

"Uнннннн," David said.

It was as good a summary of the situation as any.

"Oh," Stevie said.

Again, this about summed it up.

There was a real entombing problem at Ellingham Academy. This was undeniable. Stevie felt a vein throbbing near her ear and had the sure sense that a massive panic attack was about to level her flat. It would wipe away the world and bring her to her knees and she would die from it.

She waited. The vein continued to beat away, like the annoying sound of music from a far-off car. But there was no panic. She focused her light up on the hatch, then on David, who was himself looking a little pale.

"I didn't think that would happen," David said. "The hatch opens in."

"But it happened," she said. "How did it happen?"

"Wind's kind of blowing hard up there," David said, shining his flashlight on the flat metal hatch. "Suction? I guess?"

"Or it's designed to close," Stevie said. "Secret lair, secret door."

"There's no handle on this side," David said, a twinge of worry coming into his voice. "Why is there no handle on this side? Who builds a hatch with no way of pushing it open? *Who does that?* This is a problem. This is a *real problem.*"

He shone his light around the space, looking over the debris. He grabbed a broken shovel handle and poked it up at the hatch. It didn't reach. He threw it down.

"Calm down," she said, and then immediately regretted it. Telling someone to calm down was the worst. He hadn't seemed to notice; he was too busy freaking out.

"We need to do something a little more proactive," he said. "We can't wait this one out. The temperature will drop. We need to get that open and get the hell out of here."

"That boat," she said, taking him by the arm. "We'll get it and stand on it. There's two of us. Two of us is better than one of us. And if we can reach it, we can work out a way to get it open."

"I guess," he said, sounding a little breathless. "Yeah. Okay."

It turned out that being the calm one eased Stevie's panic. The more anxious David seemed, the more she could talk through it. She found her steps were steady and firm as she led the way back into the cavern.

They first tried to tip the boat into an upright position, which took both of them. The swan boat was heavy—*really* heavy—and looked to be made of metal and concrete. These are not generally considered to be good boat-making materials, which indicated that maybe it had not been intended to be a boat at all. Perhaps it was to be a decoration in Ellingham's weird underground grotto of love. Whatever the case, they would not be able to carry it.

"I hate this," David said. "I hate that we're down here."

Stevie scanned the area. How could there be so much crap and yet nothing useful? The rock formations couldn't exactly be pulled off the walls. The three bags of old cement had gone solid. The only thing that was left was a small pile of bricks off to one side.

"Bricks!" she said cheerfully, like bricks were fun things that you might bring to parties.

David shone his light on the meager little stack.

"Not enough," he said.

"But it's some. Some bricks are better than no bricks. There's two of us. Maybe one of us could stand on the bricks and boost the other."

"Yeah . . . maybe. I guess. Yeah."

The thing about bricks is that they are not easy to carry. One in each hand is about the limit. There was nothing in the grotto to use to wheel the bricks around.

"So we make a few trips," she said, trying not to lose the momentum of her enthusiasm. "We'll dump out our bags to carry more."

With her bag full of ten bricks and David's with about the

same, they began the journey back to the front of the cavern, David using his free hand to hold up the flashlight.

"Let's speculate," Stevie said, trying to remain cheerful. "Let's say you were planning on doing something to Hayes. Let's say you thought that since I'm the local detective that I might get ideas about it, that it wasn't an accident—which is what happened—so you do something to make me seem a little crazy. I see threatening notes on my wall at night."

"We're still talking about this?" David said. "Look at where we are."

"Hear me out. My ideas would seem less sensible, right?"

"Why are we talking about this?"

"Something to do," Stevie said, her voice strained from the effort of carrying the bricks in the cold.

"Well, let's don't. We don't have to run through your case notes every time we're alone. It doesn't always have to be about murder."

"Okay," she said.

"We have to get out of here."

"We're working on that," Stevie said.

"Don't you get sick of this place?" he snapped. "Who the fuck does this? Who builds all of these tunnels and fake grottoes?"

His words echoed around the cavern and bounced back on them.

Stevie found her body was starting to stiffen and shake from the cold. She had to keep it together. She had to be fine so that David would be fine. And she would be fine because David was there.

"You know," she said, "Disneyland is built on a slope because it also has a vast underground series of tunnels."

Nothing from David.

"They were built to keep characters in the right places. No one wants a space monster in Frontierland."

"A space monster?" David said. "Have you *been* to Disneyland?"

"No," Stevie said.

"Seriously?"

"Too expensive. But I spend my time planning my perfect Disney dream wedding, with the space monster and a . . . Mickey . . . something . . ."

They dumped their twenty bricks at the top of the ramp.

"Stop talking," he said. "It's not helping."

On their second trip, they removed another layer from the depressingly small pile of bricks. There was no way this would be enough to do anything, but she dutifully opened her bag to accept some more. Her arms ached from the cold.

"Oh my God," David said.

Stevie looked up. David was staring at the brick pile. Well—not at the pile. Something in the pool of light from his flashlight. Under the top layer of bricks there were several wooden boxes marked LIBERTY POWDER CO, PITTS-BURGH PA, HIGH EXPLOSIVES, DANGEROUS.

"Ho-ly shit," David said.

David removed a few more bricks from around the boxes. There were three in total. A bit more digging turned up a long coil of wire.

"You think this is real?" he asked.

"I think it's definitely real," Stevie said. "*This* is the treasure."

"Treasure?"

"Francis—the one who wrote the diary—she must have been stealing dynamite and stockpiling it."

"There was a student here who was stealing and stockpiling dynamite? And people bitch about a few squirrels in the library?"

They regarded the pile for a few moments. It was clear what was going to come next, though Stevie did not want to bring it up.

"I'm going to say something you won't like," David said.

Stevie said nothing.

"I mean, there is a *lot* of dynamite here," he went on. "We don't need that much. One stick is probably all we would need. Look at this. Blasting caps, wire. Everything but the plunger to set it off. I think all we'd need is an electrical charge. I probably have something in my bag . . ."

"We can't set off dynamite," she said.

"Sure we can. Haven't you ever seen cartoons?"

"We'll kill ourselves," she said.

"No we won't. We probably won't. A stick or two? That's nothing."

"It's dynamite," she pointed out. "Old dynamite. It will *blow up*."

"Dynamite," he said, looking up at her, "is a high explosive. It produces a pressure wave. Imagine a sphere—an expanding sphere. That's the pressure wave. As the sphere expands, the surface area increases by the square of the radius, therefore the pressure drops by the square of the radius. In addition, we have a wall, which means the pressure wave has to go around a corner, which it can do through diffraction, but it will lose energy in the process. I'm saying it won't be that bad."

Stevie was too stunned to reply.

"Janelle isn't the only one who knows physics," he said. "Got a few things in here that might work. Actually, the flashlight . . ."

He opened up his flashlight.

"Nine volts," he said. "That might do it. So all we need to do is wire it."

"Dynamite," she said. "They used it to blast things open. *To level the mountain*."

"Yeah, but you need a bunch for that," he said. "One stick shouldn't start an avalanche or anything. I don't think so anyway."

"You don't *think*?"

"No!" he said. "No. Probably not. No. We're not really on a slope here. There's nothing to come down."

"Except the rest of the mountain above us."

"One stick," he said. "Tiny dynamite. Cute little dynamite.

I think I can do this. Do you trust me?"

The truth was, there was no real choice. It was getting colder and darker, and no one knew they were under the ground.

And deep down, she did trust him.

"How do we do it?" she asked.

The how was not completely clear, and it was distressing to Stevie how much of this plan really did seem to be coming from cartoons. They stretched out the wire first.

"That's, what, twenty feet?" David said. "I mean, it's not enough that we could rig the hatch and get all the way in here, where it would be safe. I'll have to be closer."

"We'll have to be closer," Stevie said.

"There's no point in . . ."

"We," she said. "I'm not dying in this dumb hole alone. We."

The second problem was that they could not actually get the dynamite up to the hatch itself. They could only place it underneath and hope the force of the blast was enough. Which meant . . . more dynamite.

They decided to use two sticks.

"That should probably do some damage, right?" David said as they set it down.

"Or bring the ground down on us."

"Or that," he said.

David managed the wiring of the caps. Stevie didn't really want to watch this part, because of the terror she felt and also the fact that she suspected he was making this up as he went along. Then they both hunkered behind one of the small rock formations. This meant they had to be closer to the blast, but it provided some shelter. Stevie and David huddled under the foil blanket that Janelle had so thoughtfully packed and demanded they take.

"You're sure you won't go in the back?" David said.

"Before we do this," she said in reply. "There's something I want you to know."

"Oh boy."

"I solved it."

"You what now?"

"I solved it," she said simply. "The Ellingham case."

"You solved the crime of the century."

"Yes," she said.

"And who did it?"

"George Marsh," she said simply. "The cop, the guy from the FBI."

"And . . . that's it? You just know?"

"I don't just know," she said. "I worked the case. I researched. I sat in the stupid attic reading menus and inventories."

"You . . . solved it."

"Uh-huh," she said.

"And who knows this?"

"Nate," she said.

"Nate."

"Yup," she said. "Nate knows."

He waited a beat.

"Sure," he said. "Seems about right."

"So now tell me why I couldn't have a tablet," Stevie said. David shifted next to her.

"He got to you once," he said. "I didn't want him to be able to get near you ever again. Happy now?"

"As happy as I can be in a hole in the ground about to blast some old unstable dynamite."

"And there's this," he said. "When you took off, I was coming to show you something."

He pulled out his phone and opened up a message.

"Call Me Charles replied to Imaginary Jim," he said. Stevie read the note:

> **TO: jimmalloy@electedwardking.com**
> **Today at 3:47 p.m.**
> **FROM: cscott@ellingham.edu**
> **CC: jquinn@ellingham.edu**
>
> **Mr. Malloy,**
> **We appreciate the senator's concerns, and we certainly thank him for his help with our internal security system. Attached is a copy of Albert Ellingham's codicil. We trust that the senator will keep this strictly private.**
>
> In addition to all other bequests, the amount of ten million dollars shall be held in trust for my daughter, Alice Madeline Ellingham. Should my daughter no longer be among the living, any person,

persons, or organization that locates her earthly
remains—provided it is established that they were in
no way connected to her disappearance—shall receive
this sum. If she is not located by her ninetieth
birthday, these funds shall be released to be used
for the Ellingham Academy in any way the board
sees fit. It is further stipulated that no member of
the faculty or administration of Ellingham Academy
may claim this sum as their own.

"It's real," Stevie said. "The codicil is real."

"Apparently."

"It's *real*," she said again.

"Yeah."

She leaned her head back on the cold rock wall and laughed. The laugh quickly turned into a kind of laugh vomit, endless and rolling, to the point where she was gagging from it. David laughed too, probably because she was laughing.

"So you have your thing," he said. "Did it tell you what you needed to know?"

"No," she said, painfully coming down from the hysteria. She wiped her eyes.

They settled into each other. She wrapped her arms around his middle and he did the same to her. The foil blanket rattled.

"I've decided not to ignore you," she said. "I don't care if I promised."

"Doesn't matter. My ass is toast."

He pulled up another message, this time, a text.

Today 2:24 p.m.
I see someone named Jim Malloy now works for me. I
can only assume this is you. I also understand you have
returned to Ellingham. Be aware that I know that you
accessed my safe and our private server. If you think I
won't press charges against you, you are much mistaken.
As a public official, I need to set an example—my son will
not get special treatment. Think very carefully about what
you do next. How do you want your life to go?

"Wah-wah," David said, imitating a sad trombone. "My
life, as I once knew it, is done. Especially after I sent this."
He pulled up one more message.

Today 2:26 p.m.
Your blackmail stuff has been destroyed. I want my life to
go better than yours, and now it will. Suck it.

"You didn't wait very long," Stevie noted.

"No," he said. "There was nothing to think about. But he
is going to make my life very, very difficult."

"As opposed to now?"

"I see your point," he said.

They sat with their backs to the rock for a moment, the
wires in David's hands.

"You've really never been to Disneyland?" he said.

"Nope."

"We gotta fix that."

"When we get out of here, you can take me," she said. "You ready?"

"Sure. Why not. Shall we?"

"I guess," she said.

David took the two ends of the wire and then, with great care, touched them to the poles of the battery.

For a moment, nothing happened. Stevie looked up at the rocks and the dark and wondered if she was moving slowly through time. Maybe she was already dead. Maybe this was it. Ellingham would take her at last, like it had swallowed Hayes and Ellie.

Then, a strange noise, something angry, hissing.

Then a bang—a bang so loud it burned her ears. A cloud of white dust shot past them and there was an acrid smell. When she opened her eyes again, she found she was pressed deep into David, and David into her. She couldn't really hear because of the ringing in her ears, and she was coughing uncontrollably.

But they were alive. Dusty. Maybe with hearing damage. But alive.

They both got up and cautiously peered around the rock. There was a pile of rocky rubble under the entrance, and a tiny chink of light. They stepped forward. The ground around the explosion was pitted, and the walls were blasted. Above them, the hatch was bent upward—not completely open, but not completely closed either.

"That was amazing," she said.

"Yeah it was. Yeah it was!"

He turned to her and grabbed her in a huge, enthusiastic embrace and started jumping up and down. She started jumping too, because it was hard not to jump, and because this was something worth jumping for. They were not free, but they were not trapped either. And it was cold and snowing, and they were in a hole in the ground.

"We still can't get out!" he said. "We're still stuck! We blew it up and we're still stuck! We may freeze to death!"

The jumping was getting old, and she slowed up. He did as well. They both gasped for breath for a moment. She could see him better now that they had a tiny bit of light coming down.

"So what now?" he said.

Above them, there was a grinding noise. A pair of hands gripped the sides of the hatch and pulled it back.

Then a face appeared.

"*Germaine?*" Stevie said.

22

"Hey," Germaine said. "Did you guys blow this up? I thought I saw something blow up."

Germaine Batt was dressed head to toe in winter gear—ski pants and jacket, goggles, a massive hat, plus walking poles to help her get through the snow. She pulled back the goggles, revealing a raw red mark around her eyes where they had been. She also didn't seem that shocked about any potential explosion she may have witnessed.

"I can't believe I'm looking at you and how much I love you," David yelled up.

"What?"

"Nothing," he yelled.

"Do you have a rope?" she called down.

"No," David said. "We didn't plan to fall into this hole."

"Okay. Hold on. I'll be right back."

"We're not going anywhere," he yelled. "But can you keep the hatch propped open? We're kind of paranoid about being stuck in holes in the ground."

Germaine took off her backpack and used it as a wedge.

"Germaine," David said, turning to Stevie in wonder.

"Germaine," she repeated.

Snow poured down into the hole, but Stevie and David sat under it anyway, refusing to give up their square of sky. They squeezed together in the foil blanket. The cold was penetrating now. Her feet and hands were numb. Her skin was starting to burn all over, and she was getting tired from the effort of trying to be warm.

"What if she doesn't come back?" David said.

"She'll come back," Stevie said, pushing herself into his side. "She's Germaine. Fire and flood cannot stop her."

Germaine did come back.

She returned with some sheeting that had been on the ground where the paintballs went off on Janelle's machine. She tied these into a few knots, then tied them together. She looped the other end around the statue. Germaine dropped the sheet rope down. David gave it a test tug and nodded.

"You want to go first?" he asked Stevie. "I'll spot you."

Stevie had never climbed anything like this before. Her hands were numb with cold, and her feet slipped several times on the knots. But her determination to get out gave her the arm strength to keep pulling herself upward. The few times she lost footing, she felt David hold her up from underneath. Germaine helped pull her up into the deep snow above. She crawled out of the earth like she was coming out of her own grave. After being in the dark underground grotto, the bright whiteness of it nearly blinded her. The cold was so pure and numbing. David climbed up next, Germaine and Stevie pulling him out as he reached the top. They trudged back to the Great House. There was no worry now about anyone yelling at them. They were far beyond those kinds of cares. Pix regarded them with a weary acceptance as they dragged their snowy, wet selves in through the front door.

"You're back," she said. "And you have . . . Germaine?"

"Hey," Germaine replied.

Pix shook her head.

"Get warm," she said, pointing them to the fireplace. "I give up."

It's a funny thing about being cold—sometimes it doesn't hit you until you start to get warm again. As soon as Stevie was in front of the fire, she started to shake almost uncontrollably. Her feet and hands burned.

"H-h-how are you here too?" Stevie said through chattering teeth.

"You guys n-n-never turned up on the coach that day," Germaine said. "I f-f-figured something was up. I took the c-c-coach back when they were doing the next pickup. I told the guy I forgot something. Then I s-s-stayed. It was really easy. I wrote to my parents and said I was staying."

"You c-c-can do that?" Stevie asked.

"My parents t-t-trust me."

Stevie and David looked at her blankly.

"What's that l-l-like?" David asked.

Germaine shrugged.

The rest of the group came out to see the stragglers from the snow and were surprised to find Germaine Batt had joined their number. They had a lot of questions, but none of the three were up to answering them yet. They were covered in dust, still coughing. The ringing was getting less loud, but it had not stopped entirely.

And then, it arrived.

Anxiety does not ask your permission. Anxiety does not come when expected. It's very rude. It barges in at the strangest moments, stopping all activity, focusing everything on itself. It sucks the air out of your lungs and scrambles the world. Her vision went spotty around the edges. The ringing in her ears swelled again. Her knees buckled.

"Stevie?" someone said. She really didn't know who.

She stumbled away from them all. The Great House was turning into a hideous parody of itself. The fireplace was like a terrible maw of fire. Her friends' faces made no sense. Everything was rushing. She was on a current she could not control.

"Where's your medicine?" Janelle said, kneeling next to her.

Her medicine was in a hole in the ground, having been dumped out to carry bricks. She was going to ride this one with no help.

She stared at the grand staircase sweeping up in front of her. Anxiety, her therapist had told her many times, never killed anyone. It felt like death, but it was an illusion. A terrible illusion that inhabited your body and tried to make it its puppet. It told you nothing mattered because everything was made of fear.

"Fuck it," she mumbled, barely able to make the words.

For no reason that she could think of, she started for the steps.

"Hey, wait," Janelle said, holding her arm. "Maybe you should sit down."

"Steps," she said. The word popped out of her mouth like a strange bubble.

"Steps," Janelle repeated. "Okay. Fine. Nate, get her arm. We'll help you."

Where do you look for something that's never really there . . . Together, between her two friends, Stevie climbed the staircase.

The Ellinghams waited for her on the landing. Always on a staircase, but never on a stair. That's where they were. She needed to look for something and hold on to it—something she could wrap her head around. Any rope would do. The Ellinghams. That's why she was here. Albert. Iris. Alice. She repeated their names to herself over and over. Leonard Holmes Nair had preserved them here, in this bizarre painting, the one he had altered to include the dome, the pool of moonlight stretching over . . .

Where do you look for someone who could be anywhere?

The question popped up in the corner of her mind, distracting her for a moment.

The kid is there, Fenton had said on the phone. *The kid is there*. If George Marsh had committed the crime, what if he brought her back? What if he buried her out of guilt? What if Alice had been in the tunnel, and . . .

She looked at the painting again, forcing her eyes to

focus. The pool of light, the moonbeam, it stretched over the point where the tunnel would have been. And the form of the light—it was vaguely in the shape of . . .

"Hey," David said. He had joined them and was sitting in front of her. "It's okay. It's just panic."

"Shut up," she said. She could not articulate what was happening in her head, this massive word problem that was assembling itself in some part of her brain. Alice had been buried here. Alice was here. The kid was here. Alice had been found.

Point by point, things began to line up. Suddenly, it all made sense. All of it. The facts, which before had been falling from the sky like snow and evaporating in her memory, all sprang forth, solid, and put themselves in line. The tunnel. The excavation. Hayes in the tunnel . . . Fenton . . .

"It all makes sense," she said to David. She could feel her eyes widening.

"Are you okay?" he asked.

"Your phone!" she said. "Give it to me."

"Why?"

"*Please.*"

There must have been something in her tone. Though he looked confused, he pulled it out of his pocket and handed it to her. She scrolled through until she found what she needed.

There it was—the one discordant note.

Of course, it wasn't an accident that it ended like this. She had done the work, reading things for years. She had gotten herself to Ellingham. She had made herself a detective and put herself on this path. She had summoned this moment through work and falling down holes and running into the dark. It was time to gather the suspects, like they did at the end of every mystery.

"Get everyone," she said to him. "Everyone in the building."

"Why?" he asked. "What is going on? Are you okay?"

She looked up at him, her panic gone, her vision clear, the world starting to settle back into position.

"It's time to solve some murders," she said.

November 10, 1938

ANARCHISTS SUSPECTED IN EXPLOSION
DEATH OF ALBERT ELLINGHAM
New York Times

Police and the FBI are investigating a local anarchist group in the death of Albert Ellingham and FBI agent George Marsh.

"We believe this may have been retaliation for the death of Anton Vorachek," said Agent Patrick O'Hallahan of the FBI. "We are looking into multiple leads. We will not stop until the culprit or culprits are caught, mark my words."

Vorachek, the man convicted of the kidnapping and murder of Iris Ellingham, and the disappearance of Alice Ellingham, was murdered by a gunman outside the courtroom after his sentencing. The gunman was never found.

Albert Ellingham had been the subject of many threats. Indeed, he met Detective George

Marsh of the New York Police Department after Marsh discovered and foiled a bomb plot against him. In appreciation, Albert Ellingham hired Marsh as person security. When Marsh joined the FBI, Ellingham asked Director J. Edgar Hoover to station him in the area of Vermont around the Ellingham home and school. Despite this precaution, Iris and Alice Ellingham were taken . . .

Leonard Holmes Nair pushed the newspaper aside, but there was another underneath.

ALBERT ELLINGHAM BURIED AT MOUNTAIN RETREAT
Boston Herald

A private ceremony was held today for Albert Ellingham at his mountain retreat outside Burlington, Vt. Mr. Ellingham was killed on October 30 after a bomb exploded on his sailboat. An FBI agent, George Marsh, died with him. It is believed the two men were victims of an anarchist bomb plot. The funeral . . .

Leo got up and took his coffee to the window of the breakfast room and looked out at the kaleidoscope of color outside.

The funeral was a lie.

Parts had been found, enough to match fingerprints; the condition of the hands and the fingers the prints belonged to told authorities that the persons involved were no longer alive.

"There wasn't much," the one investigator told Leo. "We found three hands, a leg, a foot, some skin . . ."

The police could determine little about what had transpired, aside from the fact that they believed that the explosives were probably toward the back of the boat. Albert and George went out and never came back. They were most certainly dead, but there, the facts ended.

Iris had family, but Albert did not—not any he acknowledged. And while he had many employees and endless acquaintances, the only people who really counted as friends were Leo and Flora, and Robert Mackenzie, who was both secretary and confidant. The remains were still in a police mortuary, so these three were at the Ellingham Great House, going through a macabre pretense that there was some kind of remembrance ceremony going on.

So much of what was left was paperwork and packing. Like Iris before him, Albert was now being sorted into piles and boxes. Such a great life reduced to this. Leo thought about getting up and working on the family portrait some more. It was the one thing he was meant to be doing. It was only right to finish it. It sat under a sheet in the morning room. He had opened the door to the room a few times and seen it sitting there, like a ghost, frozen in a sunbeam in the center of the room. He couldn't face it, or the warm light, or the echoes of the house. The Ellingham Great House was built for parties, for families, for friends—a house made as a centerpiece to a school that sat vacant around them. This terrible quiet was hard to take, so Leo decided to spend the morning in Albert Ellingham's study, one of the few places truly set up to be quiet and soundproof. Even though the room was two stories high, with a balcony of books and shelving running around above, it managed to be snug with its rugs and leather chairs, the fire. With the curtains drawn, the room was muted. On the mantel above the fire was the green marble clock that Albert had purchased in Switzerland when they were there for Alice's birth. It had belonged to Marie Antoinette, so the story went. It was a survivor of a revolution. The reality was probably much more mundane.

"Good morning," Robert Mackenzie said, coming in. Mackenzie was a polite, serious, and deeply efficient young man, but Leo didn't hold that against him.

"There's quite a lot to be sorted," Mackenzie said. "I am going to pack the desk and have the contents taken upstairs. I hope it won't bother you if I work in here."

Leo was quite used to watching other people work as he sat and did nothing. He nodded graciously. Mackenzie set about going through Albert's desk, sifting through printed stationery, pots of ink, pens, notes. It was lulling to watch.

"Excuse me a moment," Mackenzie said, holding up a small box marked WEBSTER-CHICAGO RECORD-ING WIRE. "I want to see what's on this. It looks like Mr.

Ellingham was listening to it that morning and I need to know what's on it to file it."

"Of course," Leo said.

Mackenzie went over to a machine against the wall. He removed the heavy cover and set the wire on a spool. A moment later, Albert Ellingham's voice boomed out from the corner of the room, causing Leo's stomach to lurch.

"Dolores, sit there."

The thin, high voice of a young girl responded. She had a pronounced New York accent.

"Sit here?"

"Just there. And lean into the microphone a bit. Good. Now all you have to do is speak normally. I want to ask you about your experiences at Ellingham. I'm making some recordings—"

Mackenzie snapped the machine off and the voices fell silent. There was a whir as he rewound the wire and put it back into the box.

"Dolores," he said. "He must have been listening to this recording of her voice. He felt so bad about that girl. Apparently she was exceptional."

Leo had no reply, so the room fell silent but for the ticking of the marble clock on the mantel. Mackenzie cleared his throat and took the package with the wire recording and packed it into the box.

"It seems he was looking at the book she was reading as well," Mackenzie added. He laid a finger on a copy of *The*

Collected Stories of Sherlock Holmes, which sat on the desk. "This was with her when she died. I suppose I should put it back in the library. That's what he would want. Books in their proper places . . ."

He let the thought trail and remained as he was, one finger on the cover of the book, staring at nothing in particular. Again, the ticking clock took over the conversation. Leo began to shift in his chair uncomfortably. Perhaps it was time to seek out a cup of tea.

"Something has been bothering me," Mackenzie said. "I need to speak to someone about it. But I need your confidence. This can go no further than this room."

Leo lowered himself back into the seat and looked around as an automatic gesture, but of course, they were alone.

"Something was off that morning before he went on the boat," Mackenzie said. "I don't know what it was. He wrote a riddle, which seemed like a good thing. Then he made me promise to enjoy myself. He was saying things like—"

Mackenzie cut himself off.

"Like?" Leo prompted.

"Like he knew he wouldn't be coming back," Mackenzie answered, as if this thought was occurring to him for the first time. And then, there was the codicil."

He shuffled around in the desk for a moment and produced a long piece of legal paper. This he walked over and handed to Leo.

"Just read the top bit," he said.

"'In addition to all other bequests,'" Leo read aloud, "'the amount of ten million dollars shall be held in trust for my daughter, Alice Madeline Ellingham. Should my daughter no longer be among the living, any person, persons, or organization that locates her earthly remains—provided it is established that they were in no way connected to her disappearance—shall receive this sum. If she is not located by her ninetieth birthday, these funds shall be released to be used for the Ellingham Academy in any way the board sees fit.'"

"His mind was sound," Mackenzie said, "but his heart was broken—that's what made him do this. I have no idea where Alice is, but if she *is* out there . . ."

"This won't help," Leo said, finishing the sentiment. He set the paper down, crossed over to the window, and pulled back the curtain, revealing the pit in the ground behind the house where the lake had been. It was swampy and raw, the dome looking like an exposed sore.

He could tell Mackenzie now—tell him that Alice was there, buried in the tunnel. This terrible secret could be over. But what good would it do? She would be exhumed. There would be a frenzy. Her body would be photographed and poked and prodded. She had gone through enough. Leo had never known himself to have a single paternal instinct, but he felt one now. Alice was home.

"I can't destroy it," Mackenzie went on, "as much as I would like to. It's a legal document. But I can't let it get into the world either. It would be chaos. It would make it *harder* to find Alice, not easier. I don't know what to do with it."

"Here," Leo said, turning from the window and reaching out his hand.

"I can't let you destroy it either."

"I'm not going to," Leo said.

Mackenzie paused, then handed it over once more. Leo went over to the mantel, to the green clock. He turned it over carefully, as he had seen Albert do. It took a moment to find the button that popped out the drawer in the base. He folded the paper several times on the mantel until it was a small square, then he put it in the clock and snapped it shut.

"It is secured with Albert Ellingham's belongings," he said.

Mackenzie nodded.

"Thank you," he said. "I'm going to move these upstairs, I think."

When Mackenzie was gone, Leo found himself rippling with nervous energy. He left the study and strode across the massive main hall to the morning room. He went right to the easel and tore the sheet from the canvas. There was his work—Iris, captured one afternoon not that long ago, lounging in the cold, begging for more cocaine. Albert and Alice had been captured at different times, all stuck together in this creation of his, with the backdrop of the house. The figures were fine. The backdrop had to go.

He pulled the easel and canvas out onto the flagstone patio outside, pointed in the direction of the empty lake and the dome. Pointed toward Alice herself. He worked with swift, big strokes, covering the Great House. He painted in the dome instead, and the rising moon as the day wore on. He slashed apart the sky. Now it was every color, his grief and anger coming out, the knowledge that sat in his stomach. Over the spot where Alice was buried, he directed Iris's hand. And the moonbeam that shone down upon the spot, he crafted it into a gentle tombstone. He could do that at least. This small gesture. He worked all night, not pausing to eat, taking the canvas inside and working by the fire.

By dawn it was done. The Ellingham family looked out at him from his hallucinatory rendition—all three together, locked in mystery, but together.

23

It had to be Albert Ellingham's office—the place where it all began that night in April 1936 where a desperate man pulled money from a safe in the wall. This room, with its balcony of books as silent onlookers to the drama below, had seen so much—everything wealth had built and everything wealth had destroyed.

There were only so many seats in the office. Dr. Quinn and Hunter were in chairs by the fireplace, where no fire was lit. Call Me Charles leaned against one of the two desks in his standard *"Work can be fun!"* pose. Janelle, Nate, and Vi all sat on the floor, avoiding the trophy rug, which Vi was gazing at in horror. Germaine sat on one of the steps to the second-floor balcony, a notebook in her hand. David roamed the room a bit by the windows. Mark Parsons and Pix leaned against the wall by the door.

Stevie took the center of the floor, because that is where the detective stands.

The expressions in the room varied from confused, to

annoyed, to faintly bemused, to intensely interested. Whatever anyone felt about Stevie, she was doing a big, weird thing here in the office, where she had already once done a big, weird thing that had then led to Ellie's death.

Stevie resisted the urge to say, "I'll bet you're wondering why I called you all here." But then she realized that the reason people said that was that once you called people into one room, they *were* probably wondering why you had called them all there. So Stevie found herself vacillating between possible phrases and heard herself saying, "So, um, the reason . . . well . . ." No. Start over. Start as you mean to go on.

"People have died up here," she said, "and they didn't die in accidents."

"Okay, Stevie," Dr. Quinn said, "what is—"

"I'm serious," she said. The words came out so strongly that even Dr. Quinn was taken aback. Stevie regretted them at once, because Hercule Poirot or Sherlock Holmes never had to snap about how serious they were.

Call Me Charles, who always invited a challenge, nodded.

"We have nothing else to do," he said. "Let's hear her out."

Stevie took a deep breath, ignored the bright sparks of panic that danced on the tips of her synapses, and continued.

"They didn't die in accidents," she said again. "'They were murdered."

Nothing from the assembled. They made it look so easy in detective books—like you could just call up the suspects and expect everyone to sit on the edge of their chairs, waiting to be accused so they could walk through the motions of denial before the detective revealed that they weren't guilty. Those were the rules. The reality was that your friends looked at you with hope bordering on embarrassment, while your teachers and school staff questioned every choice they'd made in their lives to get them to this point. But even Hercule Poirot had to do this for a first time, and everyone made fun of the little Belgian detective for his fastidious ways until he smacked them down with the hammer of deductive truth, so . . .

"Stevie?" Nate said.

Her mouth was hanging open. She snapped her jaw closed and walked with purpose to the fireplace.

"Hayes Major," she said. "Right from the second I met him, all he talked about was Hollywood. He wanted to leave school and get out there as soon as possible. When all of this started, when Hayes died, when Ellie ran—I thought it was about the show, about *The End of It All*. It made sense. Why else would Hayes die? It made so much sense. Hayes was someone who took stuff that didn't belong to him. Someone looking for an easy way out. Someone who used other people to do his work. He used Gretchen, his ex-girlfriend, to write his papers. He used us to do the bulk of the work on his video project. He used someone else to write the show."

The words were putting themselves in order as fast as Stevie was saying them.

"Only one person had any motive to kill Hayes because of the show," Stevie said. "That was Ellie. But Ellie didn't care about the money. She'd been paid—five hundred dollars—

which she used to buy her saxophone. She didn't care what happened to the show because she was busy making her own art."

"Ellie ran," Vi said.

"Because she was scared," Stevie said. "She ran because I had accused her of something. But she knew something else was going on. I don't even know if she understood the extent of it, just that Hayes had gotten into something a little out of his depth. There was always a rumor that there was a codicil in Albert Ellingham's will that left a lot of money to anyone who found Alice. Most people didn't think it was real, but it was a popular theory, a grassy-knoll kind of a thing. But Dr. Fenton believed in it. She was sure it was real. She had interviewed Robert Mackenzie, Albert Ellingham's secretary, before he died. Mackenzie said it was real. And it is real."

She pulled out her phone and read the text of the codicil: "'In addition to all other bequests, the amount of ten million dollars shall be held in trust for my daughter, Alice Madeline Ellingham. Should my daughter no longer be among the living, any person, persons, or organization that locates her earthly remains—provided it is established that they were in no way connected to her disappearance—shall receive this sum. If she is not located by her ninetieth birthday, these funds shall be released to be used for the Ellingham Academy in any way the board sees fit.

"'It is further stipulated that no member of the faculty or administration of Ellingham Academy may claim this sum as their own.'"

Stevie looked at Charles.

"I asked you about it," Stevie said. "If it existed. And you lied to me and said it didn't."

Charles shrugged his cashmere-sweatered shoulders.

"Of course I said it wasn't real," he said. "That's what we tell anyone who asks. We didn't even know about the codicil until a few years ago. You know the clock I have in my office? The green marble one? We were having it cleaned and repaired, and in the process, they discovered a small drawer in the base. It was folded up in there. Clearly someone wanted it hidden away to keep the school from being overrun with treasure hunters. We felt the same way."

"That's true," Dr. Quinn said from the other side of the room. "We'd have some reality television show trying to get in here to make some kind of find-Alice-and-get-a-fortune thing."

"So the school gets the money?" Stevie asked.

"That's why we started work on the art barn," Dr. Quinn said.

"So you think someone was trying to find Alice to get all the money?" Charles said.

"It makes the most sense," Stevie went on. "We're talking about a massive fortune, worth . . . what today?"

"It's currently just under seventy million," Dr. Quinn said. "It will fund us for many years."

"Seventy million dollars is a good reason to commit a murder," Stevie said. "But there are restrictions. No faculty member can have it. Only someone outside, or a student . . .

Someone like Hayes. Or Ellie. Or Dr. Irene Fenton."

Hunter looked up.

"All three of them died in ways that were different but shared a similar aspect—their deaths seemed to be accidents where they were trapped. Hayes was trapped in a room. Ellie in a tunnel. Dr. Fenton in a house on fire. It wasn't personal or passionate. It was clinical. It could all be explained away. Somehow, Hayes, Ellie, and Dr. Fenton were all connected to getting the money. Nothing made sense until I put three things together—Janelle's pass, the message on my wall, and what Dr. Fenton said on the phone. I'll start with that last one. The night she died, Dr. Fenton was being strange when I called her. She said she couldn't talk right then, and then she said, 'The kid is there.' What if she meant Alice? That Alice was here at Ellingham. If that's true, everything starts to make sense. I had to go backward to make it all work out. Your aunt . . ."

She turned to Hunter. "She had a drinking problem," she said.

"Yes."

"She had no sense of smell."

"Yes?" Hunter replied.

"She had vulnerabilities, but how much would you say she cared about the Ellingham case, deep down, really?"

"It was everything to her," Hunter replied. "Everything."

"Everything," Stevie repeated. "On the night of her death, she stood up for the case. She stood up for Alice. And that's why she died. Because she stopped going along with the plan.

She knew that the money was real, and she knew where Alice was. That last bit, she'd just found out . . ."

The scene was incredibly clear in Stevie's head—Fenton at her table, listening, deciding, picking up her cigarettes . . .

"It all started with the art barn construction," Stevie said. "The money was coming in, and the building was being expanded. So they had to excavate the tunnel. The crew found Alice, but they didn't know it. They found a trunk. The person who opened that trunk had a problem. They had opened something that they knew was worth about seventy million dollars. Seventy million, sitting there, free to take. Except he couldn't have it."

She turned and looked at Call Me Charles.

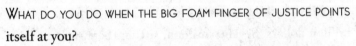

24

WHAT DO YOU DO WHEN THE BIG FOAM FINGER OF JUSTICE POINTS itself at you?

In books, the accused laughs, or mutters angrily, or knocks over their chair and starts running. That's what Ellie had done, even though she was innocent. Charles regarded Stevie with the same expression one might have upon finding a particularly bright and beautiful butterfly sitting on the tip of their nose. He almost looked delighted by this turn of events, which was weird. It made Stevie rock back on her heels anxiously.

"I saw the trunk," Stevie said to him. "You made a point of showing it to me when you took me up to the attic. You had filled it with old newspapers."

"I did show you a trunk of old newspapers," Charles said, smiling and nodding. "Yes."

Stevie walked to the window and looked out at the sunken garden, white with snow. *Don't panic. Keep going.*

"The workers pulled the trunk out of the ground and brought it to you," Stevie said, touching a finger to the frosted glass. "They probably found all kinds of things in there—junk the workmen threw in as they went. You opened it up, expecting nothing, and instead, you found a body. It was old, in bad condition. You knew it could only be one person—Alice Ellingham."

"It was a trunk full of newspapers," Charles said, "but all right."

"Maybe, before, you never thought much about the Ellingham case," she said. "Maybe you were thinking of the school at first. The school was about to get all that money. If the workmen found the body, they'd get it, and the school couldn't expand. So maybe at first you just wanted to tuck the body somewhere, bury it, let the matter go away. You take the body out of the trunk and you fill the trunk with some old newspapers. From there, you had to put the body aside until you could work out what to do next. But . . ."

Stevie began to move around the room, carefully avoiding stepping on the heads of the trophy rugs.

" . . . it's *so* much money. I mean, what would anyone do if they were handed a chance to get seventy million dollars? The codicil was clear—you couldn't collect. But what if you had a partner, someone who could locate the body and technically get the money? You could arrange to split it. You needed someone who could plausibly find something buried on the grounds, someone you could manipulate. And you found her. Dr. Irene Fenton, someone obsessed with the Ellingham case. Someone with a drinking problem. You'd arrange it so that she would find the body. She'd collect the money and you'd divide it up. Hunter, you said your aunt was talking to someone up at Ellingham, but you didn't know who."

"She was," Hunter said. "She wouldn't talk about it."

"We'll get into Fenton later. First, there's Hayes."

Stevie stopped by the mantel and looked into the face of the clock.

"Hayes was mad," Stevie said. "He was complaining all the time about not being able to go to California, about how you wouldn't let him come and go and get credit for it. All of a sudden, Hayes was all smiles. You said that Hayes could have a flexible schedule and go to California if he completed a project about the Ellingham kidnapping. What made you change your mind?"

"The fact that he was driving me nuts," Charles said. "He kept coming to my office to complain."

Stevie turned around to face him.

"Which means he must have seen or heard something he shouldn't have. Whatever happened, you worked out a deal with him—he could do a project and then he could go to Hollywood. But that wasn't enough. Did he threaten you? Did he look into things more? Something happened, because you decided that Hayes had to die. So you gave him access to the tunnel."

"Something I'll never forgive myself for."

"So here's how it worked," Stevie said. "The day before Hayes's death, you took the first necessary step. You knew Janelle's pass opened the maintenance building. When we were in yoga, you came into the art barn and slipped it out of her bag. No one would pay any attention to you walking around the art barn. No one was going to think you were going to take a pass. You made sure that at some point that day, Hayes touched the pass. Maybe called him to your office, handed him something, whatever. You had to make sure his fingerprints were on it. That night, you used the pass to access the dry ice and you put it in the room at the end of the tunnel and shut the door. The dry ice sublimated that night, filling the room with enough carbon dioxide to cause anyone to drop within a minute. The trap was set and locked. You just needed the bait."

Again, Stevie's mind traveled to the moment that night, when everyone making the video was walking to dinner, and Hayes turned back toward the sunken garden alone.

"After we had completed filming up in the garden that day," Stevie said, "Hayes said he had to do something. He wouldn't say what. What he had to do was meet with you. He went into the tunnel and he didn't come out. You made it look like Hayes died as a result of his own stupidity. Everyone assumed it was an accident, except me. But you had thought about that too."

"Thank you for thinking I did all of this well. If you're going to be in a murder mystery, you don't want to be a dud."

For the first time, his smile had a brittle, forced quality.

"You—correctly—assumed I would take an interest. I mean, it only makes sense. I was the *detective*. I'm interested in crime. So you made your first big mistake. The night before all of this happened, you snuck outside my window and projected an image on my wall, a version of the Truly Devious letter. When the police came, if I started rambling about messages on my wall, I'd seem like someone who was making things up for attention, like I was a little crazy. The Hayes matter was settled, and you could move on and take care of finding the body. But then, there was another problem, on the night of the Silent Party, the night I confronted Ellie about *The End of It All*. That night we all came here to this room. Ellie sat right there . . ."

She pointed at the low leather chair that Hunter was currently occupying.

"Did you have any idea that Hayes hadn't written the show by himself?" she asked Charles. "Were you shocked when Ellie starting crying and saying things like . . ."

She couldn't remember the exact words for a second.

"*Why did I pay attention to him?*" David chimed in. "That's what she said. *Hayes and his stupid ideas. That's what got him killed.*"

"It must have freaked you out," Stevie said, "to find out that Hayes didn't work alone, that he may have told Ellie something about what he'd seen or heard, and now Ellie was on the verge of talking. You had to think fast. So you brought the whole thing to a halt and said you had to call the school's lawyer. This seemed like the nice, responsible thing to do. When we were all leaving the room, did you whisper to her? Tell her there was a way out in the wall? Maybe you said that she should run, and wait in a place in the basement, and you would help her. She was terrified, and she bolted. She went down to the basement, down into the passageway. All you had to do was push something over the opening. Again. Impersonal. Clean. Just another accident. Ellie wouldn't even know what happened."

"Stevie," he said, "your murder mysteries are showing."

Charles's smile had slipped out of position. He tried to keep it up, but it was as if it was suspended by two nails at the corners and one of them had come loose.

"So now two students are dead," Stevie said, "and bonus! I'm gone. My parents yanked me out of school. But no matter how clean and clinical you want things to be, life happens. People walk in when they aren't supposed to. Things get left behind. Every contact leaves a trace. In this case, Edward King stepped in. He was upset because David was being an asshole and he wanted me to calm him the hell down. Edward King doesn't care that you're in charge of the school. He's an even bigger asshole."

"Fact," David said.

"He comes in with his cheap security system and flies me back on his plane and drops me right in your lap. So now you have to deal with me again. Fine. You continue with the plan of having Dr. Fenton as my adviser. When I was working with her, she had really specific things she wanted me to look into—she wanted me to find a tunnel under Minerva. I did. That's where I found Ellie. That had to be part of the plan. . . ."

This, Stevie was arranging in her head as she spoke. She gestured, assembling the picture in the air with her hand.

"I think," she said, "you realized it would be better if Ellie's body was found. The school needed to seem unsafe. It was easier if the school shut. You wouldn't have students around getting in the way anymore. You could hide the body more easily, and no one would stumble on to it accidentally. But the school rallied. Nothing was going right for you, especially since I found something that got Dr. Fenton's interest. I showed her this."

Stevie put her backpack down on a chair and removed the tin.

"You found tea?" Charles asked.

"This shows who composed the Truly Devious letter . . ."

"Stevie, how many stories—"

"It's all one story," Stevie said, and the confidence in her voice surprised her. "It was about money then, and it's about money now. They took Alice in 1936 and used her to try to get money. You had Alice now and were trying to get the fortune her father left behind. And you were almost there. You told Dr. Fenton about Alice, and she couldn't contain herself anymore. She wasn't playing along. Again, in your normal way, you set it up so that things would just happen. You turned the knob on the gas and left. Eventually there would be enough gas in that room that when she lit up, everything would go up in flames. It's smart. It's impersonal. It's not even your fault, is it? It's not a crime to bump into the knob on a stove. Anyone who messed up your plan was simply moved out of the way. Did each one get easier when you saw that you didn't get caught? You were in so deep now, you had to finish it. And thanks to Germaine, the last move was obvious."

"Thanks to me?" Germaine said, looking up from her notes.

"When Hunter got the invitation to come live here, Germaine asked why someone who wasn't a student was getting to live here, and I said because the school felt bad. She was right. Schools don't feel bad. You still needed a person unconnected with the school to collect the money for you. This time, you wanted to make sure the school was shut down. All you needed was for one more thing to happen. Again, you used something of Janelle's. You changed the pressure setting on her tank to make it shoot away from the machine. I don't think you cared who got hurt as long as something happened. A nice big accident. You like accidents. Plus, there was the storm. Clear out the school. But Hunter could stay."

"I didn't . . . " Hunter began.

"No," Stevie said. "He had to wait until the place was empty. He would make his move on you like he had your aunt. He'd play on your interests, probably say something about how you could use the money to help the environment—"

"Stevie," Dr. Quinn cut in. "This is quite a story, but it's not based on anything. Are there facts?"

"Here's one fact," Stevie said. "We sent you that email about the codicil."

"The one from Edward King's office?" she asked.

"The one from Jim Malloy," Stevie said. "The one you replied to. Then Jim wrote back, a bit more firmly, and Charles sent the codicil. But here's the thing . . ."

She turned back to Charles.

"You called the King offices. You found out there was no one there named Jim Malloy. But you answered the email anyway—*after* you made that call. David, check your phone. What time did your dad write to you?"

David pulled his phone from his pocket and the room was silent as he scanned through his texts.

"Two twenty-four."

"So by two twenty-four it was clear that Jim Malloy wasn't real. And the codicil was sent at . . ."

David did some more checking.

"Three forty-seven," he said, looking confused.

"You had taken a good guess who Jim Malloy was," Stevie said. "You wanted me to see that there was a provision in the will that said teachers and staff could not benefit."

"I think that's a pretty broad reading of the situation," Charles said. "I replied to an email from someone who may have been on Edward King's staff. Now, if you're finished, Stevie, I think we should—"

"Where did you put Alice?" she said.

"Stevie . . ." Call Me Charles half smiled. Half. The other bit was something very unpleasant. "I genuinely admire what you've done here. I think this is a real triumph of imagination. I also think the cabin fever has gotten to you a little, but no harm done. . . ."

"Like I said," Stevie went on, fighting back a tremble, "where did you put Alice?"

On that, the study doors opened and a cold snuck into the room.

"I think I have the answer to that," Larry said. "You were right, Stevie. This thing works like a charm."

He held up the wall scanner.

25

"OH MY GOD," STEVIE SAID, LETTING OUT A LONG BREATH. "WAS that enough time? Because I was running out of stuff to say."

"More than enough," Larry replied.

"That was exhausting," she said, leaning against the mantel. "Seriously. They make it seem so easy in novels, but you have to keep talking and talking..."

"Can I ask what you're doing here?" Charles said as a greeting to the former head of security. "You're no longer employed by this school."

"I'm well aware," Larry replied. "However, I've rejoined the local police department on a temporary basis. I'm up here officially, doing a welfare check on everyone. I started making plans to get here as soon as I heard the school was closing and a few idiots decided to stick around and wait out the blizzard. I definitely knew who one of those idiots would be. So I hitched a ride on an emergency vehicle with a plow, then hiked up from the road. Took me almost two days. Then that idiot emailed me to say what she was going to do, and that she'd left me a wall scanner and some very interesting instructions. It's a good thing I trust you."

Stevie looked down to keep herself from smiling.

"I've done most of the second-floor offices," Larry said. "Dr. Scott's office is the last room left to do."

"I object to an illegal police search of Ellingham property—" Charles said.

"Larry," Dr. Quinn cut in, "I authorize anything you're doing."

Charles spun around and faced Jenny Quinn, who seemed to rise out of the floor a bit.

"Jenny," he said, "this goes against—"

"My authority is equal to yours," she said simply. "And I am telling Larry he should do as he feels best."

Her words were a wall that could not be scaled.

"Fine," he said. "Go and look in my office if you want. But I would like to be there."

"We'll all go!" David said chirpily. Larry opened his mouth to object, but David was already out the door. Once David had gone, it seemed inevitable that the entire company would be coming along. Larry was not in a position to stop anyone.

The group made their way up the wide, sweeping stairs. Stevie paused a moment on the landing to acknowledge the Ellinghams. They made their way along the balcony, and through the door with the posters that had asked, so clearly, for someone to come in and issue a challenge.

Larry had emptied the bookcases and pulled them away from the walls. All of Dr. Scott's books and pictures were piled in the center of the room.

"You're going to put my office back together," Charles said to Larry.

"I'll get right on it," Larry said. "Everyone sit down and make space. Any place you want me to start in particular?" Larry asked Stevie.

Stevie shook her head. She was running on instinct at this point. If Charles had opened the trunk that day and seen Alice inside, he would have had to figure out what to do with her fairly quickly. It was most likely that he would have had to hide her in the building. He would have had months to relocate her, and Ellingham was full of places where she could be hidden, but if you had a body that was worth seventy million dollars, you'd probably want to make sure no one else found it by accident. That meant keeping it close, in a place you controlled.

Larry began on the window wall, moving section by section. From there, he did the other wall that faced the outside. Then the third wall. The atmosphere in the room thickened, and Stevie tried not to notice anyone giving her concerned side eye. Larry moved to the last wall, working around the mantel. It seemed like he was about to finish when he stopped down by the floor, in the corner.

"Something over here," he said. "It's small, maybe a foot and a half square." He stood and examined the wall up close. "There are some cuts in the wallpaper here," he said. He knocked on the wall. There was a hollow noise. He knocked around the space, making an outline that was about four feet by four feet, about three feet off the floor.

"That could be where the jewelry safe was," Stevie said. "This was Iris Ellingham's dressing room. After the Ellinghams died, the safe was taken out and it was donated to the Smithsonian with all the contents. I've seen the pictures. It's about that big."

Larry pulled a Swiss Army knife from his pocket and used it to gently work along the edges of the space. "We're going to have to take a look behind this wall," he said. "We'll need some tools. We'll have to wait . . ."

"You're not putting a hole in my wall. You have no . . ."

Without a word, Janelle stepped forward, tapped the wall, then, with one seamless movement, drew her arm back like a bow and struck the wall once with the heel of her hand. It cracked loudly. She wiggled her fingers and returned to the loveseat, where Vi put a proud arm over her shoulders.

"Holy shit," David said quietly.

"Force equals mass times acceleration," Janelle said, checking her nail polish. "Or, more importantly, force times time equals mass times the difference in velocity over that time. Basic board-breaking physics. Takes about eleven hundred newtons. It's more intention than strength."

Charles openly gaped at this. He may have anticipated many things, but Janelle Franklin bashing in his office walls with her bare hands was probably not one of them.

"I love you," Vi said.

Janelle grinned in a way that suggested this was not the first time she had heard those words.

"I gotta learn physics," Stevie mumbled to herself.

"All right," Larry said, pushing past this romantic interlude. He pulled his flashlight from a clip on his belt and stuck it into the hole. The sound of the clock drowned out everything else in the room. Stevie heard the hollow, heavy sound of her heart, thudding away in her chest. She couldn't bear watching Larry staring into the void, so she looked at the clock instead, the one that had held the codicil, the one that had survived revolutions and beheadings.

What if she was wrong?

The idea was funny. She almost laughed. She was dizzy. The room seemed to go gray and white and spin a bit. Charles had the calm expression of someone watching something happening in the far distance—a storm, maybe an accident. Something that could not be helped. Germaine, she noted, was trying to video the whole scene without being noticed.

"I need gloves," Larry said.

Stevie bolted upright like someone had yanked on her spine from above.

"Gloves," she said, pulling a handful of nitrile gloves from the front of her backpack.

"Why do you have nitrile gloves?" Janelle asked.

"Same reason you know how to break a wall," Stevie replied.

Janelle smiled with pride.

Larry put on the gloves and resumed work with the knife, picking at the cracked bit of wall until he had a large enough space to get his hand through. He reached in farther to get hold of a bit of the wall and pulled back hard, making a larger flap. He shone in his light once again, then shut it off and stepped in front of the opening.

"I need this room cleared," he said.

"I'm not going to be tossed out of my own office," Charles said. His face had lost some of its color.

"This is not your office," Larry said simply. "This is a potential crime scene. You will go next door and wait in the Peacock Room, and Mark and Dr. Pixwell will wait with you. Dr. Quinn, if you wouldn't mind taking the students downstairs?"

"I would not mind," she said.

"I don't know what's going on here," Charles said, but some of the conviction was draining from his voice. The Funko Pop! figurines on the windowsill seemed to make a mockery of him. When Pix and Mark stood up to him, he followed them without another word.

Stevie got up in a haze to follow everyone else out.

"Where are you going?" Larry asked.

"You said everyone go downstairs."

"I didn't mean you," Larry said. "Shut the door."

Stevie shut the door with a trembling hand.

"Do you want to see?" Larry said soberly.

"What . . . what's in there?"

The words came out dry. After all of that—all she had done—she was out of wind. Out of air. She knew what was in there—who—but the words were too much to say. The concept was too large.

"It's not easy to look at, but you have seen a lot."

She had no choice.

The space between Stevie and the wall was only a few feet, but it seemed to expand to the size of a grand, mad ballroom. She stepped up to the dark opening and accepted the flashlight from Larry, as well as the hand on her shoulder.

At first, Stevie thought she was looking at a large gray bag, rough, frayed with age and exposure. But as the light worked the edges and her mind and eyes adjusted, she could see the shape of a hand. A head. There was a shoe.

It was too small a space, Stevie thought.

"We need to get her out," she said.

"We will. We need to wait for the crime scene unit. We can't go in without them."

Stevie nodded numbly and turned back to the figure in the wall.

"Hello, Alice," Stevie said. "It's okay. It's over."

26

THE ELLINGHAM BALLROOM HAD BEEN BUILT TO HOLD A HUNDRED AND one dancing couples. That was Iris Ellingham's design. A hundred couples was an elegantly large number while maintaining the intimacy a ballroom should encourage. The one extra couple, she had said, was the one that counted; that couple was always the one you were in.

Iris Ellingham had been a special, creative woman. That was why she had been friends with so many artists. That was why she had such loyal friends. That was why Albert Ellingham wanted to marry her and not any other woman in the world. Stevie wanted to believe Iris would have approved of the one couple in her ballroom now, the one resting side by side in the center of the floor. Iris would have smiled at the girl who found her Alice.

After the discovery, Charles's office had been sealed. Charles himself was upstairs with Larry and the other faculty members. The seven students were downstairs and left to their own devices, as they were no longer the ones who needed to be watched for mischief. Vi and Janelle had vanished to some corner. Stevie and David had taken the ballroom, because, why not take the ballroom if the ballroom is there?

David gathered up their blankets—between them, they had four—and made a nest for the two of them in the ballroom. There they lay, in this marvelous, repeating room of mirrors and masks, looking up at the molded ceiling with its chandelier. David was brushing back her hair softly. Stevie found that she was exhausted, maybe more so than she had ever been in her life. She was between states, between worlds. The chandeliers magnified the scant bit of light in the room and dripped it across the ceiling like a smattering of stars.

"I did it," she said.

"Yup."

"You made fun of me when I first got here," she said. "But I did it."

"I was being friendly."

"You were being a dick," she said.

"Like I said, I was being friendly."

"Why do you think we like each other?" Stevie asked.

"Does it matter?"

"I don't know," she said. "I don't know how these things work."

"Neither do I. Neither does anybody."

"Some people seem to. I think Janelle does."

"Janelle," he said, "may know everything, but she doesn't know that. And I like you because . . ."

He rolled up to his side and onto one elbow, gazing

down into her face. He traced her jawline with one finger, sending such shivers down her body that she struggled not to squirm.

" . . . because you came to do something impossible and you did it. And you're smart. And you're really, really attractive."

There, on the floor that had been scuffed by a thousand dance shoes, under the eyes of the masks on the wall that had seen decades go by, they kissed, over and over, each one renewing the last.

Outside, the snow retreated slowly as if it was apologizing for the intrusion and taking silent steps back the way it had come.

Alice . . .

Stevie could hear her playing. She was running through the ballroom, her tiny patent leather shoes sliding on the floor, a ball bouncing ahead of her.

"Should we let her have the ball in here?" Iris said. "With the mirrors?"

"Of course!" said Albert. "It will be all right. Come on now, Alice! Give it a bounce! When you bounce your ball in here, you'll see a hundred bouncing balls!"

Alice put her chubby arms overhead, balancing the ball, and then she tossed it with all her might—which was not that far, but it was far enough to please her. She laughed, her voice ringing out and bouncing merrily around the room.

"It's good to be home," Iris said, putting her head on

Albert's shoulder. "We've been gone so long."

"We are all home," Albert said. "And here we will stay."

At daybreak a gentle light came through the French doors, spreading long rectangles over the dance floor. The light just reached Stevie's eyes, unsealing them. She looked around for a moment, checking to make sure the reality she remembered from the night before corresponded with the one she was in now. Yes, she'd slept in a ballroom. Yes, David was at her side, his arms over her. They were pressed together under a pile of blankets. Stevie scanned the floor for a moment, seeing the marks and joins in the wood up close. The air in the room was cold. Under the blanket, all was warm and perfect. This was where she wanted to remain, forever if possible.

But there was a murderer to deal with.

Stevie inched her way out from under David's arm, which had her wrapped in a soft, protective embrace. She set it back in the same position, then crawled away a few paces, scooping her clothes from the floor. She dressed quickly, catching her reflection as it echoed around the room. She didn't mind the girl she saw. She was the girl with the choppy blond hair, tugging on her faded black clothes. She was exactly who she wanted to be.

She opened the ballroom door gently and crept out into the hall. The Great House was still and quiet. The fire in the murderer's fireplace burned low. Larry sat by it, arms folded, nursing a tin mug of coffee. Stevie closed the door and crossed the hall to join him.

"Hey," Stevie said, gesturing above. "What's happening?"

"Mark, Dr. Pixwell, and Dr. Quinn are all up there with him in the Peacock Room. I don't think he'll try anything, but if he does, the three of them can handle it easily. I've been watching down here."

"Has he said anything?" Stevie said, sitting down in the chair opposite and holding her hands out to the fire.

"No. He's been very quiet. The police will be here soon. I told them first light was fine, that I would handle it. They're going to send someone by helicopter, and there will be some backup with a snowplow down by the main road to help get everyone out. We'll use the snowcat and then figure out how to move you all down the hill. Personally, I'd suggest sledding. That's the best sledding hill in the state, provided you don't steer into the river or a tree."

"But him," she said. "What will happen to him? Did I do it? Was it enough to put him in jail?"

"That's not for us to worry about," Larry said. "There will be an investigation. The district attorney will be involved. It's your job to present the case, remember. The DA takes it from there."

Larry was addressing Stevie like she was an actual detective, someone who could go to the DA. Stevie hid her smile by turning toward the door to the morning room. It was partway open. She could see Germaine hunched over her computer, typing feverishly. Hunter was asleep on the sofa. Nate was draped over the nearby chairs. They had all made it through the storm together.

"What's your guess, though?" Stevie asked.

"I think you've made a compelling case," Larry said. "You located a body. And I'm going to help make sure every single thing you said is fully explored. I'm coming out of retirement for this."

"You are?"

"It's not every day that you get handed a solve on a triple murder and find a body that's been missing in the case of the century," he said. "Now that Alice is known to be deceased, her case has to be looked into. No statute on murder."

"I have some thoughts on that too," she said. "But—"

They both heard it at once. The approaching helicopter.

"Come on," he said. "Let's go and bring them in."

The winter sun felt good on Stevie's face as she stood under the portico. She had to hold up her hand to shield her eyes from the glare as it bounced off the snow. It was too difficult for the helicopter to land. It hovered above the lawn and got quite low; four people in uniform jumped out into the snow. Two looked to be police, and the others were EMTs with large red medical bags. The sound roused the others. Vi and Janelle reappeared, hand in hand. Nate, Hunter, and Germaine came out of the morning room. David emerged last, pushing open the door of the ballroom and pulling a sweater over his head. The group clustered by the door as the EMTs and police conferred with Larry on the drive.

The large door was left open as the visitors brought their things inside, sending a brisk arctic breeze into the hall. They were back in the world now. Things were moving. David came and stood alongside Stevie. He dropped a casual arm over her shoulders, and she leaned in against him and tucked her head into the crook of his arm.

"Guess we're going home," Nate said.

"We'll always have this weekend," David replied, stretching out his free arm to pull Nate into the embrace. Nate sidestepped quickly.

Stevie's attention was drawn to the balcony above, where something appeared to be going on. Mark came out of the Peacock Room and hustled down the hall. Someone was pounding on a door, demanding to be let in.

"Charles!" Dr. Quinn yelled. "Charles, open this door."

"What's happening?" Janelle asked, coming over.

Larry and the police began hurrying up the grand stairs, taking them two at a time. There was a cracking noise, followed by something that sounded like a heavy sack being dropped down a chute. Whatever it was, it went past the back of the murderer's fireplace. Larry ran into the Peacock Room, then ran out to the balcony to shout to the EMTs, who were still downstairs.

"Basement!" he yelled, rushing to the stairs again. "Basement, follow me, now! Now!"

The group of students watched this mutely.

"I don't think Charles is going to jail," Stevie said quietly.

27

"WHAT A STUPID THING TO DO," DR. QUINN SAID. "WHAT A STUPID thing." For the first time, Dr. Quinn looked rattled.

The EMTs had gone down into the basement, because that was where Charles was, behind a wall. Pix had gone to help them because she was the closest thing to a medical professional from the remaining faculty, and because she had experience getting things out from difficult places. Everyone else from Ellingham was gathered in the morning room, because it was still the warmest room in the building.

"That passage was sealed," she said.

"He was going in and out of the bathroom all night," Mark said. "I assumed he was nervous. He must have been loosening the nails with a penknife or something."

"But we all know about that passage and why it's nailed shut. The stairs it connects to have been unstable for years. The ones below them are gone completely. What did he even think he was doing? That if he made it down the first flight he could jump to the basement? A whole floor? Get out that way?"

"He decided to take a chance," Stevie said.

Larry, who was leaning against the wall, nodded at Stevie. It was Larry, after all, who had said from the very beginning that people had accidents when they went into the passages.

Pix came back up from the basement and stood in the doorway. Before, there would have been a conference away from the students. They were well beyond that now.

"How is he?" Dr. Quinn asked.

Pix shook her head.

"It was a very bad fall," she said simply.

Stevie couldn't help but hear the echo of Truly Devious: *A broken head, a nasty fall . . .*

Over the next few hours, more people turned up as more vehicles were able to access the school. There was a steady flow of uniforms. Things were photographed and recorded and bagged and sealed. Everyone in the group was interviewed, but not for long. Then two individuals in dark suits with large winter coats over them appeared. They did not fit in with the other officials.

"Oh good," Nate said, looking out the window. "The Men in Black are here. Time for the brain wipe."

David looked out as well.

"I think that's my ride," he said.

Sure enough, the two suited persons were at the door of the morning room within the minute.

"We're from Senator King's office," one of the men said. "We're here to take you home, David."

"So soon?" David replied. "Gosh, I guess he really *does* love me."

The quip felt forced. Stevie found herself reaching up and grabbing David's hand, squeezing it hard.

"Are you with law enforcement?" Vi asked.

"We work for the senator," one of the men replied.

"So, that's a no," Vi said. "Which means you have no legal right to remove him."

"Vi is right," Janelle chimed in. "You have rights. You don't have to go with these two if you don't want to."

David turned in surprise. He had not expected Janelle to have his back.

"It's okay," he said. "But thanks. These nice people will give me a minute to speak to my girlfriend, won't they?"

The two men backed away from the door, and David ushered Stevie out into the hall, Stevie felt an urgency akin to panic. Her hold on his arm intensified.

"What do we do now?" she asked quietly.

"Well, my dad can't actually chain me up in the basement. Probably. I mean, he is a senator, so he might get access to some kind of chamber inside the Washington Monument . . ."

"Seriously," she said, fighting back tears.

"I don't know. We both go home. And we figure it out."

"Can your dad press charges?"

"I don't know if stealing blackmail materials from what's technically my own house is a crime, or at least one he would want to report. He's going to make my life unpleasant, and he's going to cut off my money, but that's okay. I can get a job.

It's better not taking anything from him."

He leaned down to kiss her, his lips warm against hers, his hand rubbing the nape of her neck. It was such an intimate moment, witnessed only by a dozen or so strangers, Larry, Dr. Quinn, Pix, and all her friends. As they broke their embrace, David said good-byes to the group.

Hugs were exchanged all around, except for Nate, who extended his hand for a handshake before saying, "Just . . . don't . . . do anything. Ever."

"Got it," David said, saluting. "Let me get my coat and bag."

When he had the coat and the scruffy backpack, Stevie walked with him out to where the snowmobiles were waiting. Stevie realized that she had started crying. She rubbed under her eyes roughly with the back of her hand.

"I have to go," he said, wiping her face. "Don't worry. I'll be in touch, Nancy Drew. I'm hard to get rid of."

She reluctantly relaxed her grip on his hand.

As he walked off, he turned to her one last time and smiled, his looping, half-cocked smile. Then he opened his two-thousand-dollar coat. At first, she wasn't sure why he was showing off the rich red lining. She had seen it—it was nice lining if you cared about lining.

But it wasn't the lining he was trying to show her. It was the inside pocket, or, more specifically, something peeking out of the inside pocket.

It was a stick of dynamite.

TRAGEDY STRIKES AGAIN AT ELLINGHAM

Burlington Herald

November 11

In another in a series of tragic events, Dr. Charles Scott, the head of Ellingham Academy, fell to his death yesterday morning after gaining entrance to a sealed passage in one of the school's buildings. The staircase was a remnant of a series of passages built by the school's founder, Albert Ellingham, in the early 1930s. Dr. Scott accessed the passage after being confronted about his possible involvement with the accidents at the school that resulted in two deaths, and the house fire that claimed the life of Dr. Irene Fenton.

"Dr. Scott was a person of interest in a number of recent deaths both at the school and in the Burlington area," said Detective Fatima Agiter of the Vermont State Police. "We believe the deaths of students Hayes Major and Element Walker, and the death of Dr. Irene Fenton of the University of Vermont, may all be connected. Investigations are ongoing."

KING FACES DONOR BACKLASH

PoliticsNow.com

November 27

S enator Edward King has a money problem. Over the last week, he has suffered the sudden and inexplicable loss of many of his major donors. The senator, who announced his presidential run last month, has lost the support of many of the backers who have made his candidacy possible. Recent reports have surfaced that the senator may have been keeping blackmail materials on his own donors in order to ensure their continued support.

"Complete nonsense," said spokesperson Malinda McGuire, when asked for a comment. "The media bias against the senator is astonishing. Senator King will continue to fight for what he believes in: traditional American values, personal freedoms, and a return to responsibility. We look forward to talking about all these things on the campaign trail in the following months."

IS THE TRULY DEVIOUS CASE SOLVED?

True Crime Digest

December 3

It's been called the greatest mystery of the twentieth century. In 1936, Albert Ellingham was one of the most powerful men in America, his wealth and reach similar to that of Henry Ford or William Randolph Hearst. Ellingham owned newspapers, a movie studio, and dozens of other interests. But his personal passion was for education. To this end, he built a school in the mountains of Vermont and moved there with his family. On April 13 of that year, while out on a pleasure drive, his wife, Iris, and daughter, Alice, were abducted from a country road outside of the estate. On the same day, a student from the academy, Dolores Epstein, also vanished. In the following months, both Dolores and Iris were found dead—Dolores half-buried in a field, and Iris in Lake Champlain. Alice was never recovered. She was only three years old at the time of her disappearance.

Her father dedicated himself entirely to finding his daughter, using his considerable resources on the effort. Dozens of private detectives were sent around the country and the world. A team of 150 secretaries went through the letters and tips that came in on a daily basis. The head of the FBI,

J. Edgar Hoover, took a personal interest in the case. All of this was to no avail. Albert Ellingham died on October 30, 1938, when his sailboat exploded on Lake Champlain, most likely a victim of anarchists. He had been targeted before and escaped. This time, he was not so lucky.

With the death of Albert Ellingham, some of the pressure to find Alice abated, but there have always been people looking for her. Several others came forward claiming to be Alice—all of these were found to be imposters. Alice Ellingham remained one of history's famous missing persons, like Amelia Earhart or Jimmy Hoffa, presumed dead, but with a question mark. All that was ever accepted about the culprit was that they sent a note to Albert Ellingham in the weeks before the kidnapping, a teasing riddle that warned of the danger to come. The letter, which was made of cutout letters from newspapers and magazines, was signed Truly, Devious.

Decades passed without any furtherance of the case, and then, starting last September, events began to move very quickly. Ellingham once again became the scene of tragedy, when two students— Hayes Major and Element Walker—died in accidents on the school grounds. Soon after, an adjunct faculty member of the University of Vermont, Dr. Irene Fenton, died in a house fire in Burlington.

But one student did not believe these things were accidents. She believed they were related to the disappearance of Alice—or rather, to a rumored fortune that would go to anyone who found the missing girl, dead or alive. Ellingham student Stephanie Bell, working with the school's former head of security, uncovered the body of a child in one of the walls. The child's remains are currently undergoing testing.

Bell made other significant discoveries, including physical evidence that suggests that the Truly Devious letter, long assumed to have been the work of the Ellingham kidnappers, had nothing to do with the kidnapping at all and was, in fact, a poorly timed student prank. This breaks apart decades of assumptions about the crime.

While the results of the tests and investigations are still pending, and while Ellingham Academy remains closed while the property is secured, it seems that this case may not be so cold after all. And with this most recent discovery, maybe now the spirits are at rest up on Mount Morgan.

AUDIO REVEALS EDWARD KING KNEW OF BLACKMAIL PLANS
A BATT REPORT EXCLUSIVE
DECEMBER 5th

The Batt Report has obtained exclusive audio of Senator Edward King railing against an unknown person who destroyed materials the campaign appears to have been using to blackmail donors. The audio, embedded below, contains graphic language.

"He took the [expletive] flash drives," the senator can be heard saying. "I had everything on those. We had all those [expletive] just where we needed them. That was everything we had to keep them in line. Now we have nothing. Nothing. They're all going to back out. We're [expletive]."

Stay with The Batt Report for updates on this story.

KING WITHDRAWS PRESIDENTAL BID
CNN
January 2

Following two weeks of intense speculation, Senator Edward King withdrew his candidacy in next year's presidential race.

"While it is, of course, a disappointment to withdraw," he said in a prepared statement, "I realized the toll the campaign might take on my relationship with my family."

Though the senator cites personal reasons for the withdrawal, Washington insiders have been whispering for weeks about dirty dealings in the King camp, including accusations that the senator may have been blackmailing several individuals in exchange for their financial and political support. Several weeks ago, a recording surfaced in which the senator can be heard yelling about the loss of "everything we had to keep them in line." In the recording, he laid blame for the loss of this information on his son.

It was revealed that the senator had a son from a previous marriage. In a strange twist, that son attended Ellingham Academy in Vermont, which has been in the news recently as the scene of several tragic events, including the death of

YouTube star Hayes Major. The senator's son was also the subject of a viral video in which he was beaten on a Burlington, Vermont, street . . .

ELLINGHAM ACADEMY REOPENS
THE BATT REPORT
JANUARY 11th

After a series of tragic events, Ellingham Academy, one of the country's most unusual and prestigious high schools, has opened again for classes. Once famous for the 1936 Truly Devious kidnappings and murders, the academy was again in the headlines for similar reasons this past fall.

"It's been an extraordinarily tough year," said new head of school, Dr. Jennifer Quinn. "But our students have come together. They have supported each other. I couldn't be prouder of them. They represent the true Ellingham spirit of community. We are thrilled to have the doors open again."

Police have completed their investigation into the former head of school, Dr. Charles Scott, who was accused of causing the deaths of Hayes Major, Element Walker, and Dr. Irene Fenton. Police now have substantial evidence linking Dr. Scott to the crimes, including records of phone calls between Dr. Fenton and Dr. Scott, security footage from traffic and local cameras in Burlington on the night of Dr. Fenton's house fire, and communications with banks in Switzerland and the Cayman Islands, inquiring how to open private and offshore accounts.

"We feel confident that we have identified the culprit in this case, and that this person is deceased," said Detective Fatima Agiter of the Vermont State Police. "The matter is considered closed."

For her help in the matter, Stephanie Bell was recognized in the Vermont State Assembly and was invited to visit with the governor. The Batt Report will have interviews with Stephanie Bell about her investigations, and exclusive coverage of her findings in the Ellingham kidnapping and murder case of 1936. Stay tuned.

BILLBOARD EXPLODES
Pittsburgh Press Online
February 16

An anti-immigration billboard outside of Monroeville, Pennsylvania, exploded last night in what police are calling an act of vandalism. While the billboard was completely destroyed, there were no injuries and no damage to any other property. No cars were in the area when the explosion occurred around 4 a.m.

The billboard, which was sponsored by a group associated with the now-defunct campaign of Senator Edward King, had been unpopular with many members of the community. Its unusual destruction brought about a cheer in many areas of town.

"I have no idea who did it," said local resident Sean Gibson. "But I'd like to buy them a milk shake."

DNA TEST ON REMAINS NOT A MATCH FOR ALICE ELLINGHAM

True Crime Digest
April 7

DNA testing done on the remains of a child found at the Ellingham Academy outside of Burlington, Vermont, revealed that the child was not related to either Albert Ellingham or his wife Iris, eliminating her from consideration as the long-missing Alice Ellingham. Alice disappeared in 1936, aged three, when she and her mother were kidnapped in a roadside attack. While Iris's body turned up in Lake Champlain some weeks later, Alice was never found. Her whereabouts have been the subject of intense interest since that time, many dubbing her disappearance "the case of the century."

According to forensic experts, the body found meets the description of Alice Ellingham in all other ways. "In many ways, this body comports with Alice Ellingham," said Dr. Felicia Murry of the Smithsonian National Museum of Natural History, where the body was sent to be examined alongside forensic experts from the FBI and a team from the Vermont Forensic Laboratory. "This is a child approximately three years of age, who was born and died in the period between 1928 and

1940. The clothing on the body had no labels or markings that could establish an identity or be traced, but we could date the manufacture from the materials used to between 1930 and 1940. We could not establish cause of death. We were able to collect usable DNA samples from Albert and Iris Ellinghams' personal possessions. The DNA tests performed on the remains did not prove to be a match for either parent."

If the girl in the wall is not Alice, then who is she?

28

W<small>HEN SPRING CAME TO THE</small> E<small>LLINGHAM MOUNTAIN, SHE CAME IN</small> glory, whipping her robes of fresh air and spreading fecund greenery over the mountain like a goddess on a fecund greenery-spreading binge. Life reappeared in the form of birds and buds. The cold was not fully banished, but it had a softer edge. Stevie sat in the cupola wearing her red vinyl coat. She shivered a bit underneath, but the air felt good. It kept her bright and alert—that, and the mug of coffee she had slipped out of the dining hall a few minutes before. On her lap was her new tablet, open to the article on the results of the DNA testing of the body in the wall. This, Stevie was resolutely ignoring in favor of the view.

So much had happened in the last five months. In the beginning there had been a flurry of news, stories about the case and sometimes her. She became the teen detective, the Ellingham Sherlock. There were interviews, articles—Netflix even showed interest in making a movie. It took several weeks for Ellingham to open their doors again, and when it did, not everyone came back. Before, Stevie would never have been able to return. But things were different now between her and her parents. There were no more jokes or dismissive remarks about her interest in crime. She had solved the case, and she had even made enough money from the publicity to pay for her first year of college. And now that the culprit was gone, there was the feeling—the hope—that nothing more was going to happen at Ellingham Academy for a very long time.

It had all worked out, and now Stevie was left with the beautiful view.

"What are you doing?" said a voice.

Nate, of course. He approached cautiously, his hands sunk deep into the pockets of his beaten khakis. She had been waiting for him. She knew he would come and find her in her thinking spot.

"Studying," she said. "I have a quiz on the limbic system."

Nate cast an eye on the article open on the tablet.

"That's some bullshit, huh?"

"Nah," she said, setting the tablet aside.

"*Nah?*"

"Nah."

"Are you folksy now?" he said, sitting down next to her. "*Nah?* The DNA on that body didn't match and you're . . . okay?"

Stevie tucked her knees to her chest and looked over at her friend.

"Because I knew it wasn't going to," she said, smiling.

"Wait . . . are you saying you knew that wasn't Alice?"

"Oh, it's her," Stevie said. "It's Alice."

"Not according to the tests."

"There's always been speculation that Alice was adopted," Stevie said. "There's no proof, but there was always a rumor."

"A rumor won't help you get millions of dollars."

"Nope," she said, smiling a bit.

"Now you're smiling?" he said. "Are you trying to scare me?"

"See, here's the thing that was bothering me," Stevie said. "Once I knew Alice was back on the grounds, I kept wondering why. Alice didn't die here. She died somewhere else. And the person responsible for her death was George Marsh. That much, I know. But why, if she died, would he do something so insane—bring her body back to her home and put it right under her father's nose? I had to be missing something. So I went to the library. The Ellinghams had this thing called a clipping service—it's like a human Google alert. Every time they were mentioned in an article in the news, the service would cut it out and send it to them. There's boxes and boxes and boxes of this stuff in the library here. It hasn't been digitized because no one really thought it was interesting or worth it. I had to read a lot of stuff—society reports and stuff about hats and dances and people sailing together. Did you know they used to report who was on famous ocean liners? Like, that was a whole news story. Anyway, it took me a few weeks, but I finally found this."

She reached into her pocket and pulled out a copy of a clipping from a Burlington newspaper dated December 18, 1932.

"Read it out loud," she said, handing it to Nate.

Nate took the paper cautiously and began to read.

"'Wife to Albert Ellingham'—that's nice, she's not her own person or anything—'gives birth in Switzerland. Businessman and philanthropist Albert Ellingham and his wife, Mrs. Iris Ellingham, welcomed a baby girl on Thursday, December 15, in a private hospital outside the city of Zermatt, in the Swiss Alps. Both mother and daughter are doing well, according to Robert Mackenzie, personal secretary to Mr. Ellingham. The child has been named Alice.' Why am I reading this?"

"Keep going."

"'Mr. Ellingham is of course known locally for his property on Mount Morgan, where he intends to open a school. The Ellinghams chose a different snowy mountain setting for the birth to avoid publicity, according to Mr. Mackenzie. They were accompanied on their trip abroad by Miss Flora Robinson, a friend to—'"

"There it is," she said.

"There what is?"

"I already knew that Alice was born in Switzerland," she said, her eyes glistening. "But I didn't know they went with a friend. One friend. Flora Robinson. Iris's best friend."

"Makes sense, I guess? Take your friend if you're going on a long trip to give birth?"

"Or," Stevie said, "they went away to the Alps, to a super private place, so that *Flora* could give birth and they could arrange the adoption. Adoptions are personal things. If it had happened here, the press could have leaked it. Maybe they didn't want Alice to know, or they wanted to be the ones to tell her, on their own time. People have a right to privacy, especially when it comes to their kids."

"Just because Flora went to Switzerland with them doesn't mean she gave birth to Alice, does it?" Nate asked.

Stevie closed the DNA article on her tablet and brought up a digital notebook of scans, all of long pages with neat, elaborate handwriting.

"Charles was nice enough to give me the house records, probably to keep me busy. I made copies of them for myself because I like to make my own fun. The Ellingham house was the kind of place where everything got written down, all the visitors, all the menus. So let's go back to March 1932. Who's here? Flora Robinson. So let's see what she's doing. . . ."

Stevie triumphantly showed the next pages of scans. These were of menus, daily lists of what was served at the main table and to all the guests.

"Look at Flora Robinson in March. This is her normal breakfast."

She held up one of the menu pages.

Guest, Miss Flora Robinson, breakfast tray service: coffee with milk and sugar, tomato juice, toast and marmalade, scrambled egg, sliced ham, orange slices.

"You'll see, she gets this almost every day, same thing. She loves her tomato juice and scrambled eggs and orange slices. But then, we get to mid-May, and it all changes."

Guest, Miss Flora Robinson, breakfast tray service: tea without milk, ginger ale, saltine crackers, dry toast.

"That's what she gets, if she gets anything at all," Stevie said. "All of this starts in late May and goes on through June. What does this suggest?"

"Morning sickness," Nate said, his eyes widening.

"Morning sickness," Stevie replied, smiling.

"You terrify me," Nate said quietly.

"I went through the rest of the records. Flora was here for most of 1932. Like, almost all of it. Then, in September, they all pack up and go to Switzerland. So, let's say Flora was Alice's biological mother. It means there must also be a biological father. Who is he? This is where George Marsh's actions start to make sense. . . ."

Stevie was getting that high, frenzied excitement, the one that made Nate visibly nervous.

"George Marsh is never written down as a guest, but he turns up in the records because they have to make up his room and he also gets meals. Here he is, all over March and April. In fact, for at least one weekend in April, it was the Ellinghams, George Marsh, and Flora Robinson. It's the weekend that, if you count back, would have been pretty much exactly nine months before Alice's birth. But if you want more, here is Flora . . ."

She brought up a picture of Flora Robinson.

"And here is George Marsh . . ."

One more photo.

"And here is Alice."

Nate examined the three photos together.

"Oh," he said.

"This is why he brought her back," Stevie said. "Because he was her biological father. He wanted to bury her properly, at home."

"Okay, so you're going to explain all of this so you get the money? I guess it would be hard to prove, but they could probably do it, check birth records and get DNA . . ."

"Nah," Stevie said again.

"Okay, what is this *nah* thing? You aren't going to try to prove it?"

"It wasn't about the money," she said. "If I even tried to claim it, think of the lawyers and the creeps I'd have to deal with. It would ruin my life."

"Seriously?" he said. "You're not going to fight for seventy million dollars?"

"What can I buy for seventy million dollars?"

"Anything. Almost literally anything."

"The way it is now," she said, "the money stays here, in the school. Alice's home. The one her father made. He wanted to make a place where impossible things could happen. Albert Ellingham believed in me. He let me come here, and I'm making sure it stays open. This is for Alice and Iris, and for Albert, for Hayes, and Ellie and Fenton."

She raised her mug.

"Oh my God," he said. "What are you, a saint or something?"

"I stole this mug," she said. "So, no. Besides, if the school closed down, you'd have to go home and finish your book or something. I did it for you. I'm not even telling anyone else. I mean, aside from my friends. Like you."

"Are you trying to make me have an emotion?" Nate said, his eyes reddening a bit. "Because I've spent my whole life learning how to repress and deflect and you're kind of ruining my thing."

"I have more bad news. Look behind you. The happy couples are coming out . . ."

Janelle and Vi waved back, arm in arm. Behind them, Hunter and Germaine were not quite at this level, but they were talking intently, in that way couples do. Janelle and Vi had only grown closer since the events of the fall and were even planning on how they would visit each other during the summer and coordinate their schedules. Hunter and Germaine and bonded over a mutual interest in the environment and K-dramas. Things at school had not been easy or perfect for anyone, but they were definitely pretty good. It turned out school was generally more straightforward when people weren't getting murdered all the time.

As the others reached Stevie and Nate, Stevie's phone rang. She held up a hand and stepped off a few paces to take a video call.

"Where are you?" she asked.

David was on a street somewhere, in a purple campaign T-shirt.

"Oh, um . . ." He looked around. "Iowa. We're going to

three cities today. I'm doing prep work, setting up events at some diners, stuff like that. I wanted to call early because I saw that DNA stuff. You're all good?"

"I'm great," she said. "How's the campaign going?"

"I knocked on three hundred and fifteen doors yesterday. Imagine how lucky those people were, opening their doors to see me."

"Blessed," Stevie said.

"That's the exact word. *Blessed*. I even knocked on the doors of some people who had a sign for my dad out on their lawn. Some people just won't give up on the dream."

Since leaving Ellingham, David had landed an internship with a rival presidential candidate. Ellingham had offered him the chance to return, but his father had blocked it. He was technically without a school, working on his own to finish his GED. Between the two things, he was going day and night. Stevie had never seen him at this pace, and it seemed to suit him. He looked and sounded healthier, even though she suspected he wasn't sleeping much. They spoke two or three times a day. Her parents, ironically, were absolutely delighted that she continued to have a relationship with that nice boy who turned out to be Senator King's son. Senator King's views on David's relationship with Stevie were not known and not sought out.

"I'm thinking about telling him what I'm doing," David said.

"You are?"

"I feel like he should know I'm out here, working hard for

democracy. You know, the people on the other side. I fixed their local database last night, and tonight I'm helping with social media outreach. It turns out I'm really good at this stuff."

"I always believed in you," Stevie said.

"Did you?"

"No," Stevie said. "But you have a nice ass, so I let you slide."

They smiled at each other from a thousand miles away. Stevie had never felt closer to him.

"I guess I'd better get back and finish studying," she said. "I have an anatomy quiz. Do you know anything about the limbic system?"

"What *don't* I know about the limbic system? Except what it is."

"That's about where I am," said Stevie.

"You don't get a 'the DNA sample wasn't a match' pass on that?"

"No."

"Even if you solve the case of the century, you still have to do your homework? The world is made of bullshit."

"Not everything," said Stevie.

"No," he replied, his mouth twisting into a smile. "Not everything."

When Stevie was off the phone, the group fell in together to walk toward the classroom buildings. Stevie took a long, deep breath of the fresh mountain air—the air Albert Ellingham had loved so much, he bought the side of the mountain and made his kingdom.

"Can I ask you something?" Vi said. "How did David manage to record his dad's reaction? Did he bug the office?"

"You mean, hypothetically?" Stevie said.

"Obviously."

"Say you get yourself beaten up and put up a video of it to freak out your dad and make him think you've run off to smoke pot and drop out of society, but you're really sneaking back to the house to get information."

"Seems normal," Vi replied.

"Say you also have a sister who feels the same way about your dad that you do. And that you tell that sister what you are about to do so she doesn't freak out. And that sister wants to help. So she flies from California to Pennsylvania to be at the house when you tell your dad you destroyed all his blackmail material. And she happens to be ready with her phone to record his reaction."

"Such an amazing coincidence," Vi said. "And then that recording happened to get out?"

"I know," Stevie said. "The weirdest stuff happens in this family."

"Have your parents given up on Edward King yet?" Vi asked.

"No," Stevie said. "They think it's all a plot against him or something. Some things you can't change. Anyway, I have to go or I'm going to be late. This quiz won't fail itself. Want to meet for lunch at . . ."

Her attention was drawn to a movement in the woods in the direction of the river. The trees were slowly coming back into bud, but they were still bare enough that she could make out a shape.

"Moose," she said, almost in a whisper. "Moose. *Moose.*"

She tugged Nate's sleeve.

"Moose," she repeated.

The object moved away, out of sight. Stevie blinked. It had just been there, the massive antlers moving through the trees.

"My moose," she said in a low voice. "I finally got it. The universe paid me in moose."

With one backward glance at the magical spot, Stevie Bell resumed walking toward her class. Anatomy was still ahead of her. Lots of things were ahead of her, but this one was the closest.

"That wasn't a moose, was it?" Janelle said when Stevie was out of earshot. "That's a branch, right? It moved in the wind?"

"It's a branch," Nate replied.

"Like, that's *obviously* a branch," Vi said. "Should we tell her? She seems really invested in this."

"Definitely not," Nate said as Stevie vanished in the direction of the classroom buildings, earbuds already in her ears. "Let her have her moose."

Acknowledgments

Over the past three years as I wrote these books, I have done a lot of puzzling, reworking, pacing, and internal screaming. In short, it was incredible fun, like doing a word problem for thirty-six months or more. There are many people to thank.

First, my incredible editor, Katherine Tegen—I could not have had a better advocate and editorial voice. And to everyone at Katherine Tegen books for their hard work and support. My agent, Kate Schafer Testerman, is beside me always. (And in times of extreme duress, on top of me, when I try to escape from my desk.) Beth Dunfey provided an editorial eye and helped shape the world of Ellingham Academy. My assistant, Kate Welsh, prevents me from running with scissors.

My writing life would be a flaming pile without the help of Holly Black, Cassie Clare, Robin Wasserman, Sarah Rees Brennan, and Kelly Link. My day-to-day life belongs to my beloved Oscar and my beautiful Zelda and Dexy. To all my family and friends, I am deeply grateful that you put up with me.

And thank you, most of all, for reading.